The Navigator II

Irish Revenge

Steve Coleman

This is a work of fiction. The characters and events in this story are the inventions of the author and do not depict any real persons or events. Any resemblance to actual people or incidents is entirely coincidental.

ISBN: 978-0-9850065-2-5

LCCN: 2016916055

S B Coleman

P. O. Box 130524

Birmingham, AL 35213

www.captstevestories.com

steve@captstevestories.com

This novel is dedicated to the fabulous friends in Northern Ireland with whom I had the great fortune to sail.

Many, many thanks to those who gave encouragement and criticism along the way.

A man who would dig a grave for another best take care not to fall in it himself.

—Old Irish Saying

Chapter One

While he sat alone at the bar of Eamon's Pub nursing a glass of dark brown Guinness, Joe realized that his initial efforts to uncover dissident activity had led him nowhere. In his role as a new agent in a strange place and having broken up with Mary, he felt very much alone.

"Not seen you here before," the barman said. He set a glass under the tap and began filling it.

"On vacation," Joe lied as he watched the golden liquid foam up.

"On holiday, is it? From the southern States would be my guess." Joe nodded with a shrug.

"We see Brits, Germans, French and some Dutch in here, but it's uncommon to have a Yank."

"I'll try to fit in."

"Aye," the bartender replied. "Not a bad plan."

When Joe first entered the dimly lit, varnished wood-paneled pub that smelled of beer and cigarettes and cool, damp mustiness of the harbor and the sweat of Irishmen who had been at sea all day, some of the patrons had given him the once-over. That they didn't much like strangers had been his impression since arriving in Northern Ireland a few days ago. Given his purpose for being there, he did not expect to like them much either.

He heard someone banging open the front door and turned to see a hulking figure. Rain matted the man's black hair and dripped from his seaman's foul weather jacket. The man peered around in the dim light and frowned when he apparently spotted someone. Joe watched as he strode toward a table where several women were seated, drinking and talking. One of them looked concerned as she saw him approach, and the group immediately quieted. A young woman with red hair to her shoulders, who had her back toward the door, turned to see him.

"So here y'are, Fiona," he bellowed. It brought all the customers to silence. The redhead's companions looked at her with some distress.

"Aye, Seamus, how're you keeping?"

"How would you think? Me out on the stinking trawler all day and you not at the dock to greet me?"

"I sent word, Seamus," she said with firm calmness, but there was a spark of anger in her greenish blue eyes. "I and my friends here were to have our ladies' night out. You know we come here on Tuesdays."

"And I said you were to meet me at the dock." He laid his meaty hand on her chair, jerked her back from the table and grabbed her wrist. "Now come along, I say." There was no mistaking it was a threat to the woman, and Joe stood up, feeling that someone should intervene. He could take the bully if it came to it. In his opinion, a man who would treat a woman that way and embarrass her in a room full of people surely does not deserve her.

But realizing that, as a stranger, it was not his place, he forced himself to stand still. The first rule of being undercover, he remembered, is to keep a low profile and never get involved.

"If you, Seamus O'Leary, ever want me to 'come along' as you say," she said, "it would be best for you to act the gentleman and leave us to finish our craic." She tried to pull her arm away. "Understand?"

They stared at one another for a long moment. O'Leary abruptly released her wrist, scowled at the onlookers and walked out. Mumbling a curse, he disappeared into the rainy gloom, slamming the heavy oak door behind him. Even though Joe had been in Ballycastle only a few days, he already had observed O'Leary aboard the fishing trawler that docked near his own boat. The gruff way the man ordered his crew around was indication enough of what kind of person he was, and this incident with the girl proved it.

The ladies regained their composure and once again engaged one another, but in more serious, less animated talk. Drinking several big swallows of stout to help himself calm down, Joe could not keep from glancing at the redhead named Fiona. As she spoke, a strand of hair fell across her cheek. She brushed it back, exposing the faint outline of a scar running from a high cheekbone toward her slightly upturned, thinly delicate nose. Continuing to address the women, she shook her fist, accentuating her point.

One of her companions noticed Joe's attention and nodded in his direction. Fiona turned to look directly in his eyes. It was only an instant before he looked down self-consciously. Though she continued her entreaty to her companions, he was jolted by their visual exchange and drew in a deep breath. It had been only a glimpse, a snapshot, a flash, but in it he had seen in her intense blue-green eyes an intriguingly attractive presence.

"Could you tell me who that red-haired lady is?" he asked on the publican's next trip by. The bald, bulbous man glanced over at her, and then with a raised eyebrow stared back at Joe.

"Fiona Brennan. And as you saw, O'Leary's spoken for her. That, my friend, is all you need to know."

Joe nodded and sipped his drink. Since his arrival in Ballycastle, he had made no headway in his efforts to locate anyone in the Irish Republican Army. He had singled out O'Leary as the type but had nothing more to go on. He glanced at the woman once more. Perhaps, he thought, being O'Leary's girl, she might have some peripheral connection or at least some knowledge of the IRA. So by getting to know her he could learn something. Of course, as the barman had warned, any attention he might show could be risky. Being as pretty and attractive as she was, however, seeing more of her might make life interesting.

After having escaped his rather possessive girlfriend, Mary and leaving her back home in Birmingham, Alabama, he knew this was no time to be getting involved again. Glancing over at the attractive Fiona once more, he guessed she was in her late thirties, a decade younger than himself. What this beauty saw in that Seamus character, he could not imagine. Joe noticed Eamon watching him with disapproval.

"She's O'Leary's girl," the barman repeated. "'Tis well you mind my meaning." He took Joe's glass and wiped the bar. "Another?"

Joe nodded reluctantly and watched his glass being filled. He felt a gust of wind behind him as the door opened again, and a massive figure filled the entrance.

"Evening, Big Ryan," said the bartender.

"Eamon," the man replied as he shook off his wet jacket. Joe rarely encountered someone so much taller than himself, but the newcomer, with graying blond stringy hair and great bushy eyebrows, stood at least six-feet six. Probably the result of Viking genes rather than Celtic, Joe guessed. The giant waved and exchanged brief pleasantries with one or two at the rail before taking a seat at a small table close by.

"Your usual then?"

"Oh, aye."

Joe watched Eamon draw a pint of Guinness, letting half a glass stand until the foam went down and then topping it off.

"So, how're you keeping?" the publican asked, delivering the mug of dark brown stout.

"Too idle, you know." The tall man shook his head.

"Aye, retirement's not easy. Tried it myself for a year before tending bar." Eamon wiped the table and headed back to his post behind the counter.

A couple of seaman in yellow foul-weather jackets stopped to speak to the big fellow, who greeted them with an affable smile. Joe noted they spoke to the giant with an attitude of deference and respect. When the pair left, he decided to try approaching him. If there was to be an opportunity today to meet someone local, this was it. He took his half-empty glass and walked over. The man seemed self-absorbed in thought.

"Hello. Could I bother you a moment?" The man looked up and squinted at him. "I've got a boat in the marina," Joe continued, "and I'm trying to find a mechanic."

"Well, that wouldn't be me," the big man replied, giving Joe a critical stare. "But I might give you a name or two."

"Great! I'm new around here and don't know my way around very well."

"A misplaced Johnny Reb, by your talk."

"Joe Anderson." He stuck out his hand. The big man glanced at it a full second before extending his own big rough hand that swallowed Joe's.

"Ryan McLeod."

Joe glanced at an empty chair. "May I?" he ventured, getting a slight shrug and nod in response.

"I've rented a forty-foot sloop," Joe went on, daring to sit down, "and I'm hoping to do some sailing."

"Sailing yacht, you said? And your crew?"

"All by myself," Joe replied. "Just puttering around on my own."

"Well, I hope you know these waters," Ryan said. "Seas and weather can be a might rough and changeable." He eyed Joe seriously. "Difficult for any man, especially one who doesn't know them."

"I imagine you've spent some time at sea?"

Ryan grinned. "Twenty-six years in the Merchant Marine. And I was harbourmaster here afterwards."

"I'll bet you've got some stories."

"Aye." The big man paused to finish off his stout. "Maybe one or two." He stared at Joe briefly. "And a chap all alone on a boat, is likely a tale in himself, I suspect."

Joe smiled and lifted his glass. "To good stories," he said, happy to have found someone to talk to. He beckoned to the bartender for refills. "So are you retired now?"

The question elicited a dark look. "If you'd call it that."

Joe shrugged. "It takes a while to get used to all that spare time. I take it you retired recently?"

The big man gave Joe a hard, appraising stare. Then his look softened to sadness. "If being forced out counts, then, aye, I'm a bloody pensioner."

Joe raised his eyebrows. "Forced out, you say?"

Ryan shot a look around the room and leaned closer. "The bastards claimed they needed a younger man to run the harbour," he said quietly.

"Uh, Evan Foster, you mean?"

"That's the blaggard." He stared at Joe for a moment and then sat back, looking away as if he'd said too much.

"I was running a charter boat back home," Joe offered. "But the recession pretty well retired me."

Big Ryan nodded. "It's a kick in the britches, however you get it." The conversation halted while Eamon put down the refills and took away the empties. Joe handed him a ten pound note and the barman went off for change.

"That's why I'm here," Joe went on. "I said to myself, if nothing else, I at least can go sailing—see something new, have a new life—as long as my health holds, anyway." His train of thought was lost as he saw the redhead and her friends get up to leave. They spoke to Ryan as they passed. The auburn beauty glanced at Joe as she walked by. He smiled and hoped Ryan would introduce him, but it didn't happen.

"Cheers, Fiona," Ryan said to her. Joe watched the ladies as they went out and then realized the big man was looking at him.

"So you're all by yourself, eh?" Ryan asked. "Or is your wife along?"

Joe turned his attention back to the giant and shrugged. "Divorced," he replied. But it was Mary now who came to mind and not his ex, Eileen.

"Never married, myself," the big man said. "Spent too much of my life at sea. And then the harbour job demanded lots of time, until…" His dark frown returned and they sat in silence sipping from their glasses. In the edge of the mahogany table where they sat Joe made out the words *LOYALISTS SUCK* that had been rudely carved, likely by some embittered drunk. The scrawl was barely visible. Someone, the owner maybe, had applied wood stain to try and hide it. Joe pointed it out to the big man.

"What's that all about?" he asked. Ryan grimaced and gave him a long stare.

"You don't know much about Ulster, do you," he said. Joe shrugged.

"No, but I'd like to learn."

"Oh, would you now?" The giant shook his head and gave a cynical laugh. "Oh, would you now," he repeated and looked away, his expression fading into melancholy. They fell silent again and drank.

"I'm in need of uh, a guide, I guess you'd say," Joe ventured, "someone to teach me about local tides and currents and such."

Big Ryan shrugged. "You might find someone around Belfast or thereabouts. Take your good money, too, I expect."

"I wonder if you would undertake the job. I can't pay much, but I can pay something." As he said it, Joe wondered if he was coming on too fast. "I mean, it would just be for a week or so, just long enough to get me oriented."

Ryan raised an eyebrow. "You hardly know me."

Joe grinned. "Well, since you hardly know me, that makes two of us." He widened his smile. "My boat's the *Kittiwake*, across at the marina."

The huge man wagged his head as if considering it but obviously was interested in the opportunity.

"Tomorrow, then?"

Ryan gazed at him a moment. "Half eight at the dock," he replied.

Having several drinks under his belt—well, temporarily under his belt—a sign over the urinal in the pub read *We don't sell beer. We just rent it,* —Joe made his way back to the boat through a light rain. On the way, he looked up into the window of the marina office and saw Foster's pit bulldog, Bounder, with his melon-sized ugly head peering out, barking at him.

"Love me, love my dog," he recited to himself.

The kind of dog a person owned reflected a lot about the individual's personality, he knew. And that seemed to be especially true about the new harbourmaster. Maybe there was something significant in Big Ryan's dislike, not only of Foster but maybe also of those who had given Foster his job.

As he walked down to the dock, he heard the deep guttural roar of a big diesel engine starting up. He had come to recognize Seamus O'Leary's forty-foot trawler, rigged for sport fishing, not too unlike Joe's old boat, *Tartan*, except this was an older, wooden-hulled craft.

"Hie with them ropes, Mikey!" he heard Seamus shout from the pilot house and saw the younger O'Leary cast off the mooring lines and climb aboard. Joe wondered what that lovely girl Fiona Brennan ever saw in him. The trawler, named *Red Dagger*, backed away from the dock and headed out of the pass into the sound. Joe noted the time and thought it was odd they would be going to sea at nightfall. Although he could be fishing for sharks at night, still it seemed curious. He considered sending his handler a description of *Red Dagger* so it could be tracked by the CIA/MI-5 drone surveillance campaign. He didn't want to be thought of as crying wolf, however, so he decided to wait until he had more cause for suspicion.

He thought he might ask Foster sometime about the comings and goings of O'Leary. As boss of the marina, Foster surely was in a great position to observe all the comings and goings to sea. One thing Joe had learned from his recent special training was the need to recruit people who would inform him about the situation. It was the best way to gather intelligence, they had taught him, but it was not without risks because you had to reveal something of your identity and purpose to the recruited informer. Joe realized, however, that the cold and unfriendly Evan Foster would be too unapproachable to make an ally.

Climbing aboard his boat, he gave a long look at the weathered teak deck. Would he come to love this boat as much as he had *Tartan*? Maybe he would after he put in some time maintaining and then sailing her. Experiences at sea, he understood, both the pleasant and the unpleasant, often bring a man to feel much affection for the boat he sails.

Joe took a last gaze at the light of the setting sun peeking through the passing rain shower. Looking back to the east, he saw sunlight gleaming gold on the high cliffs of Fairhead. A fabulous spot they had sent him to, this northeast corner of the Emerald Isle. But for all the beauty of this place, he had been told terrorist activities were secretly underway, and his task was to learn all about them.

Chapter Two

"I read that currents around here can be fairly swift," Joe said as he and Big Ryan left the dock the next morning.

"Aye, now that's an understatement, and you'll find many a ship has been wrecked because of it. They say more than twelve hundred have been lost in the depths along the Ulster coast. Contrary winds and tides, there be." Ryan coiled up the mooring lines and watched Joe maneuver the sloop past the rock jetties into Rathlin Sound. "You'll be finding the tide charts very valuable on this coast," he said. "There's no going against the currents in a yacht like this. And you'd be wise to keep a weather eye as well."

Joe nodded. Over the years he had developed quite a respect for wind and weather, not to mention what he had encountered aboard *MISSION* last summer. Visions of the storms and images of Mary fighting the seas at the helm came back to him, and he wondered what she would be doing today at home in Birmingham. Bridge club, he expected. Were she here and not thousands of miles away, would she like to be with him this morning, out for a sail? Or

13

was she happier at home being pursued by Wade, her dead husband's brother?

He shook off dark thoughts and focused on steering. To Joe's surprise, the little diesel had a healthy putt-putt sound without any vibration to speak of. He liked the way the boat responded, and it seemed to have a good stable feel to it. Old but experienced, he thought, just like his new Irish companion, this big man with a weather beaten face and sad eyes.

"Shall we head upwind toward the east?" Joe suggested as they approached open water.

Ryan shook his head and pointed toward a small eddy whirling near the jetty to the south. "A right good ebb running. If you want to make any headway, ye'd best turn to port."

Amused at the directness of the instruction, Joe obediently turned left beyond the jetty, which Ryan called a pier, and judged the current was nearly strong enough to double their speed over the ground. "I see what you mean."

"Lesson number one," Ryan replied.

Moving away from land they found the wind had shifted to a light breeze from the south and Joe unfurled the genoa. He was pleased to see it was a new sail, just as the marina's leasing agent had said, and it came off of its roller-furling neatly. The sail filled and Joe turned more northerly to give them a broad reach. He shut down the engine and noticed happily that the prop feathered correctly. Just on the outskirts of Ballycastle to their left a hill rose steeply, presenting a high cliff. A few miles north, across the sound, stood the monolithic Rathlin Island, its high ridges and brown basaltic cliffs shining in the sunlight.

Joe asked Ryan to take the helm, and then he climbed up on deck to remove the mainsail cover and checked to see the halyard was ready to run free. From beside the helm, Ryan slacked the mainsheet. Joe removed the halyard from the cleat on the mast and pulled. The mainsail began to fill as it was raised, and Joe asked Ryan to turn into the wind a bit to ease the pressure. Then Joe raised the main all the way and tied off the halyard, thinking one thing he would change would be to run the halyard to the cockpit so that the sail could be more easily hoisted while sailing alone. Under both main and genoa, the sloop gathered speed through the water. Watching the near shore to port, Joe realized they were making even better speed over the ground and mentioned it to Ryan.

"Aye," Ryan said, grinning. "The ebb current's reaching six knots. And soon you'll meet an amazing sight."

"What's that?"

"Look yonder in your glasses," Ryan pointed ahead of the bow. Joe picked up his binoculars and looked. "See the swirling waters about half a mile off the starboard bow?" Ryan asked.

"I think so, yes. Gosh, what is that?"

"Slough na mor," Ryan said gravely. "Swallow of the sea. That whirlpool's got a nasty nature. Forms up at two to three hours after the start of the ebb tide. And really beware when there's a spring tide. Many a fool's been capsized by it—those who ignore the power the Good Lord put into the sea."

Joe stared through the binoculars, fascinated, giving a shiver at the eerie sight. Then he noted where it was in relation to Ballycastle and Rathlin Island. "We're going to run right by it, if we stay on this course."

"Aye, and youse should take a good look." Ryan paused. "And we'd be wise to avoid her today, lest you mean to test this boat for sure."

"First one of these I've seen," Joe said. He once saw the tide pour into the Bay of Fundy, making a huge rolling wave, but this was different.

"She's doin' her dance. A great whirlpool she is. Water rushes from the Irish Sea at ebb and flows through Rathlin Sound on its way to the Atlantic. When the moon and sun are just right for a spring ebb, she can be ferocious enough, a threat to unwary boaters who venture by."

Joe watched awestruck. He had experienced riptides and strong eddies before, but this was spectacular. "Swallow of the sea—you called it?"

"Aye. 'Tis Slough na mor."

Joe took another look at the white water spinning in a 100-yard circle before them. "I guess not," he said, "since this boat still needs some work before it's ready for too much rough stuff." He realized what Ryan meant and lowered the binoculars from his eyes. "Lesson Two."

"Lesson Two," Ryan agreed.

"Let's sail toward Bull Point," Ryan suggested. "The current's takin' you to the northwest end of the sound anyway." He stood up and offered to take the wheel. "Let me take the helm while you go find them Guinnesses."

Joe started to say it was a little early for alcohol, but then what the hell? Besides, he might get this Irishman to loosen up enough to let him pry a bit. Going below, grabbing on to various handholds as Ryan brought the rolling boat around to the northwest, he took two cans of stout from the icebox and headed up. Pausing at the ladder, he glanced at Big Ryan standing behind the wheel, his blue eyes peering off in the distance, his Gaelic features and suntanned face lined from years on the oceans of the world. It was easy to imagine him being like his forefathers, an ancient captain out upon the sea.

Joe handed him the Guinness. "I guess you come from a seafaring family?"

Ryan took a swig, frowned and looked at the can as if stout never should be drunk that way. "My father was a farmer, over near the town of Ballymoney. I grew up tending sheep mostly."

"So you went to sea to get away from that, I guess," Joe leaned back, relaxed, watching Ryan expertly keeping *Kittiwake* on course.

The big man shook his head. "Wasn't the farming ran me off," he replied. "'twas more The Troubles, I suppose."

17

Joe sat up. "You mean the fighting between those loyal to Britain and those who wanted independence?"

"Aye, but more complicated than that." He looked off sadly. "I came from a mixed family."

Joe looked at Ryan in surprise. There was no sign of any mixed blood. He was nearly as purely Caucasian as anyone could appear. "I would not have thought so," he couldn't help but say.

Reading Joe's expression, Ryan laughed. "I'm not of racially mixed blood. That's your American idea of mix. Nah. Here it is a religious thing."

"Oh," Joe stammered. "I see."

"My mother was of a Catholic family. She came from County Monaghan, and my father a Presbyterian from Antrim. It caused a great row in both families. It's a wonder they ever married."

"I see," Joe said. "That can even be something of an issue for some people in the States."

"Aye, but nothing like here, I warrant. No, it was a great problem for me as a boy."

"Like how, choosing sides at school or whatever?"

Ryan sighed. "For most, there was no choice but to attend a Catholic school. And out in the world, I was forever called upon to declare which I was, Protestant or Catholic, Orange or Green. It even tore at the family. My own brother became a Catholic priest and upset all my father's kin. So at the age of sixteen, I'd had enough. I slipped off to Belfast one day and signed on a steamer hauling coal from Manchester, and that became my life."

"Saved yourself a lot of pain and misery, I guess," Joe said with a wry smile. Having married in his twenties, his own life as a young husband had become very rocky. Differences seemed to multiply, driving a wedge of misunderstanding between himself and Eileen until only divorce would solve it. "We all get separated and crossways with one another. I couldn't hold my marriage together, as much as I tried."

Ryan nodded. "Disagreement and conflict are just human nature, I'd say."

Dismissing the gloomy conversation, Joe looked to the south at the coast of Northern Ireland where a line of lower bluffs were topped with verdant meadows, accentuated by a scattering of white houses. Most prominently a white church surrounded by green pasture stood beside a road which ran toward the cliff edge and meandered down to the water's edge.

"Such a fabulous view," he said.

Ryan looked at it a moment and glanced at Joe. "Aye," he said. "Very lovely, sure enough." Then he gestured toward a high promontory further to the west. "Up there," he pointed. "That's Benbane Head. Now Point Lacada and Port na Spaniagh are just beyond, just before you reach the Giant's Causeway."

Joe shook his head. "About as pretty a place as I've ever seen."

Ryan sighed. "But not so pretty perhaps when you know the history in those rocks. Port na Spaniagh, Gaelic for 'the bay of the Spaniards', is in a depression in the cliffs. In 1588 during the war with the Spanish Armada, there was a terrific storm, the Spanish galleass, *Girona*, ran aground on a treacherous rock. A mighty wind from the north smashed them against the rocky shore. Of the 1300 Spanish aboard all but near a dozen died. A few hardy souls climbed the cliff where James McDonald, son of the infamous Sorely Boy, laird of Dunluce Castle, awaited them. It's told that McDonald helped some escape to Catholic Scotland. But legend has it that the vicious Scot and his men beheaded many poor blokes as they reached the summit. Knowing the strange things men can do, I would say that both be true."

Joe winced. "Those were cruel times."

Ryan shook his head. "No crueler then than now."

Joe lowered the binoculars and looked at the big man. "You're not referring to 'The Troubles' again, are you?" he asked. "I thought that was over."

The big man with the sad eyes shook his head again. "No meaner men lived then than can be found today in Northern Ireland."

Through his binoculars, Joe stared at the shadowy dark cliffs. "Lesson Three," he thought.

Deciding it was time to come about and head home, Joe handled the sheets as Ryan put the helm hard alee, and they came about. Expertly, Ryan turned *Kittiwake* so as to fall off from the wind and fill the genoa.

"We'll be beating to windward to reach Ballycastle," Joe said.

"Good that we've headed back before the tide turns against us," Ryan replied and asked Joe to take the helm. He went below to use the head. Alone in the cockpit, Joe thought again about that gorgeous girl Fiona he had seen in the pub and how disappointed he had felt when Eamon told him she was spoken for. While having left his last love, Mary Johnston, in Birmingham had been for the best, he realized, it was not true that he had no lingering affection for her. He hoped Mary had enough sense to understand that her former brother-in-law, Wade, was pursuing her for her money and not for any real affection. But that was not Joe's concern anymore, he supposed. Finding a girl here in Northern Ireland—even if he was on a potentially dangerous mission—would be good for his own well-being. That this red-haired girl in the bar had caught his eye was not surprising, given his unfulfilled desires.

Interrupting Joe's thoughts, Ryan came up the ladder and took a seat on the bench just forward of the helm. He glanced at Joe with a studied expression.

"You look a million miles away," he said.

Joe grinned. "I guess I was thinking about, well, about how different a place this is."

"Aye," the giant said. "So, why did you come to Ulster by yourself?"

Joe was unprepared for the abrupt question. "I just wanted a change."

21

"From what? If you don't mind my asking."

Joe felt his face redden. "Just looking for something different, you see," he said. "I, uh, well…"

"There's a lady involved, I'd wager," Ryan guessed. "Is that not so?"

Joe laughed. "How did you know?" He was happy to let that be the reason for his being here.

"I always had the sense to stay away from them," Ryan replied. "Life's a lot less trouble that way."

Joe laughed again. "Lesson Four," he said. As they tacked on in to the marina, Joe thought about that lovely lass, Fiona, he had seen in the pub and realized this was one lesson he doubted he would heed.

Chapter Three

Settling in to a routine at the Ballycastle harbor—all the
while keeping an eye out for who came and went, either by
boat or by land—Joe spent several days in port working on
Kittiwake. While she had sailed well, he did not like the
looks of the wire stays of the mast. One morning when the
wind was calm, he began releasing each one from the deck
and inspecting the cable ends. There was some corrosion but
not too serious an issue unless he got into really high winds.
How much money he should sink into boat maintenance was
the question. Someday he would have to make huge repairs
to his own wrecked trawler, *Tartan*, which he believed had
been stolen by an American-based Real IRA unit rearming
terrorists. The trawler now sat impounded in Miami and
would require lots of repair, and so he was reluctant to spend
much on this Irish boat. Even though the CIA had paid for
him to lease *Kittiwake*, he doubted the agency would
understand the need to reimburse him for renovations. They
would say it wasn't important to accomplishing his mission,
he thought, but decided he would try to convince them
anyway.

His instructions were to phone his handler, Stan Adams, at least once a week, calling at four in the afternoon, which would be 11:00 AM EDT. He recalled the time Mary's former brother in law, Wade, had introduced him to Adams, who was about 40 with rolled-up shirt sleeves, a crew cut and a mouth that seemed to settle into the hint of a permanent sneer. When they proposed the Northern Ireland project to Joe, Adams immediately had objected, right in Joe's presence, saying, "How can you expect a man as green and inexperienced as Anderson to manage this kind of assignment? Hell, within a month he'll be found lying in some ditch with his guts hanging out."

But Wade, a career operative, had managed to override any objections, convincing Hankins, the project director, as well as Joe himself, that all was not only possible but would be a walk in the park for a boat captain and former naval officer. Afterwards, Adams was assigned to be Joe's mentor and handler, a responsibility he accepted with a distinct air of condescension and a hint of pity.

"So you're Dr. Spin's good buddy?" Adams had asked sarcastically after the meeting.

"Who's Dr. Spin?" Joe asked, trying to ignore the man's acerbic tone.

"Wade Johnston, of course," Adams replied. "He's our in-house expert on propaganda and misinformation." Adams laughed. "He probably employed some of his artfulness just to get you to come here. Made it sound like you'd get to play James Bond, I imagine."

"Hardly," Joe said. He started to tell Adams he sounded like somebody who needed taking down a peg or two. But being on Adams' turf, Joe bit his tongue. *No need to get at odds with this doofus*, he thought. Joe did mentally file away the information about Wade being "Dr. Spin." It was not an original term, but from what he had seen of Mary's brother in law, it certainly was an appropriate title for him.

So at four that day at the marina in Ballycastle, he climbed into the cockpit and looked around to ascertain that no one was close by. Then he selected *Games* on his iPhone and pressed the innocuous looking little dog icon. This connected via satellite to his handler at Langley. From that point, they could talk normally, but there were some code phrases to use in case people were listening. If the operative in the field spoke the conventional "How do you do?" it meant he was in trouble.

"Hello, Joe," Adams said in an unusually genial, pleasant voice. "How's the vacation?"

"Having a good time," Joe replied. He went on to say that Ballycastle was a beautiful spot and that he'd hired a local man to sail with him once and might take him along again, just to become more acquainted with things. In the same casual tones, Adams asked the name of Joe's new acquaintance. Joe gave a casual little sketch of Big Ryan's background, saying that he seemed the sort of person who could be counted on as a friend. Then Joe mentioned the boat's need for some not inexpensive repairs and wondered if there was any allowance for that.

25

"I'll have to check with the manager." Adams reverted to his less likable tone of voice. Joe recalled that, while Adams was Joe's handler, Wade was the overall manager for the Northern Ireland project.

"Perhaps I could speak to him. Then I could explain the need better."

"Oh, he's off for the weekend. Out of town until Monday."

Joe paused, then guessed, "Gone to Birmingham, I imagine."

"Probably."

Joe paused. Damn. Wade's gone to visit Mary again, he thought. What for? Well, he supposed it wasn't his business anymore. "I'll have to be a little more cautious about the weather until I get the stays on the boat replaced."

"Well, maybe you can enjoy a good time ashore over the weekend," Adams replied. "Meet a wee lassie perhaps." He laughed.

"Yeah, okay," Joe feigned a chuckle. "I'll check back next week."

"And what about our birds? Any signs or sounds detected?"

"No," Joe replied with his mind more on Wade being with Mary, "no drones seen so far."

"By Jingo," Adams said, almost shouting in the phone. "Talk to you later."

Joe disconnected, then hit the clear button to erase all 'recent' calls on his iPhone. "Jingo," Adams had said. It was a code word meaning Joe had said something he should not have. He mentioned drones.

Hell, Joe thought. What could that have meant to anybody even if there had been someone around to hear him say *drones*? Yes, the U. S. did have a cooperative intelligence project with Britain's MI-5 with the intent to uncover weapons and drug smuggling. But at this point, no one could possibly have any idea of what that would be all about. Adams was being too cautious. And hadn't Adams become so loose-tongued as to tell him where Wade had gone for the weekend? Joe tried to dismiss it, feeling some disgust.

And then there was the email message from Mary, which had come a few days ago, and Joe kept it on his phone. He found himself re-reading it now.

> Joe, I suppose by now you're living on a boat over there, which I have to believe is where you belong. I'm trying to understand that and go on with my life, but it isn't easy, especially after first having lost Earnest and now you. But I'm not trying to lay a guilt trip on you, as they say. At Around-Town Theatre I've been given a leading role in a new play. It's a comedy, and that helps me find a few laughs in my life. Wade is coming down this weekend and promises to take me out on the town to cheer me up. He is a dear brother-in-law, after all. Sometime, if you can, email me and send a few pictures. I'd like to see where you are, at least. Love you, Mary.

27

So Wade indeed was spending time with Mary. Sleeping with her perhaps? Concerned in spite of himself, Joe put his face in his hands. What of all things was he doing here? A memory of mornings at Mary's came to him. He would slip out of bed without waking her, walk to the kitchen to fix them coffee, his bathrobe-clad otherwise naked body shivering slightly in the morning chill. When he returned to the bedside, she would awake and glance at him smiling. He would bend over to kiss her so gently with a "Good morning, my Love," throw off the robe and climb in beside her. Then he would snuggle with her, speak little nothings in her ear, and often end up making love. It was difficult to remember all that and not doubt his current mission in life. Here he was now in a foreign country, out for revenge, but going on the merest shred of evidence against an enemy he did not know and, so far, hadn't been able to identify. The thought crossed his mind he should pack up and go home. He had surrendered her to Wade, after all. And besides, he was into this now and, especially with the lease signed on *Kittiwake*, very much committed. He glanced up at the mast and realized he would have to ask for some assistance to go aloft and check the fittings at the top. Maybe he could prevail on Big Ryan for help. Meanwhile, it was late enough in the afternoon to excuse a visit to good ole Eamon's Pub.

But after a couple of Harp drafts, Joe began to sense he was slipping into that same kind of funk that overtook him in the Bahamas a year ago. Here he was in Northern Ireland, on what might turn out to be a wild goose chase, while Mary was at home, being pursued by Wade of all people. Well, whatever Mary did, it wasn't Joe's concern. He had tried out her lifestyle and had decided it wasn't for him. *Leave it alone*, he told himself.

"Another for you?" Eamon asked while collecting glasses and wiping down the bar.

"No, thanks." Joe drained his glass. "Haven't seen Big Ryan, have you?"

"Not today. He rarely comes in at midweek."

"Let me ask you something," Joe said. "That Fiona something, who was in here last week with some other women?"

"Aye, what about her?"

"Does she come in here often?"

"Not so much," Eamon replied, eyeing him.

"Wonder where I might find her," Joe ventured. "Does she live around here?"

The barman gave him a disapproving look. "Runs a wee market not far up the street," he said. "Along with her brother." He tossed his towel over his shoulder. "Seems I told you before, she's Seamus O'Leary's girl. Likely to be engaged soon, I hear." He leaned across the bar to look into Joe's face. "If you're wise, you'll remember that."

Joe met his gaze. "Thanks again for the advice," he said with a grin. Draining his glass, he stood up and asked directions. Eamon sighed, shook his head, and told him how to find Hillside Market. Joe thanked him.

"Thanks, eh, or so you may think." The older man shrugged and went on with his work.

Following the barman's directions, Joe went up the sidewalk between the hotel and the roundabout and headed up the street that sloped upward away from the harbor. In a couple of blocks among a row of businesses he saw the modest little store. When he entered, sure enough, Fiona was behind the checkout. As pretty as he recalled, she was wearing navy blue slacks and was bending over to wrestle something from under the counter. As she reached farther, her white blouse hiked up at her waist, revealing the white, white skin of her back. Joe stopped at the door, unconsciously gaping. Having heard him come in, she stood, exchanged glances with him and noted his expression. She was lovely. Her face reddened just slightly as she pulled her blouse down at the waist.

"Hi ya," she said, smiling at him.

Joe almost stumbled over a stack of shopping baskets. "Hello," he replied, taking one of the baskets. "I'm just getting some groceries…" *What a dumb thing to say*, he thought, walking past. *You wouldn't be here if you weren't buying groceries*. He went back to the cooler and picked up a carton of milk. Moving along the aisle, he picked out some dry cereal, a couple of cans of soup, and a six-pack of Coke, surreptitiously watching the girl check out groceries for an elderly lady. With the few things he picked up, he went forward and placed them on the counter.

"American you are? From the South, I think?" she asked as she scanned the milk carton with her left hand. He saw that there was no ring.

"Yes. How'd you know?"

She smiled, her greenish blue eyes glancing up at him. "I love your accent."

Joe nodded. "Well, I love yours, too." She went on scanning his groceries. Joe tried to think of something more to say. "And I guess you're Irish?" He winced. *What a dumb question!*

"Aye, how did you know?" she said with a grin and then self-consciously put her hand to the scar on her cheek. Embarrassed, Joe realized she was teasing him a bit. Well, maybe that was good. He glanced away, let his eyes search around as he tried to think of something to say. There were a couple of family-type photos taped on the wall, and beside them a Catholic crucifix, all a small hint of life lived away from the store. The thought crossed his mind that, being Catholic, she conceivably could know some IRA members. But she was too pretty to have anything to do with any of that.

"Do you see many Americans around here?"

She shook her head, auburn hair falling over the scar on her neck. "Many a Brit, some French and such sail in to the marina." She totaled his bill. "That'll be seven pounds twenty. But a rare thing is the American, although some come here after crossing the Atlantic. You can tell who they are because they always look so wind-beaten and tired."

31

Joe smiled. "I imagine so." He wondered if she really liked that Seamus O'Leary jerk. He hoped not.

He put a ten pound note on the counter. "Do you ever go sailing?"

"Good man," she recited the typical reply when one pays, picking up the bill and making change. "No, not sailing. My friend runs a fishing trawler. I've been out with him, but I've never sailed." She gave him a wistful look.

"Oh, it's great fun, having the wind in the sails, heeling the boat and making the wonderful sound of the wake in the water." He realized she had said *my friend* runs a fishing trawler instead of *my beloved* or whatever. Maybe she wasn't so attached to this Seamus as Eamon thought. But another warning flashed through his mind. In his all too abbreviated training at the Farm they told him that an agent had no business getting involved with a woman, James Bond to the contrary. He also recalled Big Ryan having said that his own secret to happiness was to stay away from women. But as he stood there looking at this gorgeous creature, he swallowed and took the plunge.

"Would you like to go sometime? I mean, I'll be taking my boat out tomorrow if you'd like to come." She looked away uncertainly.

"Or the next day, or the next," Joe stuttered. "Whenever it suits."

She bit her lip as she sacked his groceries. "Well, someday, perhaps," she said wistfully. "I don't know when I could get free…from the market, I mean." They regarded one another for a moment before she looked away.

Unhappily resigned to that answer, he looked over his purchases. There had been a big Cadbury's chocolate bar on the shelf that he'd passed up. Now it seemed he ought to indulge in something, a kind of consolation prize maybe.

"I've thought of something else," he said, laying his bag of groceries to the side of the counter. He walked back down the aisle to fetch his chocolate booby prize, and considered a few more comfort-food items, as well. While he browsed, he came upon a young man about 20 shelving some soup cans from a crate. The guy picked up the empty box and walked past, giving Joe a strange, studied glance. Joe noted his shaven scalp, hint of a goatee, and some bagginess under his dark eyes, and Joe sized him up as likely an unsavory kind of character. As Joe continued to browse, he overheard the man whispering something to Fiona. Out of the corner of his eye, Joe saw her frown and shake her head. Then the guy leaned in close to her, with a conspiratorial look, whispering angrily and squeezing her arm. She winced, lowered her head and then nodded with resignation. Joe thought this guy might be due a punch in the nose or something. He grabbed up the extra things and strode back up to the counter, giving a hard look at the punk. He saw Joe coming and released Fiona's arm. She glanced at Joe and managed a smile.

"So you found a few more goodies, I see," she said pleasantly enough. As Joe put them down on the counter, the young man walked behind Joe and made his way to the back of the store. Joe watched him go.

"Are you okay?" he asked. She nodded as if there were no cares in the world.

"Oh, that's my brother, Timothy," she explained, sacking his extra groceries. "He and I always go on that way. It's nothing. You know how brothers can be."

Joe exchanged looks with her and wasn't so sure that she was happy about whatever Timothy had said to her. She rang up his additional items and he paid. While doing so, she glanced toward the back of the store furtively. Then she looked up at Joe and smiled.

"What's your name?"

"Oh, I'm Joe Anderson."

"Anderson, 'tis a bonnie name. I'm Fiona Brennan."

"Fiona's a very pretty name. I've never known anyone named Fiona before."

"Is that invitation to go sailing still open?"

"Why sure, of course, anytime."

"I'm off day after tomorrow until four, if it suits."

"Great!" Joe was excited. "My boat's the *Kittiwake*. Just go down to the marina and I'll meet you at the gate. "Eight o'clock okay?"

She paused, then gave him a smile. "A bit early for me," she replied. "Half eight if you don't mind."

"Done," Joe gave her a big grin. He gathered up his groceries and started for the door.

"What should I bring?" she called after him.

He turned around. "A raincoat or jacket maybe," he said, heartened. "Mainly, just bring your lovely self."

Walking back to the marina, he reconsidered his motive in inviting her to go sailing. His mission, of course, was to find a way to infiltrate the IRA. Therefore, any socializing with Catholic Irish people might lead to some contact. But was he using that rationale to excuse a growing personal interest in Fiona? And was this just going to bring him trouble with O'Leary? Perhaps he was moving in the wrong direction. He paused and thought it over. Then he imagined having Fiona aboard *Kittiwake* smiling at him, her red hair blowing in the breeze.

"I also have a life," he said aloud. He glanced back for a second in the direction of the market, then jumped up and clicked his heels—something he hadn't done lately—and took a deep breath. He and Fiona were going sailing together. Amazing! He had scored!

Chapter Four

Sitting in *Kittiwake's* cockpit at 8:25 in the morning, Joe kept a lookout for Fiona. He had been up early, cleaning up the cabin and making sure he had coffee and tea at the ready. The sun was still low enough to reflect its cheery red glow off Rathlin Island and the mirror-still surface of the Sound. There were a few stratus clouds to the north, and a hint of dark cumulous to the distant west. Except for the lack of wind, it promised to be a good day to be out on the water.

Several times during the night, he had awakened, thinking about the spirited Fiona. For someone who was supposed to be spying on bad guys, Joe certainly was off track. But there's more to life than that, he thought. Forget spying. He was going to have the company of a very pretty girl, who likely was ten years younger than he. Except for Big Ryan, he had enjoyed little contact with the local people. Many of the women, in fact, seemed guarded and standoffish. Since his arrival, he had been developing a sense of loneliness, and the separation from Mary hadn't helped. He had tried to put her out of his mind, and speculating about Wade's relations with her didn't help.

The word *jealous* flashed across his consciousness, but then he spotted Fiona coming down the ramp to the floating docks, and all musing ceased. She was dressed in navy blue slacks with a white blouse and had her auburn hair under a scarf. In her left hand was a black rain jacket. He stood up and waved until she saw him. He climbed quickly over the lifelines and hurried up the dock. It was all he could do to keep from hugging her.

"What a fine boat now," she exclaimed as they walked back to *Kittiwake.* "I've never been on a yacht before." He took her jacket and helped her climb aboard.

"So many ropes," she said. "Are you going to teach me about them?"

Joe was smiling. In fact, he hadn't quit smiling. "Oh, yes…uh, aye." He was trying to pick up the colloquialisms. "I expect to make regular crew out of you."

She peered into the cabin. "Oh, just like a wee cottage in there. May I go down?"

"Of course. Make yourself at home."

She climbed down the ladder. Joe followed, and she watched as he stood bent over. "Ooh, a might tall for standing in here are you?" She grinned. "Not many Irishmen are so high as you."

"It's been my experience that Irishmen go to the pub and find another way to get high," he joked, noting that she was a good eight inches shorter.

"Too true, aye, too true," she laughed as she looked around.

She refused his offer of tea, so they climbed back on deck.

"You've done a bit of sailing in your time?"

"More than ought to be allowed, I suppose." He told her a little about being a professional boat captain, about where he was from, his former life in business, that he was divorced and so on. When he mentioned divorce, she frowned for an instant then turned away. Joe realized that, having seen the crucifix on the wall in the store, she probably was Roman Catholic and therefore might not approve of divorce.

"And do you have a boat back home?"

"Yes, but it needs some work. I've got it in storage." He raised the portside cockpit seat to pull out an inflatable personal floatation jacket.

"Would you like to wear this PFD?""

"Do you think I need it?" she asked, holding it up as if it were some strange creature. "I can swim if need be. Oh, you don't suppose I'll be needing to, do you?"

Joe grinned. "I hope not. It's a very calm day, anyway. I doubt we'll have any trouble." He took it back and stored it away. "The water here's pretty cold, as you know. So I'd hate to have to swim back in, with or without one of those."

"Only a few weeks ago, a fisherman, a dear man, fell from his boat and drowned. It was not far from here, down the coast where the eddies swirl. Out all alone, I heard. No one to help him."

Joe shook his head sadly. Going to sea, he understood, can be a dangerous business. He started the engine and began taking in the mooring lines, asking Fiona to hold the forward spring line until he could get underway. She did so with great seriousness and awaited his instruction to release it. *A good crew*, he thought, *almost as good as Mary*. But he pushed the image of Mary out of his mind and maneuvered away from the dock and out toward the pass. Fiona sat down and watched with great interest, giving him a big smile.

"Unfortunately, there's not but a breath of wind this morning," he said as they entered the Sound. In fact, it did not appear worthwhile to raise any sails at all. He glanced across at Rathlin Island six miles away. "Would you like to go to Rathlin? I've been in the harbor but haven't seen the whole island."

Fiona nodded. "I've not seen that bonnie rugged island for years. It would be a lark indeed."

"Great," Joe replied. He looked over his navigation chart and chose a course to Church Bay, checking to be sure there were no shoals to avoid. Seeing none, and because it was slack water at high tide, he steered directly toward the little group of buildings that appeared as little specks in the bright sun.

Sitting in the cockpit in front of him and taking in the view, Fiona took a more relaxed position, putting her leg across the seat, revealing her lovely white calf. She glanced at Joe, saw him looking at her, and smiled. Self-consciously, Joe looked down at the throttle, adding power and setting the RPM's to give them a pleasant cruise across the Sound.

"How did you come to visit Ireland?"

"Oh, I'd always heard how beautiful it is here, and I needed a little vacation." He stood up. "Would you like to steer?" She grimaced and looked uncertain. "Come on. I'll teach you."

Fiona crawled back to sit beside him. He showed her how he was steering a course by the compass. "But you can pick out an object on the island and just steer toward it," he instructed, becoming conscious of her hip touching his as she concentrated on the wheel.

"Seamus ne're would allow it," she said. "The steering I mean." Joe wondered briefly if it was the touching of hips she meant wouldn't be allowed.

"Seamus?" he asked, pretending he did not know about her relationship with the man.

"Seamus O'Leary, who runs the fishing trawler." She paused. "I guess you noticed him at Eamon's that night I saw you there?"

Joe nodded with a disapproving look. "Oh yeah, I saw him." They exchanged a glance of understanding, and then Fiona looked away.

"He never would let a woman touch the wheel of *his* boat," she said.

"You've known him a while, I take it?"

"An old friend to my brothers," she said. "Close to Peter and Timothy. We all grew up together."

"So you have two brothers?"

"Aye, two, but only one living, you see." She crossed herself. "Peter, the oldest, was taken to the Lord long before his time."

"I see," Joe said with sympathy. "Some kind of accident?"

She shook her head, frowning. "T'was no accident but a low, low deed by the Prods, I can tell you. Poor Peter was murdered, he was."

"I'm so sorry. The Prods, you say?"

"The bloody Protestants. Oh I don't mean all the Prods. It's the bloody Orangemen, or their like."

"Was it during The Troubles?" Joe recalled his briefing at The Farm. "What happened?"

She looked at him as if he were a naïve child. "A life of struggle we were born to, living in north Belfast."

"It's hard to imagine," he said. "Maybe you could tell me about it sometime."

Fiona shivered slightly, then forced a smile. "Now how could it be that we're on such a subject out here on this grand yacht in the fine spring air. Let's just enjoy the present and have a wee good time. And how about that tea you offered. What do y'say?"

"If you like," Joe replied, thinking it best to drop the subject, for the moment anyway. He asked if she felt comfortable steering by herself for a few minutes. Looking aft, he noticed the ferry was coming out of the harbor at Ballycastle.

"Just keep the boat pointed toward the little white church on the island, and let the ferry steer around you. He'll stay out of your way."

She anxiously looked back at the approaching ferry and then at him.

"It'll be fine," Joe smiled and dared to pat her on the shoulder on his way below.

As he lighted the little one-burner stove and put on some water, Joe pondered what it must have been like for her to experience such traumatic events in her childhood. He wondered how much he should ask about her older brother's participation in the Irish Republican Army. Perhaps he could pose his questions in a generalized kind of inquiry. It would be interesting to know what Ryan would say about Peter's murder. Would he have considered him a hero or a thug?

Waiting for the tea to brew, he stood in the shadows below and peered out at Fiona, this young lady he barely knew. From his few flirtatious advances, he certainly had made friends with her quickly. Having a boat and being able to offer a bit of fun on the water was an easy way to attract women, he had learned long ago. And if she were the poor working girl she seemed to be, then it was no wonder she had jumped at the invitation. He'd like to know more about the murdered brother, and he'd pry a little deeper at first opportunity. Then for a topic of conversation, he thought of using the Irish Republican Army medallion found on his wrecked boat *Tartan*, the boat now rotting away in the Coast Guard impoundment in Miami. Digging around in his toiletry bag, he found the object and put it in his pocket. There was a slim chance Fiona might offer some information about what the medallion signified.

"Have you run into anything yet?" he called pleasantly as he carried the tea topside.

Looking a little anxious with both hands gripping the wheel, she nodded with her head toward a wake to port. "No, but I wasn't too happy when that ferry came by."

Joe saw she had veered way to the right to keep away from the larger craft. "You've done very well," he said, slipping in beside her again. He handed her the mug of tea, with 'a wee spot o' milk' as she'd requested. As he took over steering, he noticed a bit of breeze beginning to stir. "We should be able to sail on the return trip. You have to be back to go to work at four?"

"Not to worry." She looked pleasantly comfortable now. "My brother Tim said he could fill in for me." She had taken off her scarf, and the wind blew her hair, revealing her scar. She caught Joe looking at it and met his gaze.

"Noticed my scar now, have you?" She ran a finger across it.

"I'm sorry," he replied. "I just happened to see it."

"It's a mark from childhood," she said. "A proud sign of my past."

"Oh really?" Joe said. "Tell me."

"Here now, some other time." She looked away and sipped her tea. Joe thought it better to let the subject drop.

"Is your tea okay?"

"Very nice cuppa," she said with a sly smile, "at least for one made by an American, anyway." For that, Joe gave her a little poke in the ribs. She wriggled in the seat, laughed and poked him back, their legs touching. *Now, that's fun,* Joe thought. She certainly was not standoffish.

They soon motored into Church Bay and steered for the harbor jetty, passing near a lone buoy. Fiona explained that it marked the location of the remains of *HMS Drake,* sunk by a German torpedo during the war.

"Bloody Brits should have kept their ship at home," she replied. Joe raised his eyebrows in reaction to her negative attitude toward the British but didn't comment.

He turned *Kittiwake* toward the floating docks. Fiona volunteered to handle the lines as Joe maneuvered alongside. She obviously liked boating and was more than willing to help, which pleased him greatly. As they climbed off the boat and walked ashore, the pontoon-supported dock wobbled slightly under their weight, giving Joe a chance to take her hand. Smaller than his, her hand had a surprisingly strong grip, more than he would have expected in a beautiful young woman.

A group of about 20 passengers from the ferry boarded the one available tour bus, which stood at the head of the pier just below the small stone inn. Fiona said they should take it, so they hurried over and climbed aboard. With a happy greeting and wave, the driver sat down and announced that this trip 'would be for the birds,' pun intended. He gunned the engine and started up a steep and winding incline on a narrow one-lane road. Acting also as the tour guide, he talked incessantly as the bus careered around apparently impossible curves along the ridge. After a mile or so, the driver put on a bird-beaked mask that made him look like a puffin and told his spiel of jokes, interspersed with bits of information about the island. Along the way there were ruins of houses, some mere piles of faded whitewashed stones, destroyed long ago. Once there were as many as 10,000 living on Rathlin, the driver told them, but today there were only about 100.

The bus took them to Bull Point, a high cliff at the western-most tip of the island. They followed a path and walked down steep stone stairs cut into the dark brown rock. Below them, several white gannets with six-foot wingspan soared above ocean waves that crashed against the cliff.

"They say that 250,000 sea birds nest here in June and July," Fiona said as they stood overlooking the water. "T'is a bit early in the season, but when all the birds arrive, the din of all such squawking here is enough to wake the dead." As they crossed over a few rougher steps, Joe offered Fiona his hand again. She took it with a little squeeze. He squeezed back and resisted the urge to pull her close and offer a kiss. *Don't press your luck,* he thought.

"What a wonderful spot," he commented, as they walked back to the bus.

"Aye," Fiona answered, soberly. "But the island's scarred with a terrible history as well."

"Really? That's hard to imagine."

She gave him an impatient look. "You know so little of our country."

As they rode back to the harbor, Fiona recited some of what she knew. "It was the Vikings first who landed on the island, burning and pillaging the poor native Gaelic farmers. Then centuries later, Robert the Bruce sought refuge here in a cave. Then with his brother Edward, he launched a bloody invasion."

"Was that when the Scots began to settle in Ireland?" Joe asked.

"Settle?" she repeated. "Invade's more like it. That was only the beginning. Two centuries later, when Henry VIII broke from the Church, the real problems began. There was a great massacre of Catholics on Rathlin in 1575. Perhaps as many as 3000, including women and children, were thrown over the cliffs into the sea." She sighed deeply. "The nuns who run our schools teach this to all good Catholic children."

They rode in silence back to the harbor while Joe pondered what she'd told him. Irish history evidently was important to Fiona and apparently had been taught to her like sacred doctrine. Joe wondered how differently the facts might be presented in Protestant schools.

They enjoyed a sandwich and beer at the little pub east of the docks. Afterwards, they hiked down the narrow road along the rocky beach and passed a monument commemorating Robert the Bruce.

"Just another invader," she said bitterly. "He means little to us who are the true Irish." Then she looked up at him. "Here now," she said, "I'm getting too serious on a fine day in the company of a very good man."

"I'm glad you're telling me these things," Joe replied, "sharing your feelings or whatever." They exchanged smiles, and she offered her hand as they walked back toward the docks.

On the passage back to Ballycastle, there was wind enough to hoist the mainsail, unfurl the genoa, and sail on a broad reach. Fiona was thrilled Joe let her steer while under sail. Again they sat together at the helm, and he put his arm around her, to which she snuggled a little closer. In the intimacy of the situation, he began to feel more and more relaxed in their relationship. Then he pulled the medallion from his pocket to show her. She looked at him in surprise.

"Where did you get that?"

Joe shrugged innocently. "I found it." He flipped it over as if he'd not yet examined it. He pointed to the inscription and attempted to read it. "Ogla na hhere-ann," he said in his southern drawl.

48

"Óglaigh na hÉireann," Fiona pronounced correctly. "Where did you get it now?"

Joe shrugged innocently. "I found it on the street one day. I thought someone had dropped a coin, and I just picked it up."

"I don't know that you should be carrying that on your person."

"Oh? Why not?" Joe held it up and studied it as if for the first time. "What does it mean?"

"It's an icon of one group of the IRA," she said, "the Irish Republican Army. You needn't be concerned with such as that. But if certain people saw you had it, they might not understand, so to speak."

"Back home we read lots of stories and novels about the IRA," Joe said. "But I thought that organization ended back in the '90's."

"Away with your stories," Fiona scoffed. "What do Americans know of our life?" She frowned then bit her lip sadly. Silently, she wriggled out of the helm seat and moved to the forward part of the cockpit, staring off toward Ballycastle. Joe followed her eyes, and saw Seamus O'Leary's *Red Dagger* coming out of the harbor.

"O'Leary," he said. "Your friend."

"More than a friend," she said. "I've known him ever since I was a teenager, after all." Fiona looked at Joe with great seriousness. "Such a good time I've had today. But I dare not go with you again."

"Oh, why?" Joe asked, surprised by the finality of her statement. "Did I do something wrong?"

Fiona looked down, and when she looked back up at him, he could see she was upset. "No, Joe. You've done nothing. I'm sorry. It's very complicated. That's all I can say." She sat down on the starboard seat where she would not be in view of the distantly passing trawler and stared off toward land. "I must be getting to the store soon as we can, if you don't mind."

Joe paused, then shrugged with resignation and started the engine. "This won't add but a couple of knots of speed," he said, putting it in gear and moving up the throttle. "But I'll do the best I can."

As they sailed on, Joe tried but was unable to spark much conversation. He offered to let her steer again, but she only shook her head. When they were 100 yards from the jetty, he slowed the engine, locked the wheel, and moved forward to take in the sails. When he began to prepare the mooring lines, she said she could help with them. They motored to the dock where she managed to cleat the forward lines. While he shut down the engine, she immediately began to climb ashore.

"Whatever I did, I'm so very sorry," he said.

She paused and turned to look at him. "You did nothing, Joe. 'Tis I who's in the wrong."

He sensed something he had not understood before. "I can tell that you feel trapped or something, don't you, Fiona?"

She looked at him with that same intensity in her eyes he had noted the first time he saw her. Her lips drew back as if to smile but with a sudden quiver in her chin, a spasm, nearly a sob. Her eyes expressed for only an instant a look of deep longing. And then she forced a smile.

"Thank you for a lovely day." Tears formed and she wiped a hand across her face.

He was moved by the strength of her feelings, and his own. "May I walk with you somewhere?"

"No need," she replied, turned away and hurried down the dock.

"May I see you again?" he called after her.

She did not turn to look back but merely shook her head. He watched her graceful figure striding away, and his desire for her was only increased the more.

"I'm not giving you up, sweet Fiona," he whispered. "I don't care what O'Leary thinks about it."

As he started to go below, it did occur to him that he might be losing his focus on the reason he had come to Northern Ireland in the first place.

Chapter Five

Joe took a new interest in sprucing up *Kittiwake* now that he was determined to entice Fiona to go sailing again. To make that attractive he'd have to bring the boat into topnotch condition. He washed and wiped and swabbed the decks, brought the cushions and mattresses topside to air, and inspected all the lines, stays and halyards. He found the topping lift fouled with the backstay and needed to climb the mast to fix it. In his younger years, pulling himself nearly 40 feet up a mast would not have been difficult, but being middle aged had changed all that. He phoned Big Ryan, and asked if he knew someone who could help. Ryan said he would be down himself. Clearly, the man was happy to have the opportunity to be around boats again.

Thankful for Ryan's friendship, Joe rummaged around in the forward hatch and happily found a boatswain's chair. The canvas seat was a bit mildewed and maybe not as sturdy as it should be. He rigged it to a halyard anyway and began climbing in. Hearing a rumble of boards, he looked around to see the giant perched atop an old bicycle, riding down the dock.

"So you need a wee lift up the mast, I see," Ryan said when he rode up. Joe thanked him for coming and strapped himself in. Big Ryan seized the winch handle and cranked so swiftly Joe had to ask him to slow it down a bit.

"Aye," Ryan laughed, not even close to being winded. "Don't want to give you a nose bleed."

Once the repair was complete, Ryan announced he was off to visit his brother. Joe watched as the big man was about to hop on the rusty bicycle that looked as if he'd owned it since childhood.

"Let me drive you there," Joe offered.

Ryan frowned. "My brother doesn't like seeing strangers. He's a cynical and ornery man. You could live your whole life without the profit of his acquaintance."

"It's no trouble. I'm not doing much anyway," Joe said, his curiosity peaked.

"Well now, 15 miles is not a wee venture on the bike," the giant replied. "So I'll be thanking you for it."

At Ryan's direction, Joe drove up the steep road above the harbor and took Route B17 to the west. They rode along the ridge above the coast, passing the road to Kenbane Castle, which Ryan explained was a "wee ruins" from medieval times. Soon the road snaked downward past the entrance to Carrick-a-rede rope bridge. It was a National Trust Tourist site, Ryan explained, and cautioned Joe to watch for big touring buses turning out of there. Slowing, still feeling a bit strange driving on the left, he negotiated the main street of Ballintoy. Once through the village, they passed the road to Ballintoy Harbor. Across a green meadow a white church sat perched above the cliff and was silhouetted against the blue ocean below with the dark cliffs of Rathlin Island beyond. Ryan pointed to a faint finger of land far out to sea.

"That's Islay," he said, pronouncing it *i-lee*, "the closest of the Scottish Hebrides."

"Maybe we can sail over there, one day," Joe said. "How far is it?"

"Thirty nautical miles or so," Ryan replied. "Best pick a good weather day," he said. "You cross the shipping lanes from out of the Clyde and Irish Sea, and in fog you risk collision with some huge freighter that'll never know you were there." He told Joe to slow and turn at the next left, on the road with a sign to Moss Side. Again ascending a hill, they began to pass fields of green sprouting grain, meadows of sheep and cows, the land delineated by ageless gray stone fences. After a few miles, the big man had Joe turn onto a narrow dirt lane where grass made swishes against the tires.

Joe was about to ask how much farther, when he spotted the rear of a jeep-like vehicle with a ragged canvas top. There was a small flock of sheep walking along in front of it. And there was a man's hand stuck out of the right window, waving at the sheep, herding them along.

"My brother, Jack," Ryan said. "Don't drive too close."

Joe saw there was an open gate beyond and realized the man was shooing the sheep into a pen. He slowed to a crawl but was so fascinated he drove right up behind the jeep. Suddenly, the flock bolted away *en masse*, charging past the vehicle then running wildly by Joe's car, bumping and scraping it and bleating crazily. The man opened the door of the jeep, and a black and white dog jumped out. It charged past them in a blur, galloping by the running sheep. Once in front of the flock, it turned and snarled. The sheep halted, milling around in confusion. Then bleating and ramming into one another, they came running back, the dog nipping at the feet of any that tried to stray. Within a minute, the border collie had herded every sheep inside the pen. The man, who had a slight limp, stumbled over to close the gate. The dog came out just as he did so, its tongue hanging out, panting and its tail wagging. Once the gate was secure, the man looked back at them with a scowl.

Joe and Ryan got out, and Joe followed him over to greet the sheep herder.

"What an amazing dog!" Joe said. "I wish I had taken a video of that." As he approached, he noticed the man was slightly rotund, balding but shaggy white-haired, and maybe in his sixties. Under his rumpled and dirty tan coat was a priest's clerical collar.

"I wish ye'd go away and mind yer own business," the man replied. Joe started to apologize for frightening the sheep, but realized the remark had been not for himself but for Big Ryan.

"Glad to see you, too, Brother Jackie," Ryan said. The man gave a 'whatever' wave and headed toward his vehicle. Joe and Ryan exchanged glances, Ryan shaking his head and shrugging.

Ryan followed his brother over to his vehicle. "Just came to see about you."

"Thought youse came to be spooking me sheep." Jack reached in the back seat of the jeep, pulled out a half-empty whiskey bottle and took a big swig.

"I'd hoped you'd stopped that," Ryan scolded. Jack replied by taking another big swig, wiped his mouth on his dirty sleeve, and offered the bottle to Ryan.

"Never at such an hour as this," Ryan refused, shaking his head, "and surely not poteen." The brother simply shrugged and drank again.

"And what about your mate here?" Jack offered the bottle to Joe. Joe declined politely.

"This is Joe Anderson," Ryan said, "an American that's come over to do a wee bit of sailing."

"Lost yer way, have you?" the man staggered slightly as he shook Joe's outstretched hand. "And what do you want to get out of this god forsaken land?"

"Gosh, I'm surprised to hear you call it god forsaken. I'd say this is one of the most beautiful countries I've ever seen."

"Ah, the land is lovely, beautiful indeed. T'is the men that spoil it, you know," Jack said, finally letting go of Joe's hand. He leaned against his battered car and took another swig. He glanced at Ryan. "I don't drink so much by myself. It's when you come around I feel the need."

"Oh, aye, it's me to blame for sure." Ryan shook his head. "Your blood's probably yellow as piss from all that poteen." He grabbed Jack's wrist, held it up and looked at the bottle. "Where do you get such rot-gut as this?"

"My neighbor makes it." Jack nodded toward the adjoining field. "Old family recipe." He laughed, and jerked his hand and bottle away. The two brothers stared at one another in silence.

"Is that a clerical collar you're wearing?" Joe said, hoping to change the subject. Jack gave a slight shrug.

"Once he was a grand priest," Ryan explained, "but now..."

"Aw, *now* yourself," Jack shoved Ryan in the chest with his bottle-filled hand. "And what are you, *now*, my fine brother? A man as tired of life as I? Not the mariner, not harbourmaster anymore? Why, beaten down you be, of course, just like myself. Worn down by people and their godless meanness... The evils of the Emerald Isle. Oh, thank God for sheep, and for their innocence." He stumbled over to a little bank by the gate and slumped down to sit. His dog came over and licked his hand. He patted the dog a moment and then looked at Joe and his eyes narrowed. "And as for you, American. I know you're here for something devious and wrong. I am not fooled; I know men too well."

Joe managed a smile. "I just thought a visit to Ireland would be a nice thing..."

"And what do you know about Ireland, exactly? The history? Tell me, just what do you know?"

"Not much," Joe admitted. "I know that St. Patrick brought Christianity and ran away all the snakes."

"Now see, you're already wrong," Jack said, sitting up. "Patrick may have run out the reptiles but he brought in the Christian snakes, worser beasts, and they've abounded ever since."

"The liquor's gone to your head, Jackie," Ryan warned.

"Oh, you think so, do you?" the ex-priest replied, a fiery look coming into his eyes. He focused on Joe, with an accusatory look. "I'll take yer confession now. What in the name of all the saints are you doing here?"

Joe grimaced. "Just here to learn something about Ireland, I guess."

"Learn about Ireland, is it? Well, you want the sweetness and light? The leprechauns and the shamrocks? Or do you want the real story?"

"I know a little," he said. "Ryan's been filling me in." He paused a second, wondering if he should mention Fiona and her story about The Troubles. "Just yesterday a young lady named Fiona was telling me about growing up in Belfast. She said her father and brother both were killed by the British side."

"Bejesus," Ryan interrupted, "Is it Fiona Brennan you've been after? I hoped you had better sense."

"She's a pretty girl," Joe said apologetically. "I don't know why everybody thinks she's not available."

"You don't know anything," Ryan warned. "Not about that O'Leary she goes with, and you don't know her friends. That's all I'm saying to you."

"I know she's Catholic," Joe protested. "I know she has a lot of reason to dislike the loyalists or whatever. I guess that's just her family history."

"Oh, just her history, you think?" Jack staggered to his feet. "And you think family history is a mere trifle in Ireland. Well, Mr. American, you know nothing of what her history may mean. Anyone who thinks he knows the history of Ireland, does not, you hear? Does not, does he, Ryan?"

"And I suppose you intend to tell him," Ryan said. "Might as well sit you down, Joe, till me brother gets his bloody sermon out."

The eyes of the priest, or shepherd or whatever he was, immediately took on a more sober, more intelligent expression. "For centuries," he began in a clearer voice, "this island home of ours has been subjected to the paranoia of its too-close neighbor, Britain, which has not wanted to rule Ireland so much as it wanted to deny rule and occupation of Ireland by Catholic France and other European nations. Henry II—have you heard of King Henry II?—He was granted lordship over Ireland in 1169 by a papal bull, supposedly issued by Pope Adrian IV. Now if that's true, and some scholars say it was a forgery by Henry himself, then the British who have always hated us Irish, had the pope's blessing to take lordship over us." He glanced at Ryan. "Isn't that ironical?"

Ryan shrugged. "They treat us like a stepchild, I think. Always have."

Jack nodded. "Essentially beginning in the 16th Century with Elizabeth, who was burdened with solving all the problems her father Henry VIII caused, English rulers have offered land grants to Protestant Scots and English to settle here and serve as landlords. It was all an effort to control the rebellious, untamed Celtic Catholic-leaning population. In simplest terms, this subjection of the native Irish by Scot and English landlords disenfranchised the native Irish people from the land, forcing them to live by subsistence farming. No telling how many poor wretches starved, especially during the famines."

"Here now," Ryan said. "The man didn't ask for a full-blown lecture."

"If he wants to know what a hell of a place he's come to," the priest said, "then let him hear." He looked back at Joe, took another swallow of home brewed whiskey and continued.

"The Catholic Church was strongly embedded in the hearts and minds of Gaelic-speaking Irish ever since their conversion by Saint Patrick in the 6th Century. Unwilling to relinquish its influence, even after Henry VIII's Reformation and breakaway, the Catholic Church nevertheless continued to impose its stern religion and narrow-minded education on the indigenous Irish people. As you might expect, this created a very polarized society, with native Irish segregated

61

from the Protestant Scot and English gentry." He glanced at Ryan. "You'll agree with that, won't you, brother?"

"Aye," Ryan said. "Polarized to the point of impoverishing our people."

Jack nodded. "There became two distinct ethnic groups, separated not only economically but also religiously and culturally. This division carried over from the farms to the villages and then the industrial towns. A kind of tribalism grew, particularly among the less educated, less urbane labor classes. In cities, Belfast and Londonderry mainly, Catholics and Protestants became more and more separated by misunderstanding and hatred. It was exacerbated by the fostering of traditions based upon historical heroes and myths, and fueled by economic hardship and competition for jobs."

He was interrupted when his dog jumped up and ran off barking, in pursuit of a rabbit that had unexpectedly appeared. Jack clapped his hands. "Whelan!" he shouted. "Here. You wild and silly bitch. Come here, I say."

Joe was amazed to see the dog immediately turn and trot back to her master, tongue out, panting. She came and sat at his feet. The priest reached down and stroked her head. Then he took another pull from the bottle. "Now, where was I? Oh. yes. By the 19th Century, efforts by the British government to rectify the social problems had come too-little, too-late. Ireland always was England's stepchild, offering little to increase British wealth. But because of its geographical position, Ireland was always viewed as strategically important to the defense of the larger island of

Britain." He paused and glanced at Joe. "Am I going too fast for you?" he said with muted sarcasm.

"I'm with you," Joe said. The priest raised his eyebrows in a half-mocking way, took yet another swallow of poteen and continued.

"With the advent of the French Revolution, and increasing any time that Celtic Catholics thought about independence, a kind of sociological paranoia swept over the British. But this paranoid reaction was even stronger among the Protestant population in Ireland, who recognized their own vulnerable status as a minority. While the indigenous Irish clamored for their own nation, the Protestants feared their own waning power over these people whom they had subjected to poverty for centuries. Frightened by the prospect that Britain might abandon them, Protestants formed such organizations as the Orange Order, the Ulster Volunteer Force, the breakaway Free Presbyterian Church of Ian Paisley, and other reactionary groups. On the other side, Catholics joined the Irish Republican Army and a host of equally radical separatist and nationalist sects. And you know what? It was the religious leaders, the men of the cloth, the reverend bunch of both Protestant and Catholic bigots, who led all this dissension."

"And they're the ones you were calling snakes a few minutes ago?" Joe asked.

"Oh, there be lots more snakes than those," Ryan added.

"You're coming around, are you, Brother Ryan?" Jack chuckled. "While the 20th Century partitioning of the

63

island into the Republic on one hand and six of the Ulster counties, called Northern Ireland, essentially satisfied those in the south, the north erupted into decades of civil unrest, terrorism and violence, which The Royal Ulster Constabulary, the British Army and the clandestine Security Force were unable to control. Even though significant and substantial reconciliation and compromise had been achieved by the beginning of the 21st Century, disparate organizations of extremists on both sides still operate in the undercurrent of society, disturbing the peace and creating additional mayhem and hatred. Economic recession in recent years has aggravated the discontent of the labor classes." He paused and swigged at the bottle again. "Any questions?"

Impressed and amazed at the man's recall of history, Joe thought a moment and then asked, "Why don't those who want to be Irish just move into the Republic, and those who want to be British immigrate to Northern Ireland?"

The priest smiled. "Now isn't that a sensible thing to ask?" He sighed. "An economist would simply reply that people have to remain where they own land, or hold down jobs, or believe that they have opportunities to succeed—that those things determine where people decide to live. And during the heyday of the Celtic Tiger, the time when the Republic of Ireland was one of the fastest growing economies on the earth, many did immigrate south into the new nation." He paused. "But the Irish, my friend, are not driven solely by such rational considerations. In fact, to accuse an Irishman of acting on what the British call *common sense* would be to misunderstand the Celtic race entirely. No, an Irishman is a complex tangle of love, hate, tragedy and foolhardiness that only poetry can explain. He is the crusader of lost causes and the hero of misapprehended fate... And how do I know?" He turned up the bottle and drained it dry. Then he staggered back and fell down, ending in a sitting position against the fence. "Why?" he now was slurring badly. "I know, sir, the Lord bless my soul, because I'm Irish." As the last words slurred across his lips, his eyes closed. "I know because I'm as guilty as any." He gritted his teeth in pain. "Damned I be... like all the rest." He burped loudly and slumped over in a heap. Whelan rushed over and licked his face.

"Jesus, Mary and Joseph," Ryan exclaimed, leaning over the prone figure. "He's passed entirely out!"

No amount of shaking and face slapping could awaken the man. Ryan and Joe hoisted him into the right front seat of the jeep, and then Ryan got behind the wheel and drove to a nearby farm house. Joe followed in the rental car. A strong young woman came out to help them get the priest into the house and then in bed. Introduced to Joe merely as "Breana," she thanked them for taking care of her father and said he had slept off drunkenness before and likely would sleep out this one, too.

On the way back to Ballycastle, Ryan talked about his brother. "Sometimes a man with such a brain as Jack's cannot withstand what he has lived through," Ryan said. "He left the priesthood in '98 because he simply could not abide any more of The Troubles. Something happened. It was too much, and that was when he bought the wee farm, bought some sheep to tend, and turned to drink." He shook his head

65

sadly. "Neither I nor Breana nor the Church itself have been able to help him."

"I'm sorry," Joe replied.

"Such an idealist he was as a boy, but now he's a great cynic."

"What changed him, you think?"

Ryan looked far off. "The priesthood, I think. Or perhaps taking a stand during The Troubles that was unwise. Too much power over people in any case. It finally ruined him."

"I'll have to say he surely gave one of the most impressive history lectures I've ever heard. Gosh! What an insightful interpretation!"

Ryan chuckled. "Before you hang too many accolades upon my brother, you might remember what he said about Irish history. How did he put it? 'Anyone who thinks he understands Irish history surely does not'."

They rode in silence for a while. Joe's thoughts again turned to the lovely and vivacious Fiona.

"You know," he said, "I just can't get Fiona off my mind. Know what I mean? The way her family was subjected to all that violence and everything. What a terrible amount of emotional baggage she must be carrying."

The big man wheeled around in his seat to look at Joe. "And so you want a part of it, do you? I'll say it one last time. You do not know what I know, and by all that's holy, I cannot and will not tell you." He pointed his big, gnarled finger. "You'll stay far away from Fiona and her likes if you know what's good for you."

Chapter Six

Instead of making a long list for the grocery, Joe decided to buy only a few items at a time. This would necessitate going to Hillside Market often, and that would mean more opportunities to see Fiona. Always in the back of his mind was the admonition from Adams, his handler, 'don't get involved.' Even so, Joe had to admit he couldn't get her off his mind. The way she suddenly rejected him the day they went sailing only served to make him more interested. And the way she had looked at him on more than one occasion had convinced him she might only be playing coy. But something had given him the impression that she must feel trapped, probably by her relationship with O'Leary, and surely she was not really in love with that unsavory character.

Joe tore off the top of his grocery list and went up on deck. A couple of transient sailboats had arrived in the marina, one flying the French Tricolor and the other the United Kingdom's Red Ensign. Evan Foster, with his dog Bounder on a leash, was walking down the dock toward the two transients. He spoke to two men likely in their early thirties aboard the French boat. It seemed Foster was giving them instructions about signing in for a stay. Meanwhile Bounder was very busy sniffing around the boat, almost as if attracted by a scent of some kind. He strained at the leash and halfway climbed aboard before Foster pulled him back on to the dock. The animal whimpered and then let out a deep growl.

"Twenty quid for the night if you mean to stay," Joe heard Foster say. "To be paid in advance before youse hook up to shore power and such." He didn't sound very cordial, but Joe had not found him ever to be polite or friendly anyway. He continued to watch as Foster went to the British boat, going through the same conversation with its crew. What was curious was the way Bounder continued to sniff around, pulling on the leash as if wanting to go back to the first boat. The dog's behavior reminded Joe of canines brought through the queue at British Immigration when he first had arrived in Belfast. Was Bounder a trained drug-sniffing dog? If so, then was Foster a narc? Or was it explosives he was trained to detect?

Remembering the groceries and the chance to run into Fiona at the market, Joe put his curiosity aside and headed up the dock to the street. On the way he noted that Seamus O'Leary's trawler was not at its mooring. Its curious comings and goings he had made a habit of keeping up with.

Sure enough, Fiona was behind the counter, wearing a pullover powder blue blouse that allowed just the top of the vee between her medium breasts to show. What a lovely statuesque creature, he thought, his pulse quickening. She was checking out groceries for a lady and there were a couple more people in line. Fiona looked up with a concerned expression when he came in, but glanced quickly away, continuing her work. Joe spoke as he came by. The ladies all looked up and stared at him while Fiona merely nodded. Joe walked on back to gather the things he needed.

"So how are you keeping?" he asked when he reached the counter and put the groceries in front of her.

"Learning our expressions are you. I'm keeping very well, and you?"

"More lonely than anything," he said. She looked down and didn't respond. He swallowed. "I was a little hurt when you left me so quickly last week. After our sail, I mean." There was a slight pause. She breathed deeply and then looked up.

"Merely a headache. I meant not to be rude." She smiled. "A nice outing, it was." Their eyes met, and then she began sacking his groceries.

"Could we go to dinner one night?" He almost stammered like a teenager. "I mean, tonight even, if you're not busy."

She stared at him a moment, looked away, and bit her lip. Joe realized he was holding his breath. Then she looked back. "Perhaps another night," she said. "I'll be working late today."

"Well, a drink afterwards, maybe?" He wondered how far he could push. "I could meet you at Eamon's Bar."

"I rarely go there anymore," she replied, frowning slightly. Joe recalled that, the first time he'd seen her, she looked very comfortable there with her friends, but he said nothing.

"Or we could go sailing again," he pressed.

"Someday, perhaps," she said. "Give me your wee cell number, and I'll call you." An old lady made her way to the counter and began putting a bottle of milk and some cans up to be purchased. Fiona spoke to her and concentrated on scanning her items. Joe wrote down his number and laid it on the counter. Fiona swept it up before the old lady could notice and nodded at him.

"See you soon, I hope," Joe said. Fiona frowned and shrugged, obviously not wanting to talk in front of others. Joe shrugged and headed for the door.

Leaving Fiona on that note, and heading toward the marina, he encountered her brother Timothy Brennan coming up the street. Joe glanced away, not being particularly attracted to the young man with his head recently shaved bald and a couple of ugly tattoos on both arms. Joe had not forgotten how he twisted Fiona's arm at that first meeting in the store. Joe looked for a way to avoid him, but the boy kept coming.

"Hi ya," Timothy said, giving a smile. "Fiona told me you took her sailing, showed her a good time, she said." He put out his hand. Joe rather reluctantly shifted his grocery sack to his left hand and shook hands. "Nice of you to take her out. She's been kept on a short string most of her life."

Joe nodded. "Glad to do it," he said. He tried to step on around and go but the young man blocked his way.

"Look, Joe," Timothy said. "It is Joe, right? I'd like to see me sis get a break, you know? Always hard at it at work and all. And tethered she is to that Seamus O'Leary what don't really love her nor she him."

Joe thought it extraordinary that this character would say something so direct and intimate. "So, why are you telling me this?" The brother grinned, and Joe noted he had lost a front tooth.

"Fiona's told me about you," Timothy said. "You seem a good bloke. So, I just want to encourage you, that's all." He winked. "Give my sister a run if you like, and I'll put in a good word."

Joe stared at him for a moment, not sure whether to thank him or knock him on his ass. But alienating her brother certainly wouldn't score him any points with her, and the guy genuinely did seem to have his sister's welfare at heart.

"Thanks," Joe said. "Thanks..."

"Tim, call me Tim."

"I was just asking her if I could take her sailing again, or out to dinner sometime."

"Aye," Tim replied. "I'll try to talk it up with her." He smiled and touched Joe's arm. "We'll be seeing you around, I think." He gave Joe's arm a little squeeze and headed off toward the store. Rubbing his arm where he got that unusually affectionate squeeze, Joe warily watched him

73

go, wondering exactly what this character had up his sleeve. Was he what he seemed? Or was there something more behind all this? Maybe the boy had something against Seamus O'Leary, or something. In any case, Fiona certainly was a prize worth fighting for, even if he had to tolerate her brother.

Heading on down to the marina, Joe felt encouraged, his hopes now renewed. He even spoke to Evan Foster, as the man and his dog headed toward the dock master's office. Foster gave him a cursory nod and Bounder made a slight growl.

"Nice dog," Joe couldn't help but say. He gave Foster a smile, turning to watch man and dog go on up the hill. He got no reply, and he didn't care. He soon was going to have a date with Fiona!

He thought about going over and passing the time of day with the newly arrived sailors, but no one was visible around the British boat, and the two Frenchmen were just going below. Deciding he could meet them later, Joe climbed aboard *Kittiwake*. An ugly brown spot on the deck caught his eye. Having seen it before and having put off doing anything about it, he decided now was the time. Opening a compartment in the cockpit, he found the sandpaper and went to work on the blemish. After about 15 minutes, he had it sanded down enough and went for the can of undercoating.

Two uniformed officers of Police Service of Northern Ireland (PSNI) with a German Shepard on a leash came down the gangway to the docks. They went up to the French boat and called out to the occupants to come on deck. After a brief discussion, the officers with their sniffing and agitated dog went aboard and began what appeared to be a search. The officer with the dog went below while the other officer ordered the two Frenchmen to sit down in the cockpit. The policeman down below called something to the other. He made the Frenchmen go below. In a few minutes they all came topside again, this time with the Frenchmen in handcuffs. Joe could hear a distant police-car whooper. As the prisoners were led ashore, a couple of other police vehicles arrived. More officers came to inspect the French boat and put an impounding chain on it.

After it was all over, the vehicles all drove away, and the small crowd of bystanders along the street began to go on about their business. A bit excited by it all, Joe turned back to his varnishing job, while rethinking the events. One curiously odd thing was that Foster hadn't come out of his office to witness what occurred on the dock. Why not? Perhaps he was the one who had called the police to begin with? Joe thought about how Foster had brought his dog Bounder to the Frenchmen's boat, and then the police had come with another dog. Foster must be more than just the dock master, Joe surmised. Yes, he must be a policeman or something himself. In any case, the man always was strangely distant, especially to Joe. Did that mean anything? He decided that during his next scheduled call, he'd ask his handler, Adams, if he knew anything about this guy.

In the afternoon Joe took a shower in the shore facilities and dressed, just in case Tim had come through with arranging that date with Fiona. When suppertime came, he ate a few crackers and cheese but really wasn't hungry.

Nervous anticipation, he realized. As sunset turned to dusk, he still hadn't heard from her, and it was all he could do to avoid going back to the market to find her. He sat in the cockpit and watched the last rays of sunset. Then he checked his iPhone but found no recent calls or anything. Should he call her? he wondered but hesitated because she had said she would call him, and he was reluctant to push too hard. Besides, if Brennan actually was going to be encouraging her to date him, then Joe wanted to give him time to do so. Strange, it seemed, how brothers intervene with their sisters, he thought. Here was this brother Tim helping him establish a relationship, while back in Birmingham Mary's brother-in-law, Wade, was out to interfere in another. Giving up on the date with Fiona, Joe went below and turned in for the night. Lying awake for a while, he began to recall Mary back home and how things with her had gone so awry.

Chapter Seven

Six months earlier, after inspecting his hijacked, sunken trawler in Miami, Joe had driven all night to Birmingham. When he walked in the kitchen door at Mary's house, she threw her arms around him. Before he could speak, she kissed his lips, her long blond hair tickling his cheek.

"I'm so glad you're home!"

Joe sank into her warm, comfortable embrace, wondering how he ever could question being there. He looked over her shoulder at the bright room with strawberry patterns on a yellow background, now becoming so familiar. The heat was on, just enough to warm the early morning chill of mid-December. He smiled at Mary, noting again her beautiful greenish-blue eyes, so quick, intelligent and appraising.

"Did you see your boat?"

"Oh, don't even ask," he said, giving her a sweet kiss. "It's a terrible wreck. Mold, algae, barnacles. You can't imagine." He was interrupted by the unexpected sound of someone coming down the hallway. Surprised, Joe looked up to see a man in red striped pajamas and blue bathrobe walk into the kitchen. He was about Joe's age, though shorter than Joe's 6' 3" with black hair and brown eyes that appraised Joe coolly.

She took Joe's hand. "I'd like you to meet Wade, Earnest's younger brother. He's come to stay with us a few days. Isn't that nice?" Joe managed only a nod, pausing long enough to notice that the bathrobe belonged to her deceased husband, Earnest. Previously, Mary had given the bathrobe to Joe. Reluctantly, he offered his hand to Mary's brother-in-law. He had heard of the man but never actually met him.

Wade Johnston gave him a cursory handshake with little eye contact. "Hello, Sport," he said. "I've heard a lot about you." His tone seemed slightly challenging.

"I've heard a lot about you, too," Joe said. There was an awkward pause.

"Wade arrived last night. He's here for…"

"I'm going to Maxwell for some training," Wade broke in, "starting Monday." Joe realized he meant the Air Force Base in Montgomery, about a hundred miles south.

"I thought you were with CIA," Joe said, "not the Air Force."

"Drone Ops," Wade replied.

"Drone Ops? Whatever is that?" Mary asked.

"Oh, we deploy a robot sort of aircraft that takes pictures," he said and grinned maliciously, "and it shoots a nasty little missile at you if it likes."

78

She shuddered. "Sounds awful. And you're going to learn to fly those things?"

"Part of my job." He shrugged. "Say, what about some coffee?" Mary stared at him a moment, shook her head and then invited them to sit at the breakfast table. Wade led the way, sitting at the end. Less than pleased to be associating with this character, Joe took a seat in the middle, leaving Mary her usual place.

"So, how long are you here for?" Wade asked. Joe glanced at Mary. Hadn't she told this brother-in-law about their life together? Busy getting out coffee mugs, Mary apparently had not heard the man's question.

"I don't know," Joe replied, almost without thinking. Wade gave him an intense look.

"I need to get my bag out of the Mercedes." Joe got up. "Excuse me." Irritated by Johnston's question, he headed toward the garage. As the kitchen door was closing behind him, he heard Wade say, "So you let him drive the Mercedes to Florida?" It had an accusatorial ring.

Joe paused before going down the covered walkway toward the detached garage, barely noticing the yellow chrysanthemums he and Mary together had set out along the border garden. Gardening had become one of their pleasant pastimes. He opened the door and walked toward the steel gray roadster with a black top and stone leather seats. *She insisted that I drive the car to Miami*, he thought. Opening the trunk, he grabbed his overnight bag and, somewhat agitated, he slammed the lid. Wade had followed him out.

79

"Easy on that trunk lid, okay?" Wade said. Joe looked around and saw him walking around the car, inspecting it. "Needs that damn Florida salt washed off," he said, looking at Joe.

"I'll run it through the car wash when I fill it up."

"That's the least you could do," Wade said. He peered in the car window, shook his head slightly and gave Joe an accusing glance before heading back to the kitchen. Joe stared after him.

Is this your car? Joe nearly asked, but stifled it instead. *What is it with this guy? Is he something more to Mary than a brother?* Wondering exactly what this character was up to, he picked up his bag and headed into the kitchen. As he entered, he heard Wade say that he was going to shower and dress.

"Sit down, Joe dear, and I'll fix you something." Mary headed toward the refrigerator.

"Scotch, if you don't mind." He sat at the breakfast table. "I know it's early, but I need to wind down a little." This guy's imperious complaint about the car had upset him some, adding to his general unease. During the drive back from Miami, his three options had raced around in his head, keeping him on edge, the future seeming to be a swirling merry-go-round. And now there seemed to be some competition or challenge or something to his place with Mary.

"I'll give you both coffee and scotch," she said, refilling the coffee maker. He knew she thought he drank too much whiskey. Well, he had increased to three a night during Thanksgiving. She had asked him once if it meant he was worried, or not happy about something. He had replied simply that he'd enjoyed too much holiday cheer and would try to cut down, and he had. He knew she'd insist on his drinking the coffee first and then having the scotch. Such was the way things had been going since he came to live with her.

"How long is Wade staying?"

Mary glanced toward the hallway, apparently to be sure Wade wasn't within earshot. "He said his class begins Monday, so I imagine he will drive to Maxwell on Sunday."

"I didn't see his car."

"He wants to take the Mercedes." She looked apologetic. "We can get along with just one car. I hope you don't mind."

Joe shrugged. "No, of course not. I still have my old truck." The Roadster surely wasn't his car, even though Mary had insisted he use it.

"Wade likes that car. I guess it reminds him of Earnest. They were very close. Wade is such a dear." While she poured two coffees and brought them to the table, Joe wondered just how *dear* this brother-in-law was to her.

She sat down across from him. "So tell me more about your boat."

Joe eyed the mug and then pulled it toward him. "I probably could repair it, fix it up over time," he replied, sipping politely; he really didn't want coffee at the moment. "But it might just about kill me to do it," he added.

"It's that's bad? "I'm sorry."

"You know, I climbed down in the salon to take a closer look. There's a teak bar counter in there I had finished myself, put on 20 coats of varnish, sanding each one to make it shiny as a mirror. Now it's coated with barnacles. Then I pulled open the silverware drawer and there was a dead, half-decomposed crab. The odor was unbearable."

Mary reached across the table and took his hand. "We could hire someone to clean it all up," she said. "I'd love to help pay for it." Joe smiled at her, but shook his head.

"It's my problem, but thank you for offering," he said. "If I went down there and lived on the boat, I could use the money Alex paid me to fix it all up. Of course, just the repairs to the engine, electrical system and electronics would eat up most of that cash, and you can't get charters if the boat's appearance isn't pristine."

Mary sighed. "Is it really worth all that?"

He shrugged. "It's my life. Or it was, anyway."

"Listen, Joe dear," she squeezed his hand. "Earnest left me quite a lot of money, more maybe than you realize. I could buy you a new boat, if that's what it takes." She paused, seeing him shaking his head. "Yes, I could," she urged.

"I couldn't let you do that," he insisted.

"We could even move to the coast—maybe West Palm or Charleston or somewhere, so you could continue to be a boat captain and then come home to me at night."

He patted her hand and shook his head again. "I couldn't ask you to leave your home, Mary—away from all your friends and your country club, and your acting guild, and your bridge club and all those things." He looked at her seriously. "This is your life, dear Mary. This is who you are, and where you belong. I could never take you away from this."

"I love you, Joe." Mary's eyes lightened. "I know what. We could live here in the winter and somewhere on the coast in the summer. We can find some way to make it all work. You'll see."

He met her loving gaze for a long moment and then slid his chair over to give her a huge, tender hug. "I want to show you something," he said to change the subject. He reached in his pocket and pulled out a coin-like object he had found aboard *Tartan*.

"I found this in the salon." He passed it over to her. "It's a medallion of some kind."

Mary examined it curiously, turning it over several times. "Here's a lily inscribed above some words." She held it closer. "Óglaigh na hÉireann," she read slowly, trying to pronounce the phrase. "What does that mean?"

"I've been mulling that over," he replied. "See in the last part, the letters *e-i-r-e*. That means Ireland, doesn't it."

Mary found her iPhone. "Let's google it," she said, punching in the words. "Oh, look. Here it's in Wikipedia. It's Irish. Pronounced [ˈoːɡl̠ʲiː n̪ˠə ˈheːɾʲən̪ˠ]. It means *soldiers of Ireland*."

"I never saw it before," Joe said. "So I figure it was brought aboard by the basta... the people who stole my boat. They're some kind of 'Irish soldiers' maybe?"

"The name has been used most recently by some factions of the Irish Republican Army," Mary read on. "Something about The Troubles in Northern Ireland—all fighting and bombings and everything over the struggle for independence."

"I remember," Joe said, "in the '90's mainly. When 9/11 occurred in '01, we mainly forgot about it all, or it quieted over there or something." He paused. "But what's that got to do with stealing my boat in the Bahamas?"

"Who knows? But how terrible those men were in that boat that chased us and shot at us when we were on the Smiths' boat, trying to get to Charleston." She visibly shuddered. "I still have nightmares every now and then."

"Me, too," he admitted. "We sure were lucky to survive."

"What's that about Ireland?" Wade interrupted while standing in the hall doorway, about half dressed in slacks and T-shirt. Joe realized he had been there a minute or two without announcing his presence. It seemed a bit sneaky, but then who did this guy work for, CIA?

"Joe found this medallion thing on his boat," Mary said, holding it up to show Wade. He came over and took it from her. Joe held his tongue, but he wanted to object, to ask what business was it of Wade's?

"The boat that was hijacked, huh? Mary told me your tale about being marooned on some island for days." Wade smirked. "You sure you weren't just selling it to the insurance company?" He gave Mary a sly wink.

Joe didn't think much of his sarcasm. In fact, he was just about to tell this asshole off when Mary broke in.

"Unfortunately, it was not insured," she said. "The recession had hurt Joe's business so much he couldn't afford to insure the boat."

"Too bad," Wade said. "I was just kidding of course." While silently gritting his teeth, Joe watched in silence as Wade studied the medallion.

"Óglaigh na hÉireann," Wade read the inscription. "I've heard of it before. Good chance it's from the Irish Republican Army, or some splinter group from the original one, still engaging in acts of terrorism. They get a lot of backing from sympathizers here in the U. S. so we keep an eye on 'em all the time." He smirked. "You'd probably fit right in."

"What do you mean by that?" Joe had had just about enough. If Mary hadn't been present, he would have told Wade to take his little gratuitous jibes and shove it.

"Just joking again," Wade replied. "Say, let me borrow this thing, will you? I'd like to show it to some people at CIA."

"For what?" Joe was ready to refuse.

"We've got some forensics people who just might come up with something," Wade said. You would like some help that, wouldn't you?"

Still irritated at the man, Joe agreed anyway. He had heard Wade, once a field agent, now was some sort of in-house analyst or manager or something, after all, and so this was an opportunity to learn more about who may have stolen *Tartan*. Wade pocketed the medallion, and went back to finish dressing. Joe gave Mary a look of exasperation and sighed.

"Don't let Wade's manner bother you," she whispered. "He's really very sweet, once you get to know him."

Joe shook his head and then laughed, understanding that sooner or later either he or this brother-in law would have to go. "Let's find that scotch," he said.

Early Monday morning Wade left for his course at Maxwell Air Force Base, taking the Roadster, of course. At her insistence, Joe lived on in Mary's fine home through the winter. After searching diligently for employment, he did secure a part-time job at Home Depot that provided him enough to buy their groceries and share the cost of utilities. He had his boat reclaimed and moved to a boatyard in Miami with six month's storage paid in advance, consuming the balance of his meager wages.

Mary arranged a foursome of golf for them with another couple, and Joe did not embarrass himself, at least, even though he hadn't been on the course in years. She auditioned and won the part of Ophelia in *Hamlet* at a local theater, and Joe volunteered to help paint scenery. The play ran for three Fridays and Saturdays, and he didn't miss a performance. He joined a fitness center, which gave him the opportunity to go off on his own to use the exercise machines and swim a half-mile every day. In many ways it appeared that the two of them were more or less settling in. But not completely.

The room where they spent many winter evenings was the Study. Along two walls stood walnut bookcases filled with hard backed volumes, novels, histories, biographies, classics, interspersed with fine china or vases. A fireplace was inset into the near wall with a sculptured mantel. Above it hung a large portrait of a beautiful woman—Mary's grandmother, she once had told him. On the other wall, below a bay window, was a large mahogany desk. From the masculine look of it, Joe guessed it had belonged to Earnest. It was clear that this had been his room; that Earnest had been a well-educated gentleman reserved in his tastes, and that she had not redecorated the room one bit. Joe realized he should not disturb any of Earnest's things so as to be respectful of her lingering sadness.

An ongoing irritation was more visits from Wade Johnston. There were little things. Even though Mary urged

Joe to drive Earnest's Mercedes, whenever Wade was there, he would act as if the car was his and would drive it without so much as a word to Joe about it. When Joe would have to go off to work at his menial part-time job, he would leave Mary and Wade planning some outing together—a tennis game or a matinee. Wade and Joe were in one another's way it seemed. He realized Wade thought of him as an interloper, a usurper of his dead brother's home and wife. And it was clear from the beginning there would be no love lost between them.

As irksome as it was, however, Joe's sense of being a stranger in her world stifled his complaints. It was Mary's house, after all. The answer would have been to ask Mary to marry him. The words had been on the tip of his tongue when they first returned from their harrowing sail aboard *Mission*. In those dire circumstances, having seen how she had undertaken the challenges and performed with courage, he had come to love and respect her. But the more he had seen of her lifestyle, how engaged she was in Birmingham society, the greater his doubts became. Then when Wade came into the picture, Joe began to realize that he himself did not belong there.

By the first of March his desire for a change was very strong. The situation came to a head one afternoon when he returned from a tiring day at Home Depot. The moment he walked in the door, she announced that she wanted them to attend the Beaux Arts Ball on Saturday.

"Go try on Earnest's tails," she ordered, "and if the suit doesn't fit, we have just enough time to rent one."

"I don't wear tails anymore, Mary," he replied.

"Listen, Joe," she said. "I've been looking forward to this for months. Earnest and I were founding members. I desperately need you to…"

"Take his place?" Joe interrupted. "I'm not Earnest, Mary. Why can't you understand that?"

"No, you're not Earnest," Mary fired back, upset at his recalcitrance. "You couldn't hold a candle to Earnest. But you could act like a gentleman, at least."

"Go by yourself then," Joe said, offended. "You'll never get me there now."

She came over and touched his arm. "I'm sorry, Joe dear," she said. "I didn't mean to say that."

"But you think that," Joe said, moving away from her hand. "Well, I have better things to do than Beaux Arts Balls."

He ended up taking her, of course, realizing that it meant so much, and even acting as if he enjoyed it. He danced with her a couple of times. He was a good dancer, but he felt awkward amid people she knew and he didn't. Small talk after introductions was uncomfortable because he had nothing in common with the group. Eventually, Mary realized the situation and they left early.

"I'm sorry it was no fun for you," she said on the way home.

"I didn't know anybody, that's all," he replied. "But I'm glad you got to go and be with your friends."

"I'm sorry." Mary looked out of the window, and they said little else on the way.

A few days later, Joe received a letter from Wade's office at the CIA. The envelope contained a voucher for an airline ticket to Baltimore-Washington International with instructions to come up at his earliest convenience. Research into the origin of the medallion Joe had lent him, Wade's letter said, had turned up something of interest. Dissident splinter groups from the Irish Republican Army indeed had been stealing small pleasure craft in Florida, smuggling weapons aboard them and then scuttling the boats to prevent being traced. Wade wanted him to come to his office to talk to some folks about how he might help chase down the gang that took his boat, *Tartan*.

Joe's first reaction to the incredible invitation was to doubt Wade's veracity. Considering his impression that this brother-in-law resented him for living with Mary, Joe felt very leery of the man. He wondered if this was some kind of joke. But the ticket voucher was real, no doubt about it. That night he asked Mary for Wade's home phone number and called him.

"I can't discuss anything on this phone," Wade said. "But, hell yeah, it's for real. I'm trying to do you a favor, Sport. So come on up."

So Joe did go up to CIA headquarters to meet with this man he did not care for. But with Wade's influence both on Joe and on the Agency, he was enrolled in a training period at "The Farm." Because of his special skills as a mariner and his excellent record as a naval officer in his younger years, Deputy Director Hankins assigned him as an operative. Posing as a recreational sailor on vacation, he was to rent a boat in Ballycastle where he could discover and report any smuggling that might be taking place. And he was to observe any effect or reaction among the populous to the drone intelligence program being implemented cooperatively by Britain's MI-5 and the CIA.

Receiving his final orders and a send-off by his new superior, Wade Johnston, Joe remarked that he guessed he'd "either sink or swim."

Wade had patted him on the back. "Don't worry, Sport," he said with a big grin. "You'll do just fine."

Chapter Eight

Thrilled that Fiona had agreed to go sailing again, thanks in large measure to her brother's urgings, Joe hopped over the lifelines and walked briskly up the dock to meet her. She saw him and waved. They arrived at the security gate, and he opened it for her. Noticing she had her hair pulled back in a ponytail that reflected the reddish light of early morning sun, he embraced her briefly, resisting the desire to give her a kiss.

"Are we off to Portrush?" she asked. 'I've never been by boat so far as that."

"The tide's just right to take us there, have lunch and come back before dark," Joe said. "I'm so glad you could come."

"Thanks to Tim," she replied. "He volunteered to mind the store all day so I could go."

"Fine man, that Timothy," Joe said, escorting her down the dock to where *Kittiwake* was moored. So the kid had talked her into going sailing again. It seemed he was good to his word, and Joe regretted having had a bad first impression of her brother. Carrying her rain jacket over her arm, Fiona was wearing light green knee-length pants and a white blouse tied up to reveal her slim waist. "I love your outfit," he said.

"I hope I'm properly dressed," she replied, unconsciously moving her hand across the scar on her cheek. "I'm afraid we may have some rain."

"You needn't worry," he said. "If it gets heavy, you can retreat below until it's over." Actually, the weather did look a bit dicey with occasional squalls possible. He had considered calling off the day's excursion, but Fiona may have agreed to come along today only because Seamus was off in the Hebrides for a time. If that character was around, she might not ever be willing to go. Bad weather or not, the opportunity was worth the risk.

As they neared *Kittiwake* Joe saw a familiar figure moving about on a boat moored nearby. It was Fred Gordon, a lawyer—"solicitor," he said—from a nearby town inland. Joe had met him on the dock the previous Saturday. Gordon kept his boat at the marina and often sailed with his wife on weekends. He said good morning and Joe stopped to exchange greetings. Gordon's wife, Jan, a somewhat dumpy but pleasant sounding woman in her forties, stuck her head out of the companionway. Joe introduced them. Fiona gave only a cursory nod.

"So you're off on a sail this morning, are you?" Fred asked.

"Planning to sail west down the coast and back," Joe said. "I thought we would take lunch in Portrush and come back with the tide."

"Aye, turning in the afternoon I think," Gordon said. He glanced at his wife. "Maybe we should tag along in our boat."

"Sounds like a lark," Jan replied. "Come aboard for a cuppa and let's discuss it."

"We need to be moving on," Joe said, looking at his watch.

"Coffee's already made," Jan insisted. "Here, have a seat in the cockpit and I'll fetch it in a sec." Joe looked at Fiona, who nodded with a shrug. They climbed aboard and took seats. Fred, a dark-haired, slightly-built man with a permanent grin, came aft from the bow and joined them, saying he had not decided where to sail today, so a trip along the north coast would be fun. Jan called up from the cabin, asking how they took their coffee.

"A little milk if you have it," Joe said and glanced at Fiona.

"Black is fine," she said with no enthusiasm. Joe noticed her strange reticence, wondering if she felt shy or something around the Gordons and tried to think of something to perk her up.

"I'm excited about making this trip," he said, smiling at Fiona. "I've only sailed as far as Benbane Head. If the rest of the coast is as beautiful as that part, then we're in for a treat."

"Aye," Fred replied. He took the cups from Jan one by one and passed them to his guests. "I never tire of it." He handed Fiona her cup. "Have you sailed the coast often?" he asked her.

"I don't get out much," she said and looked away. Jan climbed up the ladder into the cockpit and took a seat by Fiona.

"I know where I've seen you," Jan said, shifting around to look at Fiona. "Run the Hillside Market, don't you? We live in Armoy, but I've been in a few times, stocking the boat larder, mainly." Fiona nodded with a polite smile and sipped her coffee.

"You must have a good trade there," Jan persisted. "It's a bonnie wee shop."

Fiona gave her a quick hard look, which surprised Joe. "We do the best we can, the Brit bank near choking us at it," she said. Noting Joe's expression, Fiona dropped her glance and looked away.

"Oh, I'm sure you'll be very successful in the end," Jan replied, her face reddening a bit at Fiona's acerbic response. She exchanged glances with her husband.

"Well," Gordon said, rubbing his hands together as if to clear the air. "Best we get underway, don't you agree?"

Joe gave an apologetic look and stood up. "I guess so," he said. Fiona already was climbing out of the cockpit. He picked up their empty cups and handed them to Jan. "Thanks so much for the coffee," he said, watching Fiona climb over the lifelines and hop on the dock. "I, uh, I'm sorry…" Fiona walked briskly away.

Fred had stepped closer. "Struck a sensitive chord, I expect," he whispered. "It happens with those people sometimes." Joe looked quizzical.

"The poor dear's one of those misguided republicans, it seems," Jan explained. "Very touchy about their station in life, you know."

Joe nodded. "She has told me about growing up in hard times. I guess she's sensitive about that, as you said." With the Gordons being successful and wealthy, he thought, there might be a cultural difference between them and Fiona. He decided to broach the question.

"Would it be about The Troubles, maybe?" he asked.

"Oh, we don't talk about that," Jan said. "We just wish it into the dim and forgotten past."

"I'm keen to get underway," Fred interrupted.

"Yes, I guess we really should," Joe replied, "going with the tide and everything."

"Right-o," Fred replied. "We'll accompany you down the coast." He glanced at his wife for agreement.

"I'm happy enough," Jan said pleasantly. Joe thanked her again for the coffee and hurried after Fiona, relieved to see she was walking toward *Kittiwake*.

"Is there something wrong?" Joe asked when they were back aboard his boat.

"You don't know who he is, do you?" she asked. "Being an American, I suppose you would not." She shook her head angrily. "I recognized his name. Gordon's a bloody unionist Member Local Assembly at Stormont, or was. I can't believe I passed the time of day with them, much less drank their bloody coffee."

"I'm so sorry," Joe said. "It never occurred to me that you would have such strong feelings. Please forgive me."

She stared at him a moment and then sighed and smiled. "Never mind, you Yank," she said. "I can't expect that you would understand." She patted his arm. "Now let's get this boat going before any more Orange Order bastards trouble us."

With an apologetic look, Joe started the engine. He climbed out on the dock to take in the mooring lines and waved at Gordon who was also preparing to depart. As he jumped aboard *Kittiwake*, Fiona smiled at him, and he hoped she was over her bad mood.

He backed out of the slip, turned and steered out of the boulder-lined channel into Rathlin Sound. As he followed the Gordon's boat, he was glad the four of them were not aboard together. A surprising gust of wind blew out of the west, but the sun was rising cheerily in the east and glistened on the frilly waves. Sitting forward of him, she smiled pleasantly.

"It's so great being on the water. Thank you for inviting me."

"I'm so happy you came," Joe replied, congratulating himself on his good luck. He supposed Timothy's encouragement must have helped and wondered why her brother would favor him over Seamus O'Leary. Perhaps the novelty of having an American pursuing his sister was the answer.

"Would you come steer, so I can ready the sails?"

Appearing to have forgotten her unhappiness, she playfully pushed him out of the way and slipped in behind the helm. Undoubtedly, she was the most beautiful red-haired girl Joe had ever seen, even in spite of the scar line on her cheek. That red hair, he supposed, went with her fiery temper that had caused her to react so to the Gordons. He recalled her story about losing her father in a riot. Because she had been through that kind of childhood experience, Joe supposed, she had reason to dislike those who supported the union with Britain.

He climbed up the superstructure to the mast and began removing the tie-downs that held the furled mainsail to the boom. He was readying it for a hoist when a strong gust of wind nearly blew him off balance. He steadied himself against the mast and noted a line of dark clouds had appeared to the west. Making his way aft to the cockpit, he gave Fiona a reassuring smile, and went below. Turning the radio on, he tuned it to channel 89 to receive the Irish Coast

Guard Station at Malin Head at the northern point of the Inishowen Peninsula of Donegal. From this location west of them, a thick Irish-accented speaker began broadcasting a gale warning with Force 7 or 8 winds expected. Joe hadn't expected that, but as Ryan had said, the weather blowing in from the Atlantic was "as changeable as a wench's heart."

Switching back to channel 16, he glanced up at Fiona, wondering how she would react to bad weather. The wisest thing would be to take her back to Ballycastle and call it a day. But if he did so, would he ever convince her to go sailing with him again? Suppose they did return to port and it all blew over? He looked out the porthole at the Gordon's boat. They did not appear to be turning back, so why should he? The thing to do was to give Fiona a calm and unalarming assessment of what could be coming, discuss the options with her, and let her decide. She was as intrepid as she was beautiful, he knew, and likely would rise to the occasion. Enduring some difficulty in a storm might serve to cement their relationship, just as going through the gales aboard *Mission* had brought Mary and him together. During those perils Mary had been the perfect companion, and he hoped and believed Fiona also would measure up. If she did, although he did not want to admit it to himself, in part it would serve to justify his rejection of Mary and the life she wanted him to lead in America.

With that in mind, he went back on deck with two lifejackets and safety harnesses, which Fiona noted with an inquisitive expression. Joe nonchalantly laid them down in the cockpit, noted that the stiff breeze was from off the port bow and began raising the mainsail. The boat listed to starboard heavily, so he eased the main sheet to right her.

"How's it feel, my dear first mate?" he asked, walking back to the helm. *She'd sure make a great mate in every sense of the word,* he thought.

"Am I going right? That's the better question," she replied with a little tension in her voice.

"You're doing fine," he said, reaching down to kill the engine. "Let's put out a bit of the genoa." He looked ahead, noting the blue grey line of clouds to the west had not moved much. In the stiff breeze it required only a slight tug on the starboard sheet to unfurl the genoa. At halfway, he stopped unfurling the sail, and locked it down in this reefed position. With only that much canvas in the air, *Kittiwake* listed more and picked up speed. Up ahead he noted a slight swirling off to their left.

"In another hour," Joe said, grinning and quoting Big Ryan, "the ebbing tide will race through here at seven knots, and the whirlpool, Slough na mor, will make a mighty disturbance in the waters."

"I know many a sad tale," Fiona said. "There are stories from the old days when fisherman in small rowboats would capsize out there." She held her hand up to shield her eyes as she peered in its direction. "I hope we are safe from it."

"Oh, I think so," Joe said. Inwardly, he hoped never to have to encounter it.

As they sailed out farther from the rocky cliffs, the light breeze became disturbed with occasional gusts.

101

Scudding gray clouds continued to pour over the mainland and over the bay. The Gordons were still ahead and even slightly upwind, flying full main and jib. But even with a reefed sail in *Kittiwake,* they were catching up. About a half mile from Benbane Head, the steadily increasing wind gusted harder out of the south, and Fiona worked at the helm. As occasional gusts struck the boat, it listed hard to port.

"Please come take it," Fiona said. "I don't know how to do this." Joe reached up and massaged her shoulders, excited by how her breasts moved with the motion. She realized what he was seeing. He lowered his hands, and she gave him a coy look. Reddening, he stepped behind the wheel and took over.

"You were doing great," he fibbed, and pointed to the equipment on the seat. "I'd like for you to put on that life vest and your raincoat, too."

"Is it that bad?" she asked.

"No, not at all. It's just a precaution." He managed a confident smile. "Pass me the other one, will you?"

Fiona sat on the cockpit bench and figured out how to wear the vest. "What do I do with these straps?" she asked, indicating the two black web belts that go under the crotch.

"Hand me mine and I'll show you." She passed him the other vest. He put it on, and then pulled the web straps under his crotch and fastened them to the front of his vest. She did the same with hers, as he watched and realized he had never before thought of donning a life vest to be an exciting experience. Once all strapped in, she looked at the Gordon's boat a hundred yards or so ahead.

"Are they racing us?" she asked. Joe glanced back and waved.

"Whenever two sailboats get together, usually there's an undeclared race."

"Well let's beat them, then," she said, making a fierce look. Joe grinned. Perhaps coming in first would make her feel a little less bitter to those 'unionists,' he hoped. He thought about how strongly she had reacted to them when she realized who they were, and he wished she was not quite so conscious of political divisiveness.

"Oh, no. Here comes a real wind," Fiona said, pointing. Joe looked to see the band of ripples rolling toward them from the south. It hit them with a great "whompf" of the sails, and Joe held on to the helm through the deep heel of the boat, trying to ease the pressure without fully rounding up. This burst of wind was not just momentary, he realized, but a more permanent blast of air was rushing into the cell of low pressure charging toward them from the west. The anemometer needle wavered between 20 and 25 knots. Unfortunately, they were flying too much sail.

"I need you to come take the wheel again," he said. She nodded with uncertainty and came to the helm.

"Just hold this heading until I ask you to turn left until the sails begin to flap," he told her. "I have to make some adjustments, that's all." He lightly squeezed her hand for encouragement. Fiona gave him a skeptical look but did as he directed.

Joe climbed up on the port gunwale, clipped his harness on to the safety line and made his way to the mast. When he called to her, she correctly headed up into the wind, and Joe put a second reef in the main. When he told her to ease back to leeward, a 30-knot gust heeled them heavily, and their speed through the water increased to seven knots.

103

"You're doing great," he said and looked over to see how the Gordons were doing. "Uh oh, they've got problems."

Wind wise, *Kittiwake* was below the other yacht by 70 yards. The Gordons were struggling with their genoa, which was luffing wildly. They apparently had been reefing the sail but let it get out of hand in the high wind.

After a few minutes the other couple managed to control their sail and furl it completely. The mistake had cost them the lead, and *Kittiwake* began to outrun them.

"We've got 'em now," Joe said.

With a victorious expression, Fiona shouted, "Good riddance!" Her reaction made Joe grin. He could not believe how fabulous she looked behind the wheel.

About 600 yards offshore—"three cables distance" Ryan would have said—they could feel the wind spilling over the high headlands. The tall edifices were now dark and ominous in the mist and the rain. Millions of years of erosion had carved 100-yard wide indentations in the rock, much like the serrations in a knife blade, and this irregularity created a confusing pattern of wind gusts and shelter that made steering difficult. Expecting the wind to clock to the west as predicted, they remained fairly close in, choosing to stay upwind. Passing by the projecting headlands, the boats slowed in the lee of the cliffs only to take hard knocks as they passed the next inlet.

With the sails set properly for the time being, Joe again relieved Fiona at the helm, and she took cover under the dodger. He enjoyed watching her pull the hood of her jacket back and shaking her long red hair down over her shoulders. She noticed him looking and smiled invitingly.

"You're gorgeous when you're wet," he called to her. Soon cold rain began pelting Joe in the face. He gritted his teeth and pulled the hood of his jacket tighter, recalling once again the tortuous passage from the Bahamas to Charleston. He wondered briefly how Mary would have responded to this chilly Irish rain. She had been so courageous aboard *Mission*. But no, she was home instead, going to parties and being the socialite. Well, to each his own, Joe thought, though he had missed her on occasion. But not now. Not with this beautiful girl Fiona sitting there before him. What a trooper she was, maybe even more so than Mary. *Carpe Diem*, he thought.

They now were abreast of the depression in the high cliffs where Ryan had said the Spanish ship *Girona* had crashed upon the rocks. He pointed it out to Fiona, who said she knew the story but never had seen the spot from the sea.

"I'm glad this storm is coming out of the south," Joe said. "In this condition seas are not so rough along these cliffs."

"Perhaps if we were closer, the wind would not be so strong," she suggested.

Joe shook his head. "Eddies and overfalls from the ebbing tide could trouble us if we were nearer those rocks."

Running with the maximum ebb tide, their speed over the ground had increased significantly. Even though they were no longer in the rush of current that runs through Rathlin Bay, there was plenty of push adding to the speed from the wind. The rain slackened a bit.

Fiona pointed to the next great rock promontory. "Oh. Look. That's the Giant's Causeway, one of the eight wonders of the world. They say that the giant, Finn McCool,

105

whose severed hand is displayed in the center of the North Ireland Flag, made this huge rock edifice as a bridge to the ocean." Wiping the spray off of his binoculars, Joe peered at the sight. At its seaward end, he made out clusters of crystalline-shaped hexagonal columns of basalt and lava-baked limestone streaming out into the water.

"Amazing!" He lowered his binoculars. "There's a lot to see on this coastline." Joe spotted a bus coming down the side of the cliff, dwarfed to miniscule by the huge dark brown headland.

Fiona shook her head. "The bloody tourists keep coming, even in this weather."

Joe smiled. While he and Fiona battled the elements in a treacherous sea, ashore it was just business as usual.

"It's interesting," he remarked, "how different the world can look, all depending on your point of view."

She did not smile. "Tell that to the thousand sailors whose bones lie amid the rocks and shoals along here."

West of the causeway and set slightly inland lay the town of Bushmills, home of the famous distillery. Then beyond on a distant cliff stood the remains of Dunluce Castle, perched above the sea. They came to a line of rocky islets, known as the Skerries, lying offshore from a town.

"That's Portrush," Fiona said, "once a very fancy tourist resort in the early 20th Century. It's more a playground for locals now, and not so grand as before."

"I've heard of it," Joe said. "It has the Royal Portrush Golf Course, with some young golfers who are famous."

"Aye," she replied. "A rich man's game and not for the likes of my kin, the true Irish."

"So, what sports do you like?" he asked.

"Football," she said, meaning what Joe thought of as soccer. "Now there's a game to lose your heart and soul over."

Away from the lee of the cliffs they had left behind, it seemed they were fairly flying past the islands now, and enjoying a respite from the rain. Fiona took the occasion to come and sit beside him, and he tentatively put his arm around her. She moved closer so that their hips touched. They looked at one another and kissed. Joe could not imagine his good fortune.

First Belfast Coast Guard and then the Republic of Ireland station at Malin Head continued to broadcast warnings of impending gales. *Kittiwake* was taking occasional gusts up to 35 knots, but the steady wind was only about 20 or so. Coming around Remore Head, yet another promontory at the north end of Portrush, Joe was not happy the breeze had clocked to the northwest. Through his binoculars he could see the waves coming toward the narrow harbor entrance making it look impassable. He checked his watch and realized it would be at least two more hours until the tide turned, which made an immediate return to Ballycastle impractical. He looked at the chart of the coastline and made some mental calculations. Then he called Fred Gordon on the radio to discuss the situation.

"Let's make for the River Bann," Gordon suggested. "Our course is 240 to the river's entrance. The barmouth shouldn't be too unpleasant a passage in this wind. And if it is, we can go on to Greencastle in Lough Foyle."

Joe studied the chart and thought it sounded like a good idea. "Okay," he replied. "River Bann it is." Signing off, he went topside to explain it all to Fiona. She shrugged pleasantly.

"Why not?" she replied from the helm, her hair hanging down in strings. "You've already half drowned me anyway."

Joe gave her a thumbs up and then trimmed the mainsail. Then he fetched a couple of candy bars from the larder and brought her one.

"You're a great sport," he said.

Fiona made a face and shook the water out of her hair. "I've never had such fun in my life," she said. Joe couldn't tell for sure whether it was a sarcastic remark or not. The best thing about it was that she did not appear to be suffering from any seasickness. That would have changed her attitude considerably. She was as feisty as she was pretty, no doubt about it.

"Well, we're still ahead of those orange people," he replied, gesturing toward the Gordon's boat, which was now 300 or so yards astern.

As they passed offshore of the town of Portstewart, blue-gray clouds loomed over the green hills of the Inishowen, threatening to drench them again before they reached the barmouth. The wind continued to clock around to the north, and *Kittiwake* rolled in the waves. Joe scanned the shoreline with his binoculars and made out the entrance to the river. As they got closer, he could see it was a very narrow channel, lying between two large concrete and rock jetties. With waves breaking on the right, or western side, it would not be an easy approach.

Joe cranked up the diesel and grinned at her. "We'll take in the sails," he said. She nodded and kept on steering.

"Just head a little out from the entrance," Joe instructed. He furled the already reefed genoa and then lowered the main, wrestling with the boom to put on the tie downs.

"You do all this for fun, huh?" Fiona said as she relinquished the helm to him. Joe grinned and blew her a kiss. From the smile in her eyes, he could tell she was loving it.

"Have a seat and hang on," he said.

Then he turned his full attention to the narrow passage between the jetties—12-foot high rock walls built more than a century ago. On the low rise inshore were a pair of white towers, a *range* or *leading marks*, toward which one steers so as to visually align them for safe passage into the barmouth. About every 15 to 20 seconds a large wave broke on the right jetty, sending spray twenty feet in the air. The pass was shallow enough to make breakers. Joe realized the trick would be to pass the seaward ends of the jetties just after a breaking wave so that it would not carry the boat into the left pier. Putting one hand on the throttle and one on the helm, he jockeyed the speed to achieve the proper timing through the pass. When they were 40 yards out, he heard Gordon's voice on the radio.

"Too rough to enter there, I think, *Kittiwake*," Joe heard him say. But it was too late for Joe to turn. He was committed. He worked the wheel back and forth violently to hold the bow aligned with the range. They passed into the entrance only a few yards from the rocks, and a wave hit the high jetty to starboard, making the boat rise up like a bucking horse and surf on through. Salty sea spray splashed them, and then all was calm. They were safely inside and in the middle of the channel.

"That was exciting," Fiona said with a sigh of relief.

"I wouldn't want to do that every day," Joe replied, wiping the spray out of his eyes. He glanced back at the Gordons' boat and realized they had turned away. It appeared that they were not going to try it.

The clouds were still rolling towards them, but *Kittiwake* was inshore now, headed up the narrow river, beyond the danger. Then he heard Fred's voice on the radio again.

"Congratulations on making it in," he was saying. "We're heading for Greencastle ourselves. Seems the weather will be bad for a while. Better wait it out in the river. Cheers."

"Turning tail and running, are they?" Fiona cried triumphantly. "Orange on the outside and all yellow to their innards." She raised her fists and shook them in celebration.

"Well, I'm glad they didn't try it," Joe said. "I'd hate to be trying to rescue them off those rocks."

She waved in dismissal. "They can drown their unionist souls for all I care."

Joe, more concerned with her epithets than the course to steer, pointed the bow to pass the first red day marker down his starboard side. Intent upon listening to Gordon report that the run from Ballycastle today was a record 2 hours and 55 minutes, he failed to notice that the depth gauge was going from four meters to two.

Then as Joe looked up, he realized he was about to run aground. He spun the wheel to the right, reached down and backed the engine. The stern yawed and pointed the bow over, heading back toward the channel, but he felt the keel mush into the mud on the bottom. Joe slapped his forehead. In desperation he gunned the engine in reverse but it did no good. Disgusted, he throttled back and stopped the engine.

"What happened?" Fiona asked. "We're stuck in the mud, aren't we?"

Joe sighed and nodded. "In America," he said, "the rule is *red, right, return*. When headed inland from sea, you keep the red marks to starboard. But in this country, it's just the opposite. In other words, I should have kept that red marker to our left."

"Is the boat going to sink or anything?" Fiona looked at him with concern.

"Can't sink," Joe explained. "We're already on the bottom. And it looks like we'll be here until the tide rises." He looked at the surroundings. To the east, although Portstewart was visible in the distance, there was nothing but a stretch of desolate sand dunes in between. To the west, there was the small town of Castlerock, about a mile away but not accessible across the river. While there might be a fisherman or even birdwatchers around on a pretty day, the approaching rain storm had kept them away. He looked at Fiona and recognized the fact that they would be stranded there for several hours, alone, together.

Chapter Nine

Making a quick inspection, Joe found that, to his relief, *Kittiwake*'s hull was not damaged. The engine cooling water intakes were not blocked with mud. The rudder was not jammed. The prop wasn't bent, and the boat indeed would remain seaworthy.

"So this is the old proverbial, *the car ran out of petrol*, is it?" Fiona joked when Joe explained they would be aground until the tide turned. Joe grinned, glad she was being a good sport about it.

"I realize the circumstantial evidence goes against me," he admitted. "But this would have been a much more elaborate ruse than I could have thought up." It was good she had a bemused expression. He looked back at the barmouth a few hundred yards astern of them and watched another huge breaker crash against the jetty. "Even if we weren't stuck in the mud, we'd not get out of here until the weather calms." He did not say that if they were not aground, they could have motored upriver to the town of Coleraine where she could catch a bus or something back to Ballycastle.

"Well, I hope you've got some whiskey aboard." She unzipped the hatch cover and climbed down the ladder. Joe took another look at the dark squall line to the west. Whiskey sounded like a good idea to him, too. He made his way to the bow, got out the anchor and flung it as far as he could to the upstream side. He tied off the line, leaving some slack so that, if the boat did begin to float and drift, the anchor would have enough scope to bite in and hold them. A big black cormorant sat atop the red channel marker that he had gone the wrong way around. The bird held its wings out to dry and stared at Joe as if to comment on his foolish mistake.

"Yeah," he said to the cormorant, "but guess who I'm stuck here with?" He glanced in all directions and decided that, given the remoteness of the spot and the foreboding weather, he and Fiona would not be disturbed by any meddling rescuers. And that was good.

Making his way back to the hatch, he took off his foul weather jacket and then backed down the ladder and zipped the canvas hatch cover. "There'll be another heavy rain shower in a few minutes," he explained. Fiona was sitting on the salon couch, her rain jacket off, and was unbuttoning her wet blouse.

"Get me a towel, will you?" she said. "Can't sit around in this." With that she slipped off the shirt, exposing an equally sodden bra.

"That's wet, too," Joe dared say as he walked by.

"That's why I need the towel, you ninny," she replied in a pretending-to-be-irritated tone. Joe, getting excited, dug a towel out of a drawer and brought it to her.

"So where's my whiskey?" she demanded, reaching back to undo her bra. Joe handed her the towel, which she held across her chest, not particularly hiding her lovely white breasts. He nearly gasped and headed for his stash of liquor. Finding the bottle of Coleraine Irish Whiskey he had purchased at Eamon's off-license, he pulled out two glasses and poured a good shot in each.

"Would you like some water?"

"Water's always good," Fiona replied, "if taken in the right spirit." He laughed, added a touch of bottled water and gave her the glass.

"Cheers," she said, holding up the rudimentary cocktail. Joe clinked his against it, and they both turned them up and drained them. "Again," she said, handing him the glass with a churlish grin. He refilled their glasses and handed over hers.

"I don't know how much of a muck we're in here," she said. "But I want you to know the trip through all that rain and everything was one of the most fun times I've ever had." She gave him a loving look. "I mean that."

"I'm so glad," Joe said. "I wasn't sure if it wasn't, well, too much for you. You never know what you'll get into when you go sailing. But you're a real trooper."

"Here's to real troopers," she said, smiling and clinking glasses again, looking him up and down. "And get those wet clothes off. You want to catch your death here?"

"I hoped you'd think of that," Joe said with a grin. Realizing his face was reddening, he put his glass down and began unbuttoning his shirt, wondering just how much *wet clothes off* she meant. Shirtless, he sat beside her on the couch and watched as she lifted the towel from her shoulders and rubbed her long red hair, gazing at him. Self-consciously, he leaned over and took off his shoes and drenched socks.

A huge gust struck the boat, causing it to careen slightly as wind moaned through the mast rigging. Joe jumped up and climbed two steps up the ladder, opening the hatch cover. He could see that *Kittiwake* had pivoted around about 90 degrees but basically was in the same location.

"Is it all right?" Fiona called. She had come over and was standing behind him.

"I think so," Joe said. "Just a little wind." He stood watching the approaching line of rain when he felt her hands, first on his hips then around his waist, undoing his belt and then the snaps of his pants. She pulled them down and took hold of his underpants, pulling them down, catching on his erection on the way. He backed down the steps and turned to face her.

"More like it," she said, inspecting him with her eyes. She stepped out of her panties. "Kiss me, you lovely man."

Joe took her in his arms and they kissed, on the lips first and then with their tongues. So she was aggressively passionate, he thought, her temper matching her fiery hair. He loved it. She was unbelievably exciting. He held her breasts, touched her pink nipples, and they kissed again.
"Where can we lie down?" she breathed.

"In the after cabin," he said. Taking his erected member in her hand, she led the way with a few tugs. She opened the door and peered in at the bunk that was situated beneath the cockpit, which made a low ceiling.

"A wee spot, isn't it? Near like a bloody cave," she said. "Here, you get down first." Joe slid in and lay on his back. Fiona slipped in across him, head first, her long red hair falling down her shoulders and caressing his stomach and then his groin. He put his hands on her buttocks, and felt her lips taking him in. It was only for a few delicious seconds. Then she swung around on top and put him inside her. Though the rain drummed mightily on the deck above, Joe knew only the luscious feel of Fiona, the beautiful, fabulous, amazing body above him, moving up and down as he moved so as to increase the overwhelming, all engrossing feeling of luscious crescendo. *Ahhhh*. They lay together panting, and then she began moving away. Joe pulled her back to him in a close embrace and sighed and kissed her lovingly.

"Did you go off in me?" she whispered.

"I think so, Joe muttered. He kissed her again. "I love you, Fiona." They lay there in silence, as he caressed her. Then she sat up.

"Don't say you love me," she said. Quickly she crawled out of the bunk and went forward. "I need another drink, and, bejuzus, how about some bleeding clothes?" She went into the head and closed the door.

Joe sighed and climbed out in silence. He rummaged around in his clothes drawers, finding a long nightshirt he guessed would fit her—his feelings running the gamut of desire and frustration. He pulled on some underwear and shorts and carried the nightshirt over and put it outside the door.

"Here's the best I can find for you," he called. Then he went to make them each another whiskey. She reached out, took the shirt and closed the door again. Joe noticed that the rain was still coming down, but not so hard as before. He went to the galley for the whiskey and dug out some packaged ham and began making sandwiches. Fiona came out, wearing the nightshirt and the towel wrapped in a turban around her hair. She took the drink and sat down.

"I don't want us to do that again," she said. Joe glanced at her and then looked back down.

"I'm sorry," he said. "For whatever I did, I'm very sorry." He felt for the moment that the world was coming to an end. "I guess I should have had a condom or something."

"Condom? I'm a bleeding Catholic, don't you know?" She took a big swallow of whiskey. "It's not you," she said. "It's me...it's me and a whole bunch of things."

He brought two plates with sandwiches, handing her one and sitting down. "I wish you'd tell me," he said.

She took a bite of sandwich and chewed. "Well, there's Seamus, of course. He's been my guy forever."

Joe sucked in a quick breath. "Tim told me that you wanted out of that."

"Oh, he did, did he? As if it were any of his bloody business." She frowned. "Well, maybe he's right. But what you need to know is that I've got something I have to do, that's all. And no man can keep me from it. No man. Not even you, you lovely, sexy devil."

Joe looked at her with confusion, feeling complimented on one hand and body slammed on the other. "What? What's this 'something' you're talking about? Is it worth not being happy in life or what?"

"I have a mission," she said. "I have a duty, a thing I must do, and that is all I'm going to tell you." She drained her glass and held it up to him. "So thanks for the lovely fling, Yank," she said. "I wouldn't have missed it for the world. But that is *it*, period, end of discussion, see? Now get this boat out of the mud and take me home!"

It was only another half hour before the tide, and maybe some rainwater flooding down the River Bann, lifted *Kittiwake* off the bottom and allowed Joe to raise the anchor and maneuver back into the channel. The rain had quit and the clouds were moving on east. Passing the navigation marker correctly this time, he lined up with the range marks astern and headed for the barmouth. Noting that the breakers were much smaller, he knew passing through would still be dicey. Fiona sat forward in the cockpit, having changed to her damp but not soaking clothes under her jacket. Double-checking his alignment with the range marks, he sped up the engine enough to ensure good response from the rudder. They reached the entrance just as a wave broke on the western jetty, and the boat bucked its way through the turbulent shallow waters on the outside.

"We're on the way home," Joe said. Fiona merely gave a thumbs up.

Safely in the deeper waters of the ocean, Fiona took the helm and Joe raised the sails and set them for a broad reach. He checked the course and had her steer 060. Then he offered her another whiskey, but she said she had headache enough already. So he took the helm and she lay on her side on the starboard bench of the cockpit. Except for commenting that they were abeam of Portstewart and would pass Portrush and the Skerries around sunset, there was little said. Fiona finally drifted off to sleep, and Joe sailed on, staring at her from time to time and thinking of how sex with her had been so fabulous but so upsetting in its aftermath. He hadn't meant to allow himself to impregnate her, and he hoped it hadn't been a time that she was fertile. He did not believe a man should ever allow that to happen by accident, but he had lost his control in the ecstasy of this wonderful moment with Fiona.

"What an exotic creature you are," he whispered. Mary was exciting and fun and lovely, he recalled, but this Irish girl was dazzling with something fiery and maybe even scary about her. It was that assertiveness and then the pulling away with a total change of heart that awed him. What was this *mission* or *duty* that drove her? She seemed wound up inside, he imagined, but he was uncertain and more than a little bit concerned about what it could be.

She awoke at dusk, sat up, and stared at the dark cliffs of the Giant's Causeway off their starboard side. She went below to use the head, and when she came back, Joe asked her to take the wheel so he could do the same. Down below he put on coffee and double-checked the course on the GPS.

"We're making really good time," he told her when he handed her a cup of coffee. "Wind and tide are really giving us a push." She merely nodded and gestured for him to come steer. Silently, they changed positions. As they passed, Joe bent down and gave her a kiss on the cheek. She accepted it but did not even look at him. Resuming her place on the starboard bench, she stared up at the stars peeping out behind the dissipating clouds. Then she looked at him.

"What are you doing here in Ulster, anyway?" she asked, half accusing. Joe looked away and thought about how he should reply. "Just being here lolling about on this boat—that doesn't fully explain you, does it, Joe?" She stared at him intently through the semidarkness.

He struggled for the right answer. Now knowing her so intimately, it seemed wrong not to tell her the truth, and he came within a deuce of confessing. He swallowed and then shrugged. "I came just to find something," he stammered. "Something about myself, I suppose." He paused, realizing he was getting at the real truth about himself. "Maybe I was meant to come here to find you, dearest Fiona. Maybe we were meant to find each other."

Fiona shook her head. "I told you before, Joe. I'm not for you, you see. So just forget it before we both get hurt."

The last words came out with a stifled sob. Joe set the wheel lock and walked over to her and took her hand.

"If you…if it happens… No, even if it doesn't happen, I want so much to… care for you. I'd marry you, Fiona. We can find a way…" Their eyes met, and in hers he saw for only a second an intense longing and fear and distrust such as he had never witnessed. He pulled her strongly into his arms and she held him tightly as if the world was ending. Then he felt in her a powerful shiver, and she pushed away.

"No, you silly, stupid man," she said. "I cannot. I will not. Now go back and steer this boat before we turn over and drown." She took her hand away, pulled herself into the fetal position and closed her eyes. Joe sighed deeply and reluctantly went back to the helm.

It was dark by the time they passed Benbane Head and entered Rathlin Sound. In 20 minutes, he spotted navigation lights on a boat up ahead, peered through his binoculars and identified it as O'Leary's trawler, heading into Ballycastle. Joe wondered if O'Leary would find out Fiona had been sailing with him all day.

When he started the engine, Fiona did not awaken, so Joe set the wheel and came forward to take down the sails and rig the mooring lines. With the job accomplished, he went back to the helm and picked out the channel marker. Fiona awoke and sat up to watch.

"We're here," he said.

"Good," she replied, and offered nothing more until they were heading between jetties.

"I really did have a very good time, Joe," she said. "Everything."

Joe took in a deep breath. "So did I," he answered. He was about to tell her again how much he loved her, wanted to marry her, settle down in Ballycastle forever, and just be together. It was at that moment she saw Seamus O'Leary's trawler tied up to the dock.

"Wait!" Fiona said in a loud whisper, quickly creeping down through the hatchway. She cautiously peered out, looking in the direction of Seamus' boat. Joe became aware of voices and looked over her shoulder. Seamus and his crew were sitting on the deck of the trawler, apparently drinking and having a craic. She slipped farther below and remained in the cabin until Joe had *Kittiwake* tied up at the dock.

"I can't leave just now," Fiona said when he went below.

"What's the problem?" he asked. She swallowed and shook her head.

"He must not see me. Seamus will..."

"Seamus? To hell with Seamus." He looked out of the hatch. Seamus and his crew were still sitting on the trawler, talking loudly and laughing. Angry himself, he thought about going to confront the man right now.

"Joe, sit down, please. It will not do to cause a stir."

He grimaced, wiped a hand across his face and came back to sit beside her.

"Can we please just have a last whiskey and be quiet a wee bit?"

"But I thought… I mean, well what is it about Seamus of all things? I'm not worried about that guy."

"Trust me, Joe," she said. "'Twill not do to cross the man, for he is high up in secret republican groups. I cannot say too much. But if ye cross him, believe me, a lone man like you, a stranger here, you wouldn't stand a chance." She held his hand. "So be good now, dear one. As soon as I can, let me slip away in the dark. 'Tis better for both of us, no matter how we…" She did not finish the sentence. Instead, she stood up and peered out again. "Look, they've had their whiskey and are gone now. Here, let me borrow this jacket with the hood. I can put it over my head, and no one will be the wiser."

In frustration and disappointment, Joe watched her pull on the jacket and start up to the cockpit. "Well, the least I can do is walk you home."

Despite her protests he insisted, and they made their way down the dock. By the time they were abreast the trawler, they could see the big hulk of the man, Seamus, prostrate on the deck, apparently passed out. Fiona quickened her steps in obvious panic but was a bit tipsy from the alcohol. Just as she came up near him, she stumbled on the planking and nearly fell, exclaiming as she did. Joe caught her arm to steady her. It was just enough commotion to awaken the man on deck. He sat up, shook his head and peered at them.

"Fiona?" he muttered. "Fiona? It's you? I know yer voice. And what? With the American?" He stumbled to stand. Fiona began to run.

"Oh, Jesus," she cried and ran on.

Joe hesitated, giving the big Irishman an angry look, wanting to bust him in the mouth. The man was staggering as if to pursue them but lost his balance and fell on the deck. *Aw hell, the man is drunk*, Joe realized. Then he decided to hurry on with Fiona, who clearly was upset. Self-consciously, he looked around to see who might be witness to all this. Up the hill, in the car park outside the gate, was Evan Foster, watching the whole scene.

"I'll deal with you yet," O'Leary called after them. Joe wasn't sure whether he was threatening him or Fiona. He followed her up the road to her closed and darkened market. Without a word, she went in and locked the door. Joe shook his head and started back to his boat. For an undercover agent, he was breaking all the rules of safety. Even so, he gritted his teeth, knowing full well that one day, if he ever were to find happiness with Fiona, he would have to deal with this bastard, Seamus.

Chapter Ten

"We hear you're getting too involved," Stan Adams, the handler, said when Joe called in the next morning.

"What do you mean, too involved?" Joe was first surprised and then angered.

"Your infatuation with this Irish girl, Fiona. I hear that you've now got a row started with her boyfriend."

"Where are you getting this?" Joe squeezed the iPhone in his clenched fist. He was taking the call as planned—having driven up to the overlook on the cliff above Carrick-a-rede rope bridge, and posing as a sightseer. "How do you know anything about Fiona?"

"You didn't think the agency would be keeping tabs on you?" Adams asked. "Well, you ought to know that new, green agents get watched pretty carefully. It's to keep them from making mistakes. And you're certainly living up to the Agency's assessment of you. From what I hear, you've already got yourself in trouble with some fisherman who's likely an IRA strong man." There was a silent pause while Joe struggled to understand.

"So you actually have somebody spying on me?"

"No shit, Sherlock. And it's a good thing, too."

Joe took a deep breath and tried to calm down. "I'm just doing my job," he said, trying to imagine who had been watching him.

"Your job is simply to observe and report what you see. You're supposed to be as milk-toast anonymous as possible—a normal, average tourist, a nobody—invisible. You follow?

"Well, you have to interact with people somehow," Joe argued. "How can you learn anything if you're not doing anything?"

"Interacting doesn't have to include stealing another man's woman," the handler countered. "You've stepped in it, big time, Cowboy."

"I can take care of myself," Joe said, though he had to admit to himself that Seamus O'Leary could be a problem, especially if he was an IRA leader as Fiona had suggested.

"It's gone too far, too fast." Adams sighed. "Look, I'll have to recommend that you be recalled before you get hurt."

Joe felt desperate. He couldn't just let them order him to leave. He had come for revenge against the IRA and being called home would be a humiliating defeat. Now he and Fiona were... he didn't know what. And Fiona was in trouble with this Seamus bastard, which was his own fault. He now was bound to Fiona, in love with her maybe.

"Listen, I'm on to something," he lied. "I think I've got a lead on the smuggling. This guy O'Leary pretends to be a fisherman but never brings in a catch. If you guys will just give me a chance, I'm sure that..."

"Look, Anderson, we're in a dangerous business, in case you hadn't noticed. I've been doing this long enough to have seen field agents killed who were less vulnerable than you are. I can't be a part of letting you die because you're incompetent or foolish or whatever."

"I'm telling you, I'll be okay, if you..."

"It's not up to me to decide whether to call you home or not. I'm gonna make my recommendation and then wash my hands of it. So just hang loose until you hear from us again."

"Thanks a lot."

"One other thing," Adams went on, ignoring Joe's sarcasm. "We're now well into our drone surveillance program with the Brits. Remember, if you ever hear any talk of the drones, or learn anything that sounds like a leak in security, we want to know. So that's one little task you can focus on, anyway. That'll at least give the nation something in return for what's been spent sending you there. Got it?"

"Yeah, I got it." Joe disconnected.

He stared out at the view of Rathlin Island across the sound, absently watching a dark cloud pour rain on Bull Point. He pondered his situation. First of all, how did they know about Fiona and Seamus? Who was close enough to be watching? It was unnerving to think that CIA was capable of such surveillance. And if they were, then why was it of any value to them to send Joe there in the first place? The only person he saw much of other than Fiona was Big Ryan. But Ryan couldn't possibly be the one. Since Foster had watched the altercation on the dock last night, could he be the one? Maybe. Joe certainly didn't like the man; he was so unfriendly. Maybe he was distant just so Joe wouldn't suspect him of being anything other than an unpleasantly officious nobody. It was a curious thing how the police had shown up to arrest the Frenchmen after Foster and his dog had been there. Yes, the dog was trained to sniff out whatever it was the Frenchmen had on board. So Foster must be with the police or some UK intelligence group perhaps.

Still standing at the overlook, Joe pulled out his iPhone again and called Fiona's cell number. When it rang several times and then switched to voicemail, he left a message saying he was concerned about her and wanted her to call. He hung up and pounded his fist on the wooden railing. To alleviate his frustration, he tapped the email icon and looked at the list. There was a message from Mary. In exasperation he shut his eyes hard and held the phone at his side. Tempted merely to erase it, he finally sighed and opened the message.

> Joe, you still have not answered my last email. I'm so worried about you, even though Wade tells me you're doing fine. He came down to take me to a party at the Country Club. Remember that I would have wanted you to go with me, but you charged off to Ireland instead. Don't tell Wade, but I'd have had a much better time with you. Take care, darling. Love, Mary.

Joe read the message twice, and was struck by a great sense of sadness. Staring off into the distance, he thought about how things just hadn't worked out right with Mary. Why was it, he wondered, that he hadn't been able to accept what had seemed so happy about living with her? Then as the rain drops began falling on him, he walked swiftly back to his car, got in and started up. He focused his thoughts on his new passion which was Fiona. Whatever he was going to do about Fiona, he'd better hurry up before Adams could get him called home. He hadn't thought much about finding smugglers lately, or getting revenge against the people who had hijacked his boat *Tartan*. Now everything had changed. Now—he could not completely fathom it—Fiona might be carrying his child.

Still agitated when he arrived in Ballycastle, he wedged his car into a tight parking space near Hillside Market and wriggled out. He walked in the store but didn't see Fiona anywhere. From behind the counter, Timothy smiled at him when he asked if she was around.

"My sister is busy, you see? Off in the city, she is, for a time."

"Where? In Belfast? Is there any way I could phone or go see her?"

Her brother glanced at Joe and raised his eyebrows. "So you do have a bit of a thing for my sister?"

"I'm concerned," Joe evaded the question. "There was something of a misunderstanding last night."

131

Timothy nodded. "Aye, t'was that." He apparently had heard about O'Leary.

"Has Seamus been by to see her today?"

"Oh, aye," Timothy replied. "A bit testy he was, too. Look, my friend, he's been after Fiona for quite a few years. I know I encouraged you with my sister, but..."

"She told me about Seamus," Joe said, "how she told him to take a walk and all. Apparently, he can't get it through his head that she's not interested in him."

"And so you plan to sort it all out for him, I take it?"

"If that's what it takes." Joe realized then that he was going pretty far out on the proverbial limb, just as Adams had said. But, his commitment to Fiona was more important than anything now, and he'd have to see it through.

"She went away to keep you and Seamus from a row," the brother said. "It's best that her and youse stay apart for a while, in any event."

"Well, can't I talk to her at least? I just want to apologize and, you know, make it right, you see." He knew he was grasping for straws and tried to think of some way to ally with her more closely. "I want her to know, too, that I understand her feelings about unionists. I mean, well, I introduced her to some boaters who turned out to be on the other side—loyal to Britain, or whatever."

"Aye, now that was an error," Tim said. "We have strong feelings about that, Fiona and me. If you want her attentions, youse best stay away from the likes of them."

"She's told me about your brother and your father," Joe explained. "I want you to know that I sympathize." He paused. "I can't imagine what it's like to remember your family members having been subjected to such terrible things. I can see why you and Fiona would be so angry."

Her brother looked at Joe a long moment, as if sizing him up and considering something. He glanced around to be sure no one else was in earshot. Then Timothy leaned closer. "Look, mate," he said. "I might be able to help you...intercede with me sis, you might say." He paused. "But there be a favor I might be asking of you in return."

Joe met his gaze and grimaced. "What sort of favor?"

Timothy just leaned closer. "Before I say more, I best discuss it with me mates, you see. But there's a group, an association, sort of, and we could use the services of one like yourself."

Joe blinked. *What was this?* "Just let me know," he replied, trying to sound willing. "But I've got to hurry up and see Fiona real soon, okay?"

Timothy reached across the counter and grabbed Joe's hand. "Aye," he said, giving Joe's hand a warm shake and holding on. "We'll talk soon enough."

Joe went out to his rental car, got in and closed the door, sitting there, trying to understand what had just happened. What was it Fiona's brother had proposed to him? And who were these mates he was talking about? He shuddered slightly as he started the car and pulled out into the street. He needed to talk to somebody. Big Ryan—where

133

was Ryan today? Since it was now after four, he decided to check at the pub.

"Not seen him today," Eamon said. Joe ordered a double shot of Coleraine. He had developed a real taste for this brand of whiskey made at Bushmills and sold only around Northern Ireland. It went down pretty fast and he asked for another double. As he waited for it, he pulled out his iPhone to try calling Ryan. There was a text message there. "Call Wade." Joe stared at the screen, wondering what Wade could want. Was he the CIA official who would give Joe the proverbial axe and instruct him to come home? Joe took another big swig of whiskey, noting the barman was giving him a critical eye.

"Something wrong?" Eamon asked. Joe emptied the contents, letting it burn his throat.

"If you see Ryan," he said, wiping his mouth on his sleeve. "ask him to give me a call, will ya? Right away?" The bartender nodded, and Joe half tripped on a chair going out.

"So, call Wade," Joe muttered as he climbed in the car and rode up the hill above the town. He pulled off in a deserted spot beside a small grove on the hilltop and got out. Walking to a secluded point among the trees, he took his iPhone and called the bastard.

"Glad to hear from you, Joe," Wade said when they were connected. "I hear you're in a bit of a scrape?"

"Listen, Wade. Adams has a cob up his ass. There's no real problem here. I can handle it."

"That's good to know."

"I'm on to something here," Joe went on. "Adams said he wants to can me, but I'm just now making some important contacts." He paused, covered the mouthpiece and belched. He hoped he wasn't slurring. "You guys just need to give me some more time, that's all. I'm about to have some good info for you, really I am."

"Don't worry about a thing, Sport. Adams works for me, you know. I can replace him as your handler if he persists in this."

"Great, I'm glad to know that." Joe said, trying to disregard the fact Wade had called him *Sport* again. He tried to clear his mind. "I should communicate with you then?"

"That's right. Don't talk to anybody at the Agency but me until I assign a different handler. I'll get that all straightened out in the system here. In the meantime, you just do your job, and everything will be fine."

"Good deal," Joe replied, thinking the sooner he had someone else to talk to beside Wade the better. "And Adams said you have someone else over here that's keeping an eye on me. I didn't know that. Is it this harbormaster, Evan Foster?"

"I can't tell you anything about that, Joe," Wade said. "You're pretty new to our business. But believe me, there are some things better left alone and unsaid. Just do your job, and we'll watch your back."

"Thanks," Joe said. He noted that this was the nicest conversation he had ever had with Wade. Being a

135

professional, after all, it was not too far-fetched for him to be watching out for Joe's interests, albeit a remarkable turnaround. "By the way," he asked, "how is Mary doing?"

"Oh, fine, I guess," Wade said after a pause. "I haven't talked to her lately. But no news is good news, you know."

Joe recalled Mary's email had mentioned that Wade took her to a party, but he stopped himself from pointing out Wade's bald-faced lie. Instead, he responded very appreciatively, and they ended the call.

Mulling over the conversation, Joe walked through the trees to the top of the cliff that overlooked Rathlin Sound. Maybe Wade thought *lately* meant in the last day or two, Joe wondered. Or maybe "Dr. Spin" just didn't want Joe to know anything much about his dalliances with Mary.

Reaching the edge of the cliff, he looked down at the harbor. In the light of the waning sun peeking through the clouds, he could see the afternoon ferry making its way across and just about to enter Church Bay at the island. Coming out of Ballycastle harbor was Seamus O'Leary's trawler, making its usual evening run out to the fishing grounds. That was good news, Joe thought. At least he could get back to *Kittiwake* without having to bother with a possible encounter with that guy. Joe hoped the fishermen would stay out all night. It did cross his mind that O'Leary never seemed to unload many fish at the dock, certainly not enough to make a living on fishing.

Remembering the annoying conversation with Adams, he thought about the admonition to look for drones.

It had made Joe mad when Adams said spotting drones was the only thing Joe might be qualified to do.

"No drones out tonight," he said, mockingly putting his hand to his forehead and peering around. He supposed Adams must think drones might be better at surveillance than he was. "Bah!"

On the way back to his car, Joe decided he could use another drink at the pub. Maybe Big Ryan would have shown up by this time. If not, he could fortify himself with another whiskey and think of some way to deal with Timothy, in case the young man showed up to propose the special favor he wanted in exchange for helping Joe reach out to Fiona. As distasteful as the idea was, this Timothy very well could someday be his brother-in-law. How screwed up, he wondered, could this situation get?

Chapter Eleven

"A favor I'd be asking," Ryan said on Sunday morning, "if you still have your hire car."

"Of course," Joe replied, remembering Ryan's old bicycle. Besides, it was rare for the big man to ask for anything.

"It's my mother's birthday and, although she has long passed, I always attend the two churches of my parents in Armagh. Usually I stay with me sister there, but that's not sorting out this year. So I'll be wondering if you'd be so kind to take me over, maybe go to the churches with me."

"Churches? Plural? You go to more than one?"

"Aye. My mother's and then my father's, for to honor them both. At one time I went to Brother Jack's own parish, but no more. This annual church-going's long been my tradition."

"All right." Joe smiled. Except for going with Mary at Christmas, he hadn't been in a church in quite a while. "I haven't got much in the way of dressy clothes though."

139

Ryan shrugged. "Whatever's your best will do. I don't make a great fashion statement myself."

They agreed that Joe would arrive outside Ryan's flat at six in the morning, which he did, and they had an early ride down the M2. Not many Irish were stirring at that hour on Sunday. The Catholics would have mass at an early hour, so Joe and Ryan would attend there first.

Ryan gave directions and cursed when at one roundabout Joe nearly ran out in front of a car coming on his right. Despite his greenness at driving on the left, he did manage to get them safely to an imposing light brown stoned edifice. At Ryan's direction, he drove into the adjoining parking area. After getting out of the car, he noticed a man with a green arm band standing nearby, watching the lot and pointed him out to Ryan.

"Facilitator," Big Ryan replied. "Has an eye out for anyone parking and not going for the church."

"Limited parking, huh?"

Ryan shook his head. "He's wary for a car bomber."

Joe laughed. "A bomber? Surely not. At a church?"

The big man gave him a look as if regarding a naïve child. "T'would not be the first."

Astonished, Joe followed after him. It had been his impression, his mindset, that only Catholic republicans, IRA members, could be terrorists. Clearly, the Catholics in Northern Ireland were equally as concerned about attacks from the other side. Reprisals perhaps? Or did anyone know which side was the initiator and which was the avenger? Joe was beginning to learn more about all this than CIA had taught him.

As they walked into the crowded church yard, they encountered a talkative group of teenagers gathered to socialize. Many of them wore school blazers, and Joe noted the distinctive Catholic emblems. It struck him that these emblems immediately identified them as members of the Roman faith. On the streets of the cities, they instantly were identifiable as separate and different from the Protestant kids, who likely wore their own emblems. Otherwise, there was no difference in skin color or facial features to create a sense of separateness. They were just ordinary children with the same Gaelic features but segregated by the different embroidered badges they wore over their hearts. Many a fight must have started over nothing more than the symbols of Christianity that showed they were Catholic instead of Protestant.

Joe followed Ryan into the church and was surprised to see the big man cross himself as he entered the nave. Ryan glanced at him with a slight shrug, led the way down the aisle, genuflected, and sat down in a pew. Joe gave a self-conscious bow and followed. *When in Rome,* he thought. Sitting quietly, he surveyed the iconic sculptures of saints and the colorful stained glass windows. It occurred to him that not everyone was dressed up for church. In fact, some were quite casually dressed—a very different way of churchgoing from what he had grown up with in the Episcopal Church back home. He imagined Fiona coming to just such a church, the one in Ballycastle most likely. He wondered again about how she had acted after they had sex. That they had used no protection probably was the cause of her reaction. Of course, being Roman Catholic, she was prohibited from using anything, which seemed ludicrous, given her passion for him. Yet, he was an outsider from her religion and knew he did not know the moral influences instilled in her. Had it been a vulnerable time for her? Was she now pregnant? Was she now carrying his child? Where was she now? "In Belfast," Tim had said. Would she spurn him forever? Joe looked at the large crucifix above the altar, thinking that Christ died for the sins of all men, who like Joe himself, never had a full and clear understanding of themselves or their circumstance.

Looking around, he spotted a beautiful blond who suddenly reminded him of Mary, and he wondered if she would be going to St. Philip's today, dressed up in her finest. His face darkened as it occurred to him that Wade just might be there with her. Why should he care? Well, there seemed to be something unnatural about dating your dead brother's wife, that's all. Was Wade really interested in Mary? Or was he simply interested in Earnest's money? Joe's musings were interrupted by a sudden triumphant blast of the pipe organ and the instant rush of the congregation immediately standing. The procession began, led by a finely robed priest, swinging an incense censor. As he came by, the unguent cloud wafted toward Joe. *Damn!* He sneezed, pulled out his handkerchief to put to his nose, but too late. This allergic reaction hadn't happened since he was a teenage acolyte at a high-Episcopal service. He sneezed again. Big Ryan looked over at him and grinned.

"As we all know, the Orange Order soon will begin their Marching Season," the priest said in his homily. "The bishop has called for an increase in the ranks of our Safeguarding Facilitators in order to meet the demands that will be forthcoming in the summer. So I urge all able-bodied men to volunteer. Application forms will be made available at the door." He paused, and Joe noted a few murmurs around the congregation. He recalled that the Protestant Orange Order organized numerous pipe and drum bands that marched in the cities during the summer. While the nominal aim of such marches were to honor William of Orange, they were designed to show the Republicans that the Orange Order was strictly loyal, too, and would defend the union with the United Kingdom at any cost. Joe leaned toward Ryan.

"What are facilitators?" he whispered.

"Bodyguards," Ryan whispered back, "or such as the man in the car park."

"While we're on this subject," the priest continued, "I'm here to remind you of your Christian duty. Now I know it's hard to abide the Orangemen marching in the streets, beating on their big drums and shrilly piping, provoking the ire of good Catholics. Not but a lad among you remembers the history of violence and hatred. But remember this, dear friends, their marches say nothing, mean nothing, prove nothing, so long as we of the true faith ignore their foolishness."

There was more low murmuring and a feeling of tenseness. A young man to Joe's left made a fist and banged on the pew. A mother two rows ahead put her arm around a little girl and pulled her close.

"I'm aware of the ill will that so many of us feel inside," the priest went on, "especially among so many of our young men." He glanced around, fixing his gaze on some younger members here and there. "But those of us who recall the days of The Troubles know that there is nothing to gain by vengeance. There is no room for violence in our society today."

Joe glanced around, noting some stony expressions. One elderly lady put a handkerchief to her eyes. Another crossed herself. A pair of men in their twenties whispered to one another. Ryan glanced at Joe and shook his head. So, where were the terrorists who bomb indiscriminately, Joe wondered, or the hijackers who took *Tartan* in order to smuggle weapons, the people Joe had sworn to seek out for vengeance? Likely these IRA members sat among the congregations, apparently espousing Catholicism, crossing themselves and devoutly praying. Did they really hear their priest's message? Would they heed it? Or would they, like typical churchgoers, leave the Christian message at the door as they departed the sanctuary?

Later, in the car on the way to the Protestant church that had been the other religious home for Ryan in his boyhood, Joe asked him what he thought of the priest's remarks.

"Very appropriate," Ryan replied. "Suited to the times and suited to our patron, Saint Columcille. *Colum* means dove. *Columcille* means dove of the church. But as a young man, even Columba was as wild and bloody as many other adolescents. It was only in his mature years that he converted and stood for peace."

"I see. That made the priest's sermon very appropriate for his congregation, didn't it?"

"There's only one problem." Ryan looked grave. "Did you notice? It's the young men, the ones whose balls be their brains. They're the ones not listening."

As he drove, Joe pondered what he had seen and heard while Ryan directed him to the second place of worship. Arriving a little early, they parked on the street near the more modern building of the Free Presbyterian Church.

"This was your father's church?" Joe asked. "It looks a bit too new for your childhood."

"'Twas not till me teenage years that my father dragged me here." Ryan stared out of the window in silence. "It was this church's teaching ran me to sea," he said finally. "Took me out of my youth and sent me away."

"I'm sorry?" Joe said, not quite understanding.

Ryan opened the car door. "Come ahead. You'll get it soon enough, I warrant."

Growing up as an Episcopalian, Joe had never really heard a fire and brimstone sermon in person. But in this comparatively stark barn of a sanctuary, he was hearing one today. The preacher, a thin, almost emaciated looking gray-haired man, in coat and tie—a far cry from the grand robes of the Catholic clergy—glared at the congregation and raised his fist.

"The devil is in ye," he suddenly shouted, and paused to look around at them. "Make no mistake," he continued in a softer voice. "Oh aye, a wily creature he is, with a bag of tricks to discourage even the best of Christians." He shook his head sadly. "This world is no friend to Christ, my brothers. It was our own race of humans who put him to death. The work of the devil, make no mistake."

Joe dared to glance around at the people nearby. A young couple sat rigidly to his right. Their small son wriggled nervously between them, and his mother put out a firm hand to restrain him. Beyond them sat an older gentlemen in a brown suit and dark tie who looked as somber as if he were attending a funeral.

"In our own city," the preacher continued, "the ungodly live in our midst. We find them in our own stores, rub elbows with them at the counter, and meet them walking in the streets. They appear on television—the devil's own contrivance—speaking lies, making sexual displays, and subject us to all kinds of evil. Some even engage in the filth of homosexuality." There were murmurs of disgust from the congregation. "The devil is out there, my brothers, and not only ourselves but our children are in peril from the temptations of the ungodly." The preacher closed his eyes as if in pain and anguish.

"How do we guard against them, my friends? Read the Bible. Take refuge from the temptations of sin that the

146

evil ones put before you. They are the devil's own, working to destroy your peace of mind and your righteous soul."

"And we are tempted, Oh Lord are we tempted, by those who would have us unite in harmony with those who do not profess our faith. Aye, we are asked, invited by certain would-be reconcilers who ask us to join in so-called ecumenical meetings with the papists. And yet, my brothers, how could we as righteous, followers of the one true Bible, allow ourselves to mix with the misguided and foully flawed Romans? Refuse! Refuse, my friends. Live separately. Shun the wrongdoers and wrong thinkers."

"We members of the Free Presbyterian Church will never countenance the ecumenical movement. We never will join in fellowship with those who mistakenly compromise our beliefs as if somehow it was the Christian thing to do. No. We are the only true Christians, the only ones who will be saved. And why? Because we live our lives in faith, faith based in the truth of the Bible as the only word of God."

The preacher paused, reached down for a glass of water, took a sip, and for the first time, he smiled. "My dear friends, remember what Saint Paul tells us in his epistle to the Romans. 'If God be for us, who can be against us?' I'll say it again. No matter what the devil and the devil's own people may do, no matter what terrors or republican violence may befall, remember this, my brothers, 'If God be for us, who can be against us?'"

He surveyed the congregation with hawkish eyes, happened to see Joe's incredulous expression and stared with a look of disdainful unwelcome. Joe returned the look with

147

an unwavering stare. Clearly, he'd never bother to come back to listen to this kind of vitriolic tirade. Then the old preacher broke his stare, looked away, turned and stepped down from the pulpit. Joe felt suddenly sad, a sense of pity for the old man. He exchanged glances with Ryan, who merely shook his head.

"Want to leave?" Ryan whispered. Joe realized his own feelings were plainly obvious and tried to smile.

"Only if you do," he whispered back. "Otherwise, I'm okay with staying."

In a few minutes while a hymn, "Let All Mortal Flesh Keep Silence," was being sung, Ryan gestured to Joe. They got up and slipped to the aisle, attempting to be inconspicuous as possible—a very difficult task for two tall men. With a last glance at the preacher, Joe noted a "to hell with you" look, and it made him grin as they reached the door.

"Whew!" Joe said as they walked to the car. It occurred to him that while his mission was to find a devil or two among the IRA who were Catholic, it seemed that the meaner people likely were among these fire-breathing loyalist Protestants, or this sect anyway. He grimaced. "I'm coming out of there feeling a little scorched or something. No wonder you go to that church only once a year."

Ryan sighed deeply. "'A sad day indeed,' me mother would say, when my father joined Ian Paisley's church." He wiped his hand across his eyes. "She marked it a sad day; a sad day, in fact, for all of Ireland."

"One detour on the way, if you will," Ryan said as they approached Ballycastle. "We'll not go in. I just want you to see."

"Sure," Joe said, "if it won't take too long." He was weary of the car and even wearier of all he had seen and heard that morning.

"It will lighten your day a bit." Ryan gestured to a side road. "Turn up here." The road climbed the hill and overlooked the sea. They came to a group of white buildings and parked in front near a few other vehicles.

"Corrymeela Centre for Reconciliation," Ryan said. "Founded in 1965 by a man of great vision, Reverend Doctor Ray Davey, it was. He hoped to create a bridge between the Protestants and the Catholics, the loyalists and the republicans. For almost 50 years now, brave Christian leaders have struggled to bring peace and harmony to Northern Ireland."

"How successful has it been?" Joe asked, following Ryan out of the car. "From what I heard in those two churches this morning, I can't see that there's been a whole lot accomplished." They went over to the main building and peered in the window. There was a meeting in progress, and someone was leading a discussion.

"I hear that the Center has done well in many ways," Ryan said. "But the Troubles are like an epidemic. If you can't vaccinate everyone, then the illness continues. It's the young bucks, the teens and the 20-year-olds, full of new mischief and their own piss and vinegar, that carry on the infection of hatred and violence."

As he continued watching, Joe pondered that idea. "Well, they have to get it from somewhere," he said. "I don't think each generation dreams up prejudice all on its own."

"Right on," the big man replied. "It's their fathers and mothers that feed them the poison." He got back in the car, Joe followed and drove down the drive.

"It's passed down from the fathers, in a tribal sort of way," Ryan went on. "The fathers and even the mothers will pass stories of terrible things done by the other side. Hatred is taught to children, a sorry heritage for the young."

"Did you hear those kind of stories, Ryan, when you were a boy?"

"Aye, but it was different, my mother being Catholic and my father a Protestant. In our case, we caught it from both directions. While Brother Jack threw his lot in with the Catholics and became a priest, the whole business drove my sister near to distraction. As for me, I escaped by going to sea." As he drove down the mountain, Joe tried to imagine the extent of the conflict that must have torn the family.

"Seems to me that, by going to sea, you would have gained a better perspective on all that," Joe suggested.

Ryan shook his head. "I just learned to shun both sides," he said.

Chapter Twelve

"Can ye meet me at half ten tonight?" Tim had called Joe's iPhone. "I'll be closing down the market and we can visit with me friends."

Just about to drive away from the Ballymoney Leisure Center where he had been swimming laps for exercise, Joe found himself nervously squeezing the iPhone again. He wished he hadn't given Tim his number.

"Can't we meet at Eamon's Bar?" he suggested, not liking the idea of confronting Timothy in any other than a public place.

"We'll be attending a meeting," Timothy explained. "And a bit on the *q-t* as well."

"Will Fiona be there?" Joe asked. There was a pause.

"She has no part in this," was the curt reply. Then there was another pause.

"Me and youse'll speak about me sister later," Timothy said.

"I see," Joe said, noting an unpleasantness in the brother's voice. It appeared that if Joe was to get this guy to tell him where his sister was, then he'd just have to do things his way.

"I'll pick you up at the marina car park," Timothy instructed.

Joe frowned. "Uh, maybe down the street would be wiser?" He had no idea where he would be going or what he would be asked to do, but Joe didn't want Foster to know, or anybody else for that matter. "Better still," he said." I'll just walk up to your store."

"Aye," Timothy agreed. "Make it half ten, sharp."

"You got it. Do I need to bring anything?"

"Just keep all this to yerself," Tim said and disconnected.

Joe grimaced, turned off his iPhone and realized his pulse was racing. He already had pegged Fiona's brother as a devious character, and the idea of a clandestine meeting with him was more than worrisome. Joe decided to find the closest pub where he could think things over. Once or twice on his way into Ballymoney, he had noticed The King William, a pub with lots of cars parked nearby. He found a narrow spot on the street for his car, squeezed it in by jockeying back and forth several times, wishing the government would paint dividing lines between places. It seemed people didn't mind parking in the middle of two vacant spaces, getting their own car parked and never mind the next driver.

He got out and walked down to The King William, pushed open its ornate heavy wooden door and went in. It was around six in the evening and the place was crowded, even though it was a week day. A number of people eyed him in silence as he made his way to the bar, and he realized they were not just curious but somewhat suspicious of strangers. The bartender gave him a smile, however, and the Irish horizontal nod. Joe asked for a scotch on the rocks.

"Must be an American," the publican said with a hint of disdain. "I'll see to finding a wee bit of ice." He disappeared in the back room and took time returning with two small lumps in the glass, over which he poured whiskey. By the time it was set before Joe there was not a trace of ice left.

"On the rocks; that's you," the man said with a smile. Joe put his three pounds fifty on the bar and smiled back.

Still edgy about his upcoming meeting with Timothy, he unconsciously gulped down the smooth whiskey in four swallows. All he really wanted from the guy was a way to further his relationship with Fiona. The idea that in the process he would have to associate with her brother was not what he considered desirable. But anyway he had agreed to go to whatever Tim had on his mind.

Waiting for a chance to order another scotch, Joe gazed about the room. There was a faded banner hanging prominently on the wall to the right of the bar. It was orange and blue with the figure of a man on a white horse leading a company of soldiers whose dress appeared to be 17th

Century. The next time the publican came by, Joe asked him about it.

"That's a banner of the Orange Order," the man replied, "carried in many a parade for nigh on to a hundred years, it was. And it has hung there for most of my lifetime." He turned to admire it. "Heard of the Orange Order, have you?"

"Yes, but I don't know much about it," Joe said, pretending ignorance. "Sort of a fraternity or something, isn't it?" Actually, he had read a good bit on the subject but wanted to hear firsthand.

The barkeep smiled. "Much more to it than that." He scooped up a couple of empty glasses and put them in the sink under the bar.

"Are there many members here in town?"

The man gestured with a sweep of his hand. "Near every man here belongs. Has been the tradition of many for generations." Someone signaled him down the bar, and he went to fill the man's glass.

As he sat sipping the whiskey, with two more small ice cubes doing their best to disappear, he noticed a group of three middle-aged men down near the Orange Order banner, drinking and talking and becoming louder by the minute. He indicated them to the publican. "They must come here often."

The publican glanced at them and nodded. "Aye. Own those stools from half three to ten or later, or think they do."

"Don't they have jobs?" Joe asked, although he could see they were very casually dressed. "I mean, how can a man of 50 or so spend so much time here?" They watched as the man in a black tam spoke some punch line, and all three laughed uproariously.

"Political pensioners. Paid off by the government." He pulled a white towel off his shoulder and wiped the counter.

"How do you mean, *political*?

The bar tender smiled thinly. "Man threw a rock in a street riot, or helped set off a bomb or two. Or maybe tipped off the police once. The government gives 'em a pension to behave themselves. Think it keeps such rowdies off the streets, you know."

Joe was amazed. "You mean they get a pension just to behave themselves? I can't imagine."

"Saves lives. Protects the peace." The bartender shook his head. "What gets me is their craic," he said. "Forever telling the same stories, night after night. It begins to make my head go hurting." They watched as the three raised their glasses and toasted King William's image on the banner.

"Loyalists, obviously," Joe said.

"Oh, aye, of course. And no doubt but they know which side of their bread the butter's on." Someone hailed him across the room, and he went off to fill yet another glass.

157

A man about Joe's height and size, about 50 or so, wearing a Spandex cycling suit entered and took a place at the bar beside Joe. He hailed Alex, the bartender, who answered, "Hi ya, Johnny," and brought over a pint of Guinness without asking. Johnny noticed Joe and nodded. Joe motioned to the man's clothing.

"Out riding a bike?"

"Aye," Johnny replied. Giving Joe a careful, sizing-up stare.

"Do you ride far?" Often he had seen bicyclers on the narrow roads, all but oblivious to the car traffic.

"From Portstewart to Portrush to Ballymoney and back," the man replied. "Keeps me fit."

"I swim myself," Joe said. "I do laps for a half mile or so. Nice pool at the Leisure Center here."

"Canadian, are you?"

Joe grinned. "From a little farther south."

"On holiday?"

"Aye," Joe said, smiling at himself for unconsciously employing the term in his vocabulary. "I've got a boat in Ballycastle. Just doing some sailing." Johnny nodded and sipped his Guinness.

"Do you work in Portrush?"

"Retired 12 years ago," Johnny said.

"What sort of work?"

The man took a swig of his ale before answering with apparent reluctance, "the R.U.C."

"Royal Ulster Constabulary?" Joe said. "Policeman?"

"Aye, that I was," he shook his head. "No more."

"Now you have the PSNI?" Joe asked. "Why did they change the name?" The question brought a dark look across the man's face.

"Too much of the past carried in the old name, so they said." He glanced at the Orange banner, sighed and gulped his ale.

"I guess you saw a lot of The Troubles."

The former policeman shot him a hard glance. "More than you'd believe," he said. Joe nodded. He recalled Fiona's critical remarks about the RUC and realized that, as the old adage says, there must be two sides to every story.

"I've only heard the Catholic side," Joe said.

The man gave him another hard look. "Catholic are you?"

Joe shook his head. "Episcopalian, I guess, if anything. That's Anglican in the U.S."

"We lost many a good man to the bloody Catholics." The policeman took a gulp of his dark stout.

"I've heard it was really terrible," Joe said. He received a look of mild disgust, and realized his comment must have seemed pretty lame. "I'm sorry," he added.

159

He stared at Joe a moment, then looked away and shrugged. "Over the years, many of my fellow officers were killed, 13 of them close friends. Bombs, guns, bricks, ambushes, you name it." His eyes closed in painful memory. "Don't talk to me about the Papist animals."

Joe nodded and drank his whiskey. "I'm sorry," he said. "I suppose you were trying to protect the Protestant population, who wanted to be a part of the U. K.?" His question drew another look of hard disdain. Joe thought for a moment the man might even throw a punch. But the man's eyes softened to sadness as he looked away.

"There were thugs among the Loyalists as well," Johnny said. "Still are." He shook his head. "A constable who tries to be fair has to watch his back." He gave Joe another long stare and then turned to his drink.

"Well, I'm glad you're out of all that," Joe offered gently.

Johnny glanced at him and gave a cynical laugh. "Oh aye, out of it, indeed, were that possible."

"You mean it may not be over?" Joe dared to ask.

Johnny held his glass at an angle and gazed at the contents. "Some of the bastards have long memories." He shook his head. "I keep an eye out."

Joe realized he was talking to a man likely still suffering from his experiences. He'd had a friend, Frank, from childhood who joined the Marines and served in combat in Vietnam. Afterwards, Frank suffered for years with PTSD until one day he took his own life.

"Bicycling must help you," Joe said. "Deal with things, I mean."

Johnny suddenly turned and faced Joe squarely. "Look here," he said. "What business is it of yours? You know nothing of what the RUC was to me. A proud force we were. Kept the whole bloody society from falling into civil war. We were disbanded, but not for lack of dedication or weakness or incompetence, I'll tell you. No, they renamed our force "the service, the Police Service of Northern Ireland, as you said. Made it 40% Catholic, and took away the shields and vests." He shook his head. "Well, the liberal politicians will learn that this weak new 'service' will fold and fail in time."

"Because things aren't really settled between the different sides, you mean?"

The policeman shook his head. "It's history."

Joe smiled kindly. "You were heroes, I think."

The man closed his eyes for a moment. "The heroes are dead."

Silently, they stood at the bar for a long moment before Joe nodded his understanding. "May I buy you another round?"

Johnny stared at him briefly, gave a shrug and shook his head. "Take care, mate." He drained his glass, then abruptly turned and walked out.

Joe watched him go and then glanced back at the Orange banner. There must have been not two but three sides fighting one another in The Troubles, he realized. Now he would have a different view of Fiona's stories. He checked his watch. It was getting close to time to go meet Timothy. What kind of meeting it was going to be was anybody's guess. Despite the alcohol, however, Joe wasn't feeling as fortified for it as he would have liked. In fact, he realized as he walked out to his car, it was making him downright nervous.

Chapter Thirteen

At 10:30 that night—"half ten," as Timothy had said—Joe walked up to the market. In the twilight he made out Tim waiting outside by an old rusted red Opel.

"We have a wee drive," he said, climbing in. Joe slipped as he stepped off the curb and caught himself on the car boot.

"A bit tipsy perhaps?" Timothy noted but did not laugh. Joe shrugged and crossed his arms. He might seem 'tipsy,' but mentally he was concerned and alert. They rode in silence a few minutes, heading out into the Glens of Moyne.

"What's our destination?" Joe asked, trying to sound casual.

"A farm near Cushendun." Timothy gave no more explanation. In fact, he seemed unusually distant. He drove at better than 80 KPH even around the sharp curves, which made Joe even more nervous, but the locals always seemed to do that, and Joe supposed the boy knew the mountainous

163

roads, anyway. At a remote intersection in the moors, Timothy pulled off and stopped the car.

"What's the matter?" Joe asked, startled by the sudden stop. Tim turned toward him and made an open-hand gesture.

"I'm sorry to ask this, Joe, but me mates insist that I blindfold you for the rest of the way."

"What for?" Joe was about ready to jump out of the car.

"We're going to a secret meeting," Timothy explained. "I cannot divulge its location until you're in with us. Better for you that you don't learn too much at first, 'til you're agreed. Else there'd be no way for you to…" He paused. "Just better, that's all." He pulled out a black hood. "I'll need you to wear this." Tim reached over to place the hood on him, Joe grabbed his wrist. "Look," he said. "I've got to uh… explain something to you. I want you to know that I'm not interested…uh, in you."

Tim pulled the hood back away from Joe, took in a breath, and then laughed. "You think I'm out after you? No, you ugly bloke. Bejuzus! What gave you that idea?"

"Well, Fiona, Fiona told me about well…you and her one-time fiancé. I thought that maybe you were taking me to some sort of party, or whatever."

"Not on your life, mate," the young man said. "We're off on serious business." He laughed again. "Now be a good lad and put this on."

Joe managed a laugh, too, releasing some of his tension. He took the hood and placed it over his head. Tim shifted the car into first and took off again. They rode in silence for a few minutes before Joe spoke.

"Look here, Tim. If you want me to stay blindfolded, you're gonna have to tell me something about what we're doing here. "

Tim sighed. "It's to a meeting we're going, political of sorts."

"Political?" Joe repeated. "What kind of politics?"

"Well, I don't know what you understand about Ulster, mate, but there's many of us who are republican. We're fighting to become part of the Republic of Ireland."

"I see. And that has to be a secret?"

"Aye, mate. There's no other way."

"And you want me to join in?" Joe tensed a little.

"There's just a favor from you, we'd be asking," Tim explained. "Look, you can trust me, Joe. Fiona would have my head if anything happened to you."

The idea that Fiona might care about him heartened Joe somewhat. He sighed and nodded, "Okay." As they drove on, he tried to relax, but his mind was racing, trying to figure out several plans of action, either to knock Timothy out and then run, or just run. *What had he gotten into now?*

In about 15 minutes Timothy stopped the car, reached over and helped Joe slip the hood off. Through bleary eyes he could see they were at a stone cottage that had a barn nearby. They got out, and a brown and white spotted hound ran up and barked. Tim led the way to the kitchen door. Joe followed with the dog sniffing at his leg. Tim knocked three raps, paused and then two more. In a moment, a matronly woman let them in. Joe nodded politely to her, but she merely replied with a tight-lipped stare. Seated in the kitchen at a wooden table near a fireplace were two men.

"This is Joe Anderson," Timothy said. "And this is our leader, Tom. And Ned here is our... sergeant at arms, you might say." He laughed.

Joe nodded to them. Neither got up nor smiled. Tom, a man of about 60, dressed in coveralls and smoking a pipe, indicated a wooden chair for Joe. Joe sat down, realizing that he was in really deep now.

"So," said the older man, "tell us what you're doing in Northern Ireland."

Joe took a breath and began his rehearsed cover story about being recently retired and on vacation, renting a sailboat with plans to cruise around the coast and maybe up to the Scottish Hebrides in the summer. As he talked, he tried to appraise the two men, hoping to figure out what they were up to. The second man was in his twenties perhaps, like Timothy. He wore a tight green t-shirt that revealed his farmhand muscles. On his left arm just below the shoulder was a tattoo of a cross with pointed ends to make it look more like a dagger. When Joe finished his story, they continued to stare at him in silence.

166

"And why would ye be wanting to help us?" the older man asked finally.

Joe shrugged. "I don't know. I mean, I have no idea who you are or what you want, so I don't know why I'd help do... whatever."

The man puffed on his pipe for a moment. The smoke had a honey-sweet smell, but it did not make Joe feel any better. The man locked his eyes on him. "What's your religion?"

Joe shrugged again. "Religion? Uh, well I was brought up an Episcopalian. But I'm not real religious, I guess." He paused. "You know, in the U.S. nobody much cares what you are. Well, maybe some do, but I'm not much for church-going myself." He was just a little bit irritated about being asked such a question. Of course, the whole situation was beginning to seem outrageous. He gave Timothy a reproachful look.

"Joe's taken a liking to my sister," Tim said. "I think he'd be willing to help us..."

"You already said that when you rang us up," the one with the tattoo interrupted. He looked at Joe. "Are ye at all acquainted with the IRA?"

Joe's pulse quickened. He forced himself to remain calm. "I've heard of it," he said. "I mean, I've read a little history about Ireland, but I don't claim to be an expert at all."

"And do you know how the Brits have treated the Irish?" the older man asked, leaning forward, his finger

167

waving at Joe. "Do you know that for centuries the Brits and their Scot Presbyterian lackeys have oppressed our people, taken away our lands, starved us, kept us down and nary a tuppence for it?"

"Yes," Joe said. "I've read Sean O'Casey and…"

"Bah!" the man pulled the pipe from his mouth. "You can't understand it by reading a bloody book. It's in the sweat and the blood of the Irish that such tales are written, I'll tell you. I don't know your heritage, Anderson, but where there are Irish, there's kin that suffered." He glanced at the younger man for agreement.

"Aye, 'tis so," Ned said, giving Joe a savage look.

"You know, in America," Joe said, trying to keep his voice even. "We're likely to have lots of different ancestry and kinships. My sister married a Catholic, and they get along quite happily."

"And did she convert?"

"Oh no," Joe replied. "Some of their children are Catholic and some are Protestant. It's their own choice, really."

"Couldn't happen here," the older man said, gripping the pipe stem tightly in his teeth. He puffed a couple of times. "You might bear that in mind if you've an eye on Fiona."

"I wouldn't forget about Seamus O'Leary, if I were you," the tattooed Ned added, with a chuckle.

Joe shrugged. "That's my problem," he said, thinking that it wasn't any of their business anyway. "So, let's get back to why I'm sitting here." He had just about had enough of this browbeating treatment.

The man with the pipe smiled. "I like your spirit at least." He glanced at the others, then he looked at Joe. "We'd like to use your boat," he said. "And you, too, of course." He glanced around at the others again. "We need you to make a run for us, you see. Pick up a wee bit of cargo and deliver it."

Joe waved it off with his hand. "I'm not in the hauling business," he said, realizing full well that he had landed right in the middle of what he had come to Northern Ireland for. "I'd think there'd be some commercial type boat around, like that small steamer that seems to be making deliveries around or whatever." *Don't say too much*, he told himself.

"They're watched, day and night," Ned said.

"But now you, a tourist here among us," Tom explained, "you could sail in and out entirely unnoticed. The fact that you're a neutral would make it work."

"Because I don't have a dog in your fight, so to speak," Joe said, attempting to sound flippant. "And what's in it for me?"

"We have resources," Tom replied. "I'm sure we can come to an amicable agreement."

"For some kind of smuggling, I take it?" Joe asked. "What kind of stuff is it?"

169

Ned started to speak. Tom put up his hand to silence him. "Just a few wee things we need in our business," he replied. "Industrial chemicals, like."

"Well, if it's no more than that, then why sneak it in?"

"The Brits don't think it's environmentally safe," Tom replied with a smirk, and the three Irishmen laughed.

Joe nodded soberly. Inside, he was about to burst. "You're talking about weapons or explosives and the like?" Joe guessed, still trying to keep his voice even.

"Why, nothing more than you can buy in American gun shows," Tom replied. "Rocket launchers, AK-47s and the like. Or maybe a wee bit of explosives. No more than what you'd find in any household in the States." Timothy and Ned laughed again. Joe smiled politely.

"Look," Tom continued. "You'd make a wee short run and soon be done with it."

"Don't forget Fiona, Joe," Timothy said. "If you help us, Fiona will be pleased."

Joe hadn't thought about Fiona being in favor of all this. But there wasn't time right now to consider that. He had to play along. Besides, what would they do with him now if he didn't play along. *Don't think about that either*, he told himself.

"When?" he asked, keeping his voice as even as possible.

"Oh, soon," Tom said. He tapped his burnt tobacco in a saucer. "We don't yet know the schedule." He looked at Ned.

"Within the week," Ned said. "We'll let you know the details in a day or so."

"And how much pay for my time?"

"Five hundred quid," Tom said.

"Two thousand," Joe said, thinking he had to bargain so as not to sound too eager.

"For a few hours' work? Blarney," Tom exclaimed. "A thousand and not a penny more."

Joe paused as if considering it, mentally counting to ten to make it convincing. "Okay," he said with a shrug. "I'm in."

"Well, good on ya," Timothy said, looking relieved. Joe realized that Tim had stuck his own neck out some by bringing him here.

"One other wee concern," Ned added, giving Joe a stare. "No one crosses the Real IRA. Any bloke who does gets his balls cut off and stuffed into his bloody mouth, you see." His lips formed a thin smile. "Just thought you ought to know."

Joe returned his stare and let out a gasp of a laugh.

"Oh, it's no joke," Tom said, "a matter best remembered."

Knowing clearly there was no way out, Joe mustered his nerve. "As I told you," he said evenly, "I'm in."

Timothy insisted Joe wear the blindfold for the first ten minutes of the ride back to Ballycastle. Joe complied without question, deciding that it didn't matter much where they had held the meeting. He thought about Fiona again and wondered what she might know about all this. Meanwhile as Tim drove, he talked excitedly about Joe's new role.

"I knew you'd like joining in," he said. "It's a great cause we're about. You'll see."

Joe nodded politely. "Thanks for the opportunity," he replied, thinking to himself that Tim sounded a bit like a boy inviting a friend to play soldier. "Say, Tim," he said as if making conversation, "what's your job in all of this?"

"I'm an explosives man," Tim said proudly, "well, learning how anyways."

"Making bombs, you mean?"

"It's quite an art, actually, and not without its hazards." Tim went on to tell of a friend in Derry who lost a hand trying to arm a car bomb. "It pays to be very careful, so that the device goes off only when you mean it."

"How do you know it's not going to harm somebody who's just a bystander?" Joe asked, trying to keep his tone matter of fact. Timothy hesitated before replying.

"In our pursuit of the cause," he said, sounding as if he were reciting, "innocents on occasion must be sacrificed. It's for the ultimate good."

"And you don't see that as murder then?" Joe said with more vigor. "Look, can I take this blindfold off now?"

"Sure," Tim reached over to help Joe pull it off his head. "Is it murder when soldiers fire at one another across a battlefield? We're in a war, I'll tell you."

"Because the loyalists have done bad things, then your side does them, too?"

"Oh, aye. I wager you'll see," Timothy insisted. "We have more than a wee bit of reason for seeking revenge."

"And so you're gonna keep fighting on?"

"For sure, mate. We'll not stop until the British and their Protestant lackeys are driven into the sea." He grinned. "And that's why we need the explosives you'll be helping us smuggle in."

"Explosives?" That was even worse than guns he realized.

"Aye, explosives," Tim sounded almost excited by the prospect.

"To maim and kill even more people?" Joe asked in disbelief. He and Tim glanced at one another in the darkness.

"To fight the Orange bastards and the frigging police. It's what it takes, mate."

Joe felt revulsion and anger at this terrorist beside him, even while realizing this was Fiona's own brother, who had the same sad dark memories of childhood she had spoken of. Tim looked back at the road and drove silently a few minutes.

"There's a lot you know now, Joe," Tim said soberly. "A man would be wise to keep it all to himself." He paused. "And that also goes for what Fiona told you about me, know what I mean?"

"Of course," Joe said, fully knowing it was his duty to defeat this terrorist gang. But he could not help but feel some sympathy for this guy. Joe thought again about Fiona.

"Look, Tim, I'm really worried about your sister. I hope she's not involved in all of this."

"I told you no. Not this anyways."

"Well, where is she?" Joe pressed. "Why won't she call me? What have I done wrong?"

Tim abruptly stopped the car in the middle of the deserted road and turned to stare at Joe. "I know what you've done," he said.

Joe looked away. Had she told him about their tryst aboard *Kittiwake?*

"You've got her pregnant, that's what you've done," he said. "She tells me everything." Then he exploded, pounding his fist on the wheel. "You took her on that boat of yours and did me sister, that's what. Knocked her up good."

He gritted his teeth. "Well, didn't youse? Aye. Was you. Sailing youse call it. Sailin' me arse."

Even though he had suspected it, Joe gaped at him in shock. Of course, it was true. He had known it from the moment it happened. But now to find out it was so... Joe laughed. He did not mean to; it just came out.

Tim glared and threw open his door. "Get out. I'm goin' to beat your friggin' arse." He stormed around to the front of the car. "Get out!" he shouted, making fists.

Joe was a whole lot bigger than Timothy ever dreamed of being. For an instant he imagined himself beating the little punk into a pulp and leaving him lying beside the road. He started to get out, but then he regained his senses. He grimaced and rolled down his window. "Listen, Tim. I didn't mean to laugh. It just meant that I'm so glad. I mean. Come on now."

After a moment, Timothy lowered his fists, obviously not anxious to take him on.

"Look, Tim," Joe said. "I love Fiona, I swear. I'll marry her. I want to marry her. I love her so much. We'll get married, and I'll make Fiona happy, you'll see." Neither spoke or moved for a full minute. Then Timothy let out a big breath.

"Bejezus!" he said and walked back around the car. He grabbed the door handle, held it a moment, then jerked it open and got in.

"And what of Seamus?" he said. "You're a bloody idiot if you think he'll allow it." Tim stared at the windshield. "Had I known of it before I first told Tom about you, then things would be different. But now you're in it for good, you see, and there'll be no way out." He shook his head and stared at Joe in the darkness. "You do right by her, you hear?"

"For sure," Joe replied. "I meant what I said."

Tim let out his breath, abruptly started the car and began driving down the road again.

Joe sat in stunned silence, realizing the full meaning of the situation. Could he somehow find Fiona and escape with her? Would she go? Of course she would; she was just as trapped as he. Surely she could be persuaded. He believed she had some feelings for him, and then there was to be a child between them. But how could he find her and devise an escape for them? He knew he would have to play along with Tim and his gang, go through with this smuggling deal and somehow set a trap for the IRA and then escape. Was it possible? Or were both he and Fiona condemned by the situation?

His worries were interrupted as they entered the outskirts of Ballycastle. Tim drove up to the marina and stopped. Just as Joe was about to get out, Tim put a firm hand on his arm.

"A word to the wise, Anderson," Tim said. "Your loyalty to the cause is counted on now. Don't forget about what Ned told you. Your life is on the line over it."

Chapter Fourteen

"Who should I tell?" Joe asked himself, after a nearly sleepless night. He had been so keyed up that now he had a splitting headache. No doubt, CIA should know immediately. But since Wade Johnston was now his only contact, he would be the only one to call, and Joe was reluctant at the moment to discuss anything with him. Wade had said he might assign another handler, so perhaps he could wait until that happened. While Stan Adams had mentioned there was some other agent in the area who was keeping an eye on Joe, he did not know who it was. There was that Evan Foster character. Joe suspected he was an agent of the British government, but Wade had refused to confirm it, and there was no proof one way or the other. He certainly was an unpleasant guy, and Joe hoped he wasn't his only ally.

And finally, there was Big Ryan, who obviously had no political or governmental connections. No, he was simply Joe's one friend. Confiding in Ryan would only serve to draw him in and jeopardize Ryan's safety. If Joe had been on his own before, he felt extremely alone now. Getting out of his bunk, he stumbled into the galley to make coffee, his head swimmingly pounding with a hangover.

Making his way topside, he sat down in the cockpit to drink his coffee and try to recover. Tension added to his misery, he realized, and thought about how easy it all would have been just to settle down to life with Mary. But that hadn't worked and besides, she had Wade. Why was he thinking of that?

When he first came to Northern Ireland, he had not expected to feel so at home. Probably as a result of being displaced from his old life, however, he was becoming attached to this new setting. Now there seemed to be a new possibility. If he hadn't come to Ballycastle, then he'd never have met Fiona. Just thinking about Fiona and her lovely marble-white complexion and beautiful smile got him excited. But their relationship was far deeper than that now.

And where was she? Somewhere in Belfast? And now he knew that her brother was clearly a terrorist who would have to be brought to justice. How could he do in this Timothy and not make Fiona hate him for it?

He noted that Seamus O'Leary's trawler was tied up at the dock. No one aboard was stirring, so Joe supposed they had been out all night. After his own experiences last night, the one thing he did not want was to have any altercation with O'Leary, which would complicate matters, to say the least. Perhaps the best thing would be to leave Ballycastle for a while, stay away until the IRA punks wanted him to go into action. He went below to his chart table and looked up the tides for the day. It appeared a flood current would be running in the morning, and would take him east and south. That, along with an easterly wind, would make for a fine sail down the coast toward Belfast. Too bad Fiona was not available to go with him. He wondered if he should invite Big Ryan and decided it was a good idea.

"Just like that?" Ryan grumbled into the phone. "A good Irishman is not even out of bed at this devilish hour?"

"Oh, come on," Joe encouraged. "It's a beautiful morning for a sail. And I'll pay you to go with me."

"Pay me? Jesus, Joseph and Mary! And your lovely boat being my only chance to sail these days? Away with your paying talk! Friendship's not figured in money."

"I know one thing," Joe said. "You're priceless to me."

"Fools talk." Ryan snorted and cleared his throat. "And sailing on the turned tide, you'll be wanting, I suppose?"

"Yes, right away, actually," Joe replied, smiling at the fact that Ryan, a lifelong professional seaman, always was aware of the present state of tidal activity. "Between the wind and the tide, we should easily make Belfast by dark, if you can come now."

"Oh, aye," Ryan grumbled in his raspy voice. "It'll take me a bit, but I'll come along."

With a "thank you" Joe disconnected and began making preparations for getting underway, suddenly feeling

179

somewhat relieved if not entirely happy. It was good to have such a friend, and he was glad to be providing the old salt an opportunity to go to sea again.

True to his word, Big Ryan arrived within the half hour, grip in hand. Joe greeted him at the rail, took his bag and went to the helm to start the engine.

"In a blasted hurry, are you?" Ryan said, apparently still not beyond the morning grumbles. He took in the lines, climbed aboard and Joe began backing out of the slip.

"I'd like to get away before O'Leary and his crew get up," Joe explained as he turned *Kittiwake* around and headed out. As they approached the pier where the trawler was docked, sure enough Seamus O'Leary climbed out on deck. He spied Joe motoring past, put his hands on his hips and watched them go by. Joe put on a big grin and waved. Seamus didn't wave back, but he gave Joe a strange look, a knowing evil grin, which seemed very curious of him.

"An enduring friend of yours, I take it," Ryan said as he coiled the mooring lines.

"We've had a bit of a disagreement," Joe replied. "He knows I'm after his girl."

Ryan looked at Joe with reproach. "Not a man to be crossing, I'd say. Someone your age ought to know better."

"I'm not *that* old," Joe countered, though he agreed that once having been through an unpleasant divorce, and then a breakup with Mary, chasing yet another woman seemed like a rather foolhardy occupation.

"A lesson I learned early in life," Ryan said. "It was another thing drove me to sea for 40 odd years."

Coming around the jetty and turning east, they had the bright morning sun in their eyes. The promontory, Fairhead, cast a giant shadow to starboard as they headed out of the Sound. *Kittiwake* began to pitch gently and Joe tasted the salt spray on his cheek. Ryan took the helm, and Joe went up to the mast to remove the sail cover. In a few moments they had the mainsheet flying in the headwind and reefed in tight. Joe released the furler on the genoa as Ryan eased on around to the south. When Joe reefed in the sails, *Kittiwake* heeled to starboard and picked up speed. Soon they were making seven knots through the water and, with the help of current, 11 over the ground. Looking west, Joe could see the sunlight reflecting off the cliffs of Northern Ireland, providing a grand sight.

With the engine off, Joe heard another engine sound, higher pitched, coming from overhead. He gazed back aft, but could see nothing. Ryan picked up the binoculars and looked up as well.

"Airplane?" he asked. "Looks like a small one. A peculiar thing, like a plane with a down-pointing tail. "There it is." He pointed and handed Joe the binoculars. "Look for yourself."

"A strange aircraft," Joe agreed. "Never seen one like that before." It was his first sighting of a drone, and he wondered if it was spying on them. No doubt it belonged to that combined operation between MI5 and CIA. He decided that next time he called in to CIA, he would report having spotted it. Realizing that perhaps the drone operator on the ground somewhere was actually watching *Kittiwake*, he looked toward the thing, made a big grin and waved.

"Smile, you're on Candid Camera," he said sarcastically.

"What's that?" Ryan asked.

"Oh, nothing," Joe replied. "Just joking." The sound faded and they sailed on in silence for a while as he pondered things.

"Tell me something, Ryan," he said. "This Irish Republican Army bunch—I've heard there are different groups of them?"

"Aye," Ryan replied. They're so cantankerous that they cannot agree among themselves. Over the years, there's been the 'Provos', that's the Provisional IRA, the Continuity IRA, the New IRA, and now we have these who call themselves the Real IRA." He shook his head. "A mean lot, all of them."

"Interesting," Joe said. "All of them wanting independence from Britain, is that it?"

"Oh aye, and now we also have the R-A-A-D, Republican Action Against Drugs, or some such. Vigilantes, they are, fighting the drug runners, they do. It could be a good service, were they not such outlaws themselves."

Evan Foster and the Frenchmen came to mind. Joe had assumed that Foster's having his dog sniff their boat and then sic'ing the police on them had proven him to be an undercover intelligence type. But now there was a new possibility—could he be in this R-A-A-D organization?

"Too many organizations," Joe said.

"Oh, there're many more, past and present," Ryan replied, "and we haven't even begun to name the loyalist ones. Most are no better, if you want my thoughts."

"Sounds like a mess, if you ask me."

"A great tangled web, Ulster is," Ryan said.

Trying to dismiss it all from his mind, Joe took out his iPhone to check for a signal, and he found he had an email. It was from Mary.

> "Dear Joe, I have no idea about how you are or what you are doing, and I worry about you every day. Wade came to visit me for the weekend, again, and I finally had to have it out with him. I told him that, even though you seem not to love me, I still am very much in love with you. I said that until I know for sure that you no longer will be in my life, I cannot even imagine continuing to consider his expressions of love and affection. So, in fear and trembling, I need to ask you to tell me where things stand between us. I surely hope you'll say that you'll be coming home to me. I love you so much, dearest Joe. Please remember all the wonderful times we've had together and come home to me. And please be safe. I'm so worried about you. Much, much love, Mary."

Joe looked up and stared at the horizon. Life with Mary seemed so distant and far away. He had come to believe that her relationship with Wade would be growing, which cut him out of the picture. Now here was Mary saying she had had it out with Wade? And she was very much in love with Joe? He looked up in confusion.

"Did the main boom jibe over and strike your noggin?" Ryan interrupted his thoughts. "You look as at-sea as ya are, me lad. What's come over?"

Joe glanced at Ryan and it took him a second or two to come to his senses. "Mary Johnston," he said. "I think I've mentioned her to you before." Joe gave a brief account of his relationship with Mary, their experiences aboard *Mission* and how they had lived together for a few months.

"So what in the name of all goodness are you doing here?" Big Ryan asked. "Would that I had such a lass myself. I'd know which side of the scone the jam was spread."

Joe shook his head. "I thought she was in love with…" He paused. "Well, it's complicated." He felt a strong urge to tell Ryan everything and get his advice. But he was afraid that, if Ryan learned that he was a spy, he might lose Ryan's friendship. He noticed the big man was gazing intently at him.

"You're a strange man," Ryan said. "Makes me wonder why I fool about with you."

Joe grinned. "May be," he agreed. He thought again about replying immediately to Mary's email. Hearing from her left him with ambivalent feelings. He focused his mind on Fiona. He believed he had a duty to her now. Deciding to

184

think it over a while, he offered to take the helm. They swapped seats and Ryan studied the coast of Northern Ireland to their west.

"All my life, I've enjoyed the view of land from the sea," Ryan said. "It's cleansing somehow to be out here looking back at the towns and the homes and the farms, seeming so wee in the distance." He took a deep breath. "Makes all of man's troubles seem so much without importance and meaning." He looked at Joe. "You get what I'm saying?"

Joe smiled. "You're quite a philosopher." Then he gazed at the coastline and thought about his encounter with the IRA members the previous night. Perhaps it took place inside one of those farmhouses visible to the south of the distant promontory, Torr Head, just tiny spots of white amid the green fields. Weapons, explosives, guns, violence, spying—all of those things were dwarfed to insignificance by the waves and the sun and the wind of the sea. The problem, of course, was that he'd have to go ashore again and deal with the dangerous situation. He was now deeply involved.

"I really don't know what I'm doing here," he found himself saying aloud. Then self-consciously he glanced at Ryan. The giant met his gaze.

"None of us do, really," he replied. "Not in this life, we don't."

Chapter Fifteen

Kittiwake entered Belfast Lough just before sunset that Saturday and soon was moored at the marina in Carrickfergus. Joe checked his iPhone to see if, as promised, Timothy had texted the number where Fiona was staying. Tim had not done so. Frustrated by the way things were going, Joe suggested to Ryan that they take a taxi downtown—just to see the sights—but really his motive was to find Fiona, wherever she was.

A cab, driven by a balding middle-age man, picked them up and headed down the coast road toward Belfast. Because of slow traffic, the driver took a right at a light and headed down into the Ardoyne section. Without warning they came up to a line of stopped cars behind a police barricade at Crumlin Road with a number of yellow striped PSNI vehicles with their blue lights flashing.

"Can you turn around and go another way?" Joe asked with irritation.

The cabbie shook his head and pointed. Through the night's gloom, they could see policemen coming down the line of stopped cars, making people get out. The police had a couple of leashed dogs that were climbing in each successive vehicle and sniffing. Another policeman walked down the line with a device on a long pole that he ran up under each car. Joe wondered aloud what might be going on.

"Bomb scare, I'd think," the cabbie said. He opened his glove compartment, pulled out a handheld scanner radio and turned it on. It locked in on a voice transmission. The communication seemed to be about calling in a special unit. Between the accents and the police jargon, Joe couldn't quite catch it all.

"Is it about a bomb?"

"Aye," Big Ryan said. "We're certainly in the thick of it here."

"A terrorist bomb?" Joe asked. "An IED or something?" He was aware of roadside bombs being used in Iraq and Afghanistan, but he hadn't expected such a thing here, not in today's Northern Ireland anyway.

Two policemen walked up, the one behind carrying an automatic rifle. "Get out and stand beside the vehicle," the first one ordered. Joe, Ryan and the taxi driver got out and lined up on the left side. The cop asked the driver for his license and then Ryan and Joe for identification. For the first time since going through British immigration and customs, Joe produced his passport, which he was awfully glad he had remembered to bring along from the boat.

While their papers were examined under a flashlight, a third policeman arrived with one of the dogs. Without asking, the policeman opened the door and let the dog climb in and sniff around.

"American," said the policeman checking Joe's passport. "Here for long?"

"Just a few months," Joe replied.

The policeman shined his light on Joe's face, compared it with the passport photo, and then handed the document back to him. "Enjoy your visit."

"Thanks," Joe replied, trying not to sound sarcastic.

"Open the boot," the dog handler ordered.

"An illegal search," the cabbie said, but opened the rear compartment anyway.

"Aye, and ye'll thank me for it when we find the bombing buggar," the cop replied, shining his light and letting the dog sniff around.

"Is there really a bomb nearby?" Joe asked. "Or is this inconvenience just a routine kind of search?"

The one with the dog brushed brusquely past him without giving an answer. But the one who had checked the identifications said, "There's a bomb under a car a couple of blocks from here. People are being called out of their homes over there. No sir, I don't think you're the ones so inconvenienced, as you call it."

The police dismissed them with instructions about how to detour around the area. They got back in and the cabbie drove off.

"Who'd plant a bomb under a car?" Joe asked as they rode on.

"UVF parade tomorrow," the driver said. "Could be either a loyalist or a nationalist done it. Just a wee preview for the event," he chuckled.

"Ulster Volunteer Force," Ryan explained, "founded in 1913 to combat a rebellion by the Republicans who wanted to make all of Ireland an independent state."

"I heard on the scanner of another one over in Newry," the cabbie said. "They've called in the army to deal with it. A bugger of a bomb, it is, near 50 pounds of explosive, they said."

"That's huge!" Joe said. "What for?"

"Politics, they call it. Death and destruction it is," Ryan said. "Making the devil's own statement is what it's all for."

Joe shivered and pondered in silence the fact he had agreed to help smuggle in more arms or explosives to aid the Real IRA. His true task, of course, was to figure out some way to thwart the operation. Then he thought of the skinhead, Ned, with his dagger-like-cross tattoo. The question would be how to avoid delivering weapons without getting tortured, maimed and killed.

"Ryan," he said. "Do you know a good pub around here? I need a drink."

Ryan knew of a place up near the shipyard and docks that he had frequented in his merchant marine days. The taxi stopped outside of McHugh's, an old, traditional Irish pub, and Joe paid the cabbie. They found the place packed and noisy. As they elbowed their way to the bar, Joe noticed a lot of orange shirts and arm bands. Joe ordered a Bushmills and soda, Ryan a pint of Guinness. A couple of guys in their thirties or forties standing near them at the bar gave them the onceover.

"Loyalist crowd," Ryan said. "Gearing up for tomorrow's parade, I wager."

"Reminds me of the night before an Alabama football game," Joe replied. He was thinking how nice it would be to be back in the States where the major conflict would be on the playing field and not in the streets. Not far from here the police had found bombs? This was not a Middle Eastern country, he thought. Even though he had heard Timothy talk about learning to make bombs, it still was difficult to accept the idea they actually would be used here. Then he recalled there had been bombings back home during the sixties, and later the federal courthouse in Oklahoma City, 9/11 in New York, and the Boston Marathon. He shivered and took a big swig of his whiskey.

"How're you keeping?" Big Ryan asked.

"I could use another drink." Joe caught the publican's eye, drained his glass and ordered another.

Ryan refused a refill. "You seem a bit nervous, I think."

Joe shrugged. "I'm just not used to this."

There were banners all around, photos of marching men in black suits with orange vestments over their coats. "Defend, preserve, protect" seemed to be the watchwords. What did they want to preserve? Joe wondered. Was it the union with Britain? Was it the way the British and Scottish landlords had dominated and oppressed the Gaelic Irish for so many centuries? Were they protecting their majority rule in Northern Ireland? Recalling what he learned from Fiona the day they toured Rathlin Island, Joe understood the bitterness felt by the Catholic Irish. In the corner someone struck a couple of chords on a piano, banged on it for attention and began a song. Soon the entire crowd was singing some kind of raucous anthem, the words slurred enough to make it hard for Joe to understand.

"They gave their today so that we could have a tomorrow," he heard. Then there was a refrain, "Ulster is free." People pounded on the bar, sloshing beer, eyes nearly blazing with drunken fervor. Joe looked away feeling even worse. When the song and the ensuing cheers and clapping ended, the two men beside him at the bar moved over close.

The skinhead jabbed his elbow into Joe's arm on the counter. "What about it, mate? Didn't hear youse singing." There was nothing friendly about it.

"Maybe you don't like the anthem?" the other said, staring.

"I don't know the song," Joe said. He took another swallow of whiskey. "Maybe you'd like to teach me?" Ryan was watching. He suddenly put his big frame between Joe and the men.

"He's an American," Ryan said. "Just here to see the sights. I am, too, if ye get me drift." The two men eased back a little.

"Just being sure he ain't no bloody repub," the older of them said. "Where in the States?"

"Alabama," Joe said, as he took a big swig.

"Never heard of it," the skinhead said.

"Oh, aye," the other said. "Football."

"American style? Ha," the man went on. "Rugby's the real football."

Joe was about to carry it further, but another song drowned out all talking—something about William of Orange. Distracted by the music the two men turned away and began singing.

Joe downed the rest of his drink and turned toward the singers. "So I guess William of Orange played Rugby, huh?"

Skin head stared at him. "What'd ye say?" he shouted over the singing.

"Come on," Ryan said, grabbing Joe and shoving him roughly toward the door. "As the old saying goes, many a mouth broke the nose."

They took a cab back to the marina in Carrickfergus and spent the night on the boat. Joe tried to get Ryan to explain what all the celebrating was about, but Ryan insisted they go back to town the next day to let Joe see for himself.

"You've yet to witness a parade."

The next morning Joe apologized for how he acted at the pub. "I don't know what made me so belligerent," he apologized while holding his pounding forehead.

"Often a man gets that way, chasing a woman," Ryan replied.

Joe tried to contact Timothy to see if he had any word from Fiona, but there was no such message. He was very frustrated to think that she must be somewhere around the city but couldn't be found. Joe and Ryan returned to Belfast, arriving in time to see people lining the street. Coming from the city center came ranks of marching men in black suits, carrying banners with a drum and flute band booming along behind. It was an anniversary celebration of the 1913 founding of the Ulster Volunteer Force, Ryan had said. The lead banner, so large it was carried by two men, had an oval symbol with a red hand in its center. The inscription read, "For God and Ulster." More ranks of black-suited men of all ages followed, very somber and dignified in their demeanor. Another band came next with a meaty-fisted man beating a base drum hard enough to bust it. And then came more companies of marching men. Joe recalled their visit to the Free Presbyterian Church and realized many of these marchers sat in those churches Sunday after Sunday being indoctrinated with that same warped message so removed from the real loving generosity of Christianity. And likely, on the other side many of the Roman Catholics were subjected to yet another kind of distortion.

Ryan called his attention back to the marchers. "Many are sons and grandsons of the original UVF."

"And they're marching to commemorate the struggles in the early 20th century?" Joe asked, nearly shouting to be heard over the booming base drums.

"More than just a celebration," Big Ryan said gravely. "It's also a warning to the other side." They watched the marchers going by. "Now look at this bunch, would you?" Ryan pointed to another formation in the parade—this one being led by a banner that had the UVF red-hand symbol but with the faces of five men painted above it. Below the symbol were two masked figures in black combat gear holding machine guns at the ready.

"Shankill Butchers," Ryan said. "A bloody gang from the 1970's that slaughtered many Catholic nationalists, and some Protestants, too, who were believed to be disloyal. I hear they will be in the parade."

Joe stared at the procession in disbelief. "Don't they know that all they're doing is stirring up trouble? Feeding people's paranoia?"

"Aye, paranoia it is," Ryan said. "But there's nothing imaginary about it. These Shankill Butchers are here to show the Catholics that the terrorist gang has not gone away."

Joe sighed, thinking that Fiona and her family were on the other side of all this conflict. "How is it possible for anyone to live here and not take sides?"

Ryan shook his head. "If you're educated and wealthy, a businessman or professional like a doctor or lawyer, then you're above the fray. But if you live in the towns, like Belfast or Newry or Derry, and make your living by your labor, then it's hard to escape the struggle. It's a curse upon Ulster for certain and sure."

From the sheer number of people, Joe observed, he supposed nearly the whole town was there—well, the Protestants anyway. Then he spotted a red-haired young woman in the crowd who resembled Fiona. He focused on her and realized it was Fiona. He quickly pushed his way through the spectators until he was about ten feet away and called out to her.

She looked up at him and instantly looked terrified. "Stay away, stay away!" she cried. "My God, get away." She shoved through the crowd to escape him. Joe stopped, perplexed at her reaction. He barely could see her moving through the throng of people. A young man near Joe looked up at him with a threatening frown and then pushed off in Fiona's direction. Joe stood there in amazement, supposing this guy must be her with her. *A new boyfriend maybe?*

Disappointed to say the least, Joe stared blankly out at the parade, contemplating what Fiona's actions might mean. Coming along in the parade behind a band that was playing the same "Unity" song from the pub was a convertible with a couple of older men standing up in it, waving to the crowd. On the door of the car was the symbol he had seen on the banner for the Shankill Butchers. He supposed these characters in the car were some of the original gang.

There were gunshots, shouts and cries from the crowd. It came from down near where Fiona had gone. Then he saw the shooter in the crowd near the car. It was the man who had followed Fiona. The man turned and shoved his way through the spectators. There was Fiona. The man ran right beside her, making a pass with his hand as he brushed by. She turned and went back into the crowd. A couple of policemen were running toward the man. The first policeman tackled him, and the second came to help throw the man to the sidewalk. It was not the shooter, whom Joe had seen hand something to Fiona. Meanwhile, the convertible sped by, honking its horn. The men in the convertible were crouched down inside, shot or not, Joe couldn't tell, but there were bullet holes in the side of the car.

Frantically, Joe tried to get close, to spot Fiona and see if she was okay. But because of the morass of startled and escaping spectators he couldn't get to her. He pushed on, trying to get close. Then he realized the actual shooter had passed off the gun to Fiona, who then had faded into the crowd. It was slick, like two pickpockets working a busy street corner. The realization made Joe sick at his stomach. He had just witnessed Fiona being involved in an assassination attempt on the Shankill Butchers.

He had to reach Fiona, help her somehow, find out how and why. He spotted the shooter again and went toward him, expecting Fiona to be with him. Policemen were converging on the spot where the gun had been fired, but he was far away from there by now. Joe pushed on toward them.

"Stop, Joe," he heard Ryan call from behind him. "What are you doing?" Joe waved him off with his hand. He caught a glimpse of the shooter and headed for him, almost running, weaving through the crowd. Then someone tackled Joe from behind, and the two of them went down on the pavement, knocking Joe's breath out. A heavy foot stepped on his neck. Someone shouted at him to lie still. In pain he turned his head to see who had attacked him. Rough hands grabbed his arms, pulling them behind his back, and he felt ropes or manacles or something being fastened to his wrists.

"Who are you?" Joe gasped.

"UVF, you bastard," one of his attackers said. "Get up."

Joe was dragged to his feet. He looked around at a ring of angry men surrounding him.

"He's not involved," he heard Ryan say from behind him. Joe looked back to see the big man confronting his attackers.

"Don't give me that, mate. He was running away with the other bloke." The speaker, who had on a black armband with the letters UVF, nodded to the right. Joe looked and saw the shooter, also surrounded and with his hands tied. His head was bleeding and a stream of blood ran down the side of his face.

"Take 'em to the cars," the man with the armband commanded. Joe felt himself being pushed and dragged through a crowd of people, who merely stood and watched. If there were any police around, they were not coming to his

198

aid. He was roughly shoved into the back seat of a black sedan.

"You'd best take me, too," he heard Ryan saying. Then the giant abruptly sat down in the seat beside Joe.

"Have it your way, mate," the leader said. Two men leaned in over Ryan with plastic manacles. Ryan calmly put out his hands and let them shackle him. Joe gave him a look of surprised disbelief. Ryan merely gave Joe a frown and disgusted shake of the head. One of the thugs climbed in behind the wheel. The leader got in on the other side. The driver blew the horn at the crowd that had gathered to watch. They parted and the car started off. Joe could see the shooter being loaded in another vehicle. There was no sign of Fiona anywhere.

"You've got this wrong, you know," Ryan said. "This man's an American, a tourist. He has nothing to do with IRA or…"

"We'll sort it out soon enough," the leader interrupted. He turned to the driver. "Slow down, Angus. We don't want to attract the PSNI."

"Where are you taking us?" Joe asked.

"To an interrogation," the man said. "To a place where we can talk about your little assassination attempt."

"We didn't do anything…"

"Oh, we have ways of finding out just what you did or didn't do. All in due time." Joe looked at Ryan and saw a grim expression. He had heard stories of brutal beatings.

Kneecapping, shooting a man in the knee, was one of the favored techniques. He glanced at Ryan again, in wonderment and admiration for how the big man had stuck with him instead of merely standing back and watching the thugs haul him away.

"We're not Catholics, or republicans, or whatever," Joe said. "I'm an American tourist. Looks like my accent would have told you that by now." The UVF leader glanced back at Joe with an uncertain expression. Then he and the driver exchanged a look, which Joe hoped showed some doubt.

Alongside a grassy meadow, the driver abruptly turned the car onto an unpaved lane. They jostled down through the field and stopped at an abandoned old stone barn. Joe and Ryan were helped out. The second car pulled up beside them, and the shooter was dragged out. All of them went inside. The thugs went through Joe's and Ryan's pockets and removed wallets and Joe's cell phone and passport. The leader took Joe's iPhone and studied the icons on it. Joe silently hoped he didn't find the app for calling CIA. Then he hoped maybe he would find it and somehow make a call that would send a distress signal.

The shooter had no wallet or other identification. He was wearing a crucifix on a chain around his neck, which was confiscated. Joe got a good look at him finally. The man appeared to be in his twenties. His head was shaven revealing only the fuzz of brown hair. Above his ashen cheeks his greenish eyes showed real fear of his captors. No telling what they had been saying to him during the car ride from the parade. Once he was thoroughly frisked, he was shoved over in a corner and kicked in the groin. Moaning, gasping, he fell in a heap, looking up with defiance in his teary eyes.

"My mates'll pay you back for that," he cried. "You'll get yours."

The man who had kicked him gave him another boot to the hip.

"Enough for now," the leader commanded. Then he turned to Joe, giving him a long, appraising look.

"So Joseph Anderson, you are an American," he said as he looked at Joe's passport. "Why would an American be involved in this shooting? Are you a Fenian sympathizer?"

"What's that?" Joe answered, knowing full well that the Fenian Society recruited many U.S. citizens of Irish descent who sympathized with their struggle for independence.

"He's no Fenian," Ryan said. "He's only a rather foolish American who can't seem to mind his own business."

"And what about you?" the leader demanded. "How do I know you're not a bloody republican?"

"If I were in any way involved with your enemies, would you think now that I would have volunteered to come along to this wee gathering?" The big man held out his manacled hands. "Take these off now and take us back to town." He gave his captor a long stern look, until the man averted his gaze, exchanged glances with the others and shrugged.

"Take these two downtown," the leader said to the driver. "Let them off wherever they like, but use the blindfolds and don't release their shackles until there." He turned to address Ryan and Joe. "You're fortunate to have met a reasonable man," he said. "But remember now we know your names and where we can find you. If you have too much to say about what happened here, we won't be so easy next time."

And what of that poor bloke over there?" Ryan asked, nodding at the shooter lying crouched in the corner.

"Oh, we'll have a few questions for him before the PSNI get him," the leader replied with a wry smile. Joe looked at the poor boy and realized he was not going to share their good fortune of being freed. Of course, he was the one who tried to assassinate the old men in the car—Shankill Butchers or not.

The thugs put Joe's wallet, passport and iPhone back in his pockets, put the blindfolds back on both of them, and led them to the car. He realized he was feeling weak in the knees and had been perspiring through it all. A mile or two down the road, the man in the front seat turned and took off their blindfolds. Joe wondered what may have saved them from the fate befalling the luckless shooter they had left behind.

Soon they turned on to a street bordered by a high wall with chain-link fencing atop. It stretched for many blocks, painted with numerous murals and graphics, some skillfully done and some merely crude graffiti.

"The Peace Wall," Ryan commented, "separates Catholic from Protestant neighborhoods." They passed one roughly scrawled sign that read "Berlin 1961-1989, Belfast 1969-?" Other murals were beautifully rendered, some with expressions of peace, some with threats of continued violence and war.

"The walls keep the two sides from being at one another's throats all the time," Ryan explained.

"But the Catholic bastards slip out, don't they?" the UVF man interrupted. "Like today when we try to have a peaceful parade and that piece of shit what fired at our Shankill Butchers. Thank God none were hurt."

"And what can you expect?" Ryan retorted. "Parading down the streets lauding men who called themselves 'butchers' during The Troubles? You keep fanning the flames of hate, don't you?"

"It's the other side what does it," the man insisted. "We have to pay them back."

Ryan told the driver to take them to the bus station so they could get a ride out to the marina. The car stopped in front, and they were uncuffed and freed, just left at the curb like some ordinary passengers who had been given a ride.

"Let's get out of here," Joe said.

"What's wrong with you?" Ryan asked sarcastically. "Don't you like the sights here in Belfast?"

They finally found a cab a couple of blocks from the parade route. On the way back to Carrickfergus, Ryan supposed the shooter surely was a republican, likely some member of the IRA.

"The Real IRA," Joe corrected, feeling overwhelmed.

"You okay?" Ryan asked.

"I'll be okay," he apologized, not wanting to explain.

They rode in silence until Ryan and the taxi driver struck up a conversation about what had happened at the parade. Joe hardly heard them, the revelation of Fiona being involved weighing heavily on him. Then his iPhone chimed. He pulled it out of his pocket and found a new email and a new text. The email was from Mary.

"Dear Joe, You haven't replied to my last message and I'm so worried about you. I'm thinking of buying a ticket to Belfast. But I told Wade, and he emphatically said I must not. Would you like for me to come anyway? Much love, Mary."

The text message was from Tom. "North side of Rathlin Island. Meet ship at 0200 tonight. Deliver the cargo to Ballycastle before dawn. Acknowledge."

Chapter Sixteen

"You have to take the bus back home," Joe told Big Ryan when they returned to Carrickfergus. "I have to insist. I'm sorry but it's real important."

The man's face turned red. "No good sorry you be, if you strand me here. I'm flabbergasted, I am." He studied Joe a moment. "It's not me but your senses you'd be taking leave of. What's with this carrying on? Are you suddenly daft?"

"I must be," Joe replied, "or something like that."

"And you've taken note of the weather, have ya?" Ryan said, waving toward the west. "It's turning off to a stormy blow for the afternoon. Any sane sailor can see that."

Joe glanced at the dark cumulous in the distance. A storm would make it even harder if not downright dangerous to try and negotiate one of the narrow little harbors between Belfast and Rathlin Island. So it was better all-around to leave Ryan here.

"Look, my friend, here's 50 pounds." He pulled out his wallet and offered the bill. "Please just take this and go back by train or bus or whatever. I've got something I have to do, and I don't want you involved." He grabbed Ryan's big rough hand and thrust the money in it. "Please don't argue. I have to do this."

"Out of your head or had by the devil," Ryan said, staring quizzically at him. "Thousands of miles from your home and you're wanting to go off on your own, and likely it is into a storm." He wadded up the bill and threw it on the deck. "Here's your filthy 50 quid. I'll take nothing from a crazy man." He gave Joe a last stare and then went below to collect his things.

Joe paced the deck, looking at his watch. Even with the tide running north, he'd be cutting it close on time unless the wind was favorable. Ryan threw his duffle up on deck and followed it out of the hatch.

"Would you cast off the lines for me?" Joe asked. He started the engine and then offered the money to Ryan again. Ryan shook his head, climbed onto the dock and began releasing the mooring lines.

"Are ye sure, Joe? Going off half-cocked, you are."

Joe put the engine in reverse and began backing out. "Don't worry," he called. He held up the bank note. "We'll spend this in the Harbor Bar when I see you there. I'll wine you and dine you like a king to make up for this."

"That you'll live so long, I'll be hoping."

Joe turned his attention to the harbor traffic ahead. A huge black oil tanker was standing out the channel from Belfast and a red-hulled freighter was entering from sea. Joe

206

hugged the northern bank to give them plenty of room. Once past, he steered away from shore and out into the channel. *Kittiwake* began to pitch in a light chop of waves from seaward. Soon he rounded the point and headed north.

Despite an occasional gust from the approaching weather, there was only enough steady breeze to justify flying the mainsail. He locked the wheel, regretting that there was no autopilot, and rushed about raising the main. With it set way out, he managed to get a little push from the wind, but knew he'd have to motor-sail. Luckily, he had topped off his diesel in Ballycastle. Still, there was no great supply of fuel, maybe not enough to reach the north side of Rathlin Island, let alone arriving by one in the morning.

"Suppose I can't even make the rendezvous?" he asked himself aloud. "Wouldn't that be a hell of a deal?" He laughed. *Sorry fellows, smuggling called off on account of weather. Now just how would you explain that to your new buddies of the Real IRA?* One thing he knew for sure was that he could see no way out of it.

He considered again whom he could tell. Perhaps he should have explained it to Ryan, but that would mean breaking his cover. Surely he could trust the man, who was his only friend here, really. But then suppose Ryan, hoping to be helpful, decided to take it upon himself to notify the police? Any unusual police presence in Ballycastle probably would cause the whole smuggling operation to be cancelled. And if the IRA thugs got the idea that Joe had leaked the plan to anyone, there'd be hell to pay.

Seeing the wind had increased and shifted more to the west, he decided to unfurl the genoa. He turned the bow to port and walked forward in the cockpit to release the furling line. His sense of caution told him to let the sail out only half-way, keeping it reefed in case of higher gusts. But, impatient to get on, he let the entire sail out and sheeted it in tight. Returning to the helm, he turned back on the northerly course. The boat heeled to starboard and picked up a couple of knots. A gust of wind whistled in the rigging, increasing his creeping anxiety, and he peered at the western sky. Dark blue clouds approached, creating an accentuated background for Knocklade Mountain that rose from the distant landscape.

Unfortunately, no new CIA handler had contacted him, so he decided to call Wade. He had to call Wade. There was no other way. He locked the wheel and climbed down into the cabin to get his iPhone. With a quick inspection to be sure everything was secure for heavy weather, he grabbed up a box of crackers and his foul-weather jacket and climbed topside. *Kittiwake* had come up into the wind so that the sails were flapping with violent snaps. Ducking below the wildly swinging boom of the mainsail, he made his way to the wheel and steered back on course. A light, blowing drizzle began to fall. He reached down on the steering console and flipped on the running lights and then activated the special app on the phone.

"Leave a message and I'll call you back," Wade's recorded voice said. Reaching only voicemail was highly irritating to say the least. There was a good chance Wade was off in Birmingham, chasing after Mary again.

"Things are going down, Wade," Joe said to the recorder. "I'm headed to do some smuggling for IRA terrorists. Call me ASAP." Joe disconnected, realizing the message was bone-chilling enough to get anybody's immediate attention. Still, he felt a deep sense of distrust toward Wade if not the whole organization. He wiped the rain off the phone with his hand and put it in his pocket. Then he zipped up the jacket and raised the hood over his head, pulling the left side of the hood around to protect his cheek from the blowing, stinging rain.

He could not forget the image of the shooting at the parade, of the man firing at the convertible and turning, brushing by Fiona to slip her the gun, and then Fiona melting away in the crowd. Even though on the day at Rathlin Island when she related the sad history of the oppression of Irish Catholics, and had told him about her older brother being brutally murdered by loyalists, it never had dawned on Joe that Fiona could be a terrorist herself. Of course, Timothy was a member of the Real IRA and had gotten Joe into all this smuggling mess, but the idea of such a sweet, beautiful girl being involved was hard to accept. Joe wondered if his own willingness to participate in the smuggling deal in part was to gain her favor—although who knew what the consequences would have been for him if he had refused Tom and Ned the other night? Or was he truly carrying out his mission as a CIA spy, helping to catch the bad guys, gain revenge against the IRA for hijacking his boat *Tartan*? Only a year ago, in the Bahamas aboard *Mission*, he had found himself unwittingly trapped into aiding and abetting Alex Smith in smuggling offshore cash into the states. Now, here was Joe Anderson again, caught in a somewhat similar, but far more dangerous situation.

"And who are the good guys, anyway?" he asked aloud. "Is it the loyalists, who want to protect and defend the union with the United Kingdom? Or is it the republicans of Ulster, who want to become part of the Republic of Ireland? Or is it the police, the secretive British intelligence agents and the cooperating CIA that are helping to bring about order and peace? And what of his own selfishness in wanting to get revenge against the IRA? One thing Joe was sure of was his present mission didn't feel very righteous and good or in the best interest of all.

During his musings, the wind hit *Kittiwake* with a sudden fierce blast, snapping the genoa, heeling the boat and turning it uncontrollably. He was unable to steer, fighting the wheel as the boat gyrated wildly. He reached over and released the starboard sheet, which helped bring the boat upright. He locked down the wheel and stumbled forward to try to furl the genoa, which flapped crazily in the wind. A new onslaught of hard-blown rain stung his face and clouded his vision. He began tugging on the furling line, hoping nothing would jam the sail. Slowly, painfully, the genoa began to wrap around the forestay, but the line fouled and jammed in the cleat. Working his way back to the helm, he brought the boat up into the wind again, locked the wheel, and went back to the furling line. With a hand-hurting tug he got the knot out of the line and began furling the flapping sail again. After a five-minute struggle, he reefed it to three-quarters and then hauled in the lee sheet.

Going back to the helm, he wrestled the boat back on course. He should have been paying more attention, he realized, and begun shortening the sails before he got into high winds. It sure would have been nice, he was thinking, to have Ryan aboard to help. But all of this was his to do alone.

After about an hour, the wind subsided some and the rain dwindled to a fine mist. Being able to relax, he got out his phone to reread Mary's email. He read the message over several times before resting the phone in his lap and sighing deeply. Yes, he had thought about Mary more than once a day, too. It usually came in flashbacks of their perilous passage from the Bahamas aboard *Mission*. Or it was some of the wonderful times they'd made love. And always it was with Mary as the beautiful but strong and brave character she was, so admirable and so lovable.

And then he thought of Fiona, the gorgeous, marble-skinned, red-haired girl who had captivated him, infatuated him, his passion nearly having taken away his reason. By their one brief act of love, they now were bound to one another by the possibility of having a child. The sensation of nausea returned as he recalled the parade, the way she ran from him, the shooting, and how she took the pistol and melted away in the crowd. How could she be a part of all that terrible violence? Her older brother had died in violence, tortured and murdered perhaps by the Shankill Butchers. If so, then her role in the shooting at the parade was an act of revenge. Fiona came from a Catholic family who had lived under oppression and in near poverty for centuries. No wonder she was involved in creating the same kind of terror and violence to which her kin had been subjected. Yes, it

211

was for revenge. And yet, how could she, such a delicate beautiful person, join in such awful acts against humanity?

So here he was, about to aid and abet their revolution by smuggling explosives into the country. And yet, here he was a spy whose task was to betray them, lay the trap to catch them in the act—all because he had joined the CIA to seek personal revenge. *Who are you? What are you?* he asked himself.

Or perhaps there was another way. He looked to the east at the distant hills of Scotland, appearing blue in the afternoon light. He just as easily could sail to the east, up into the Firth of Clyde, away from Northern Ireland and all of its problems. The temptation to do so was great. Hadn't Adams told him he was incompetent, incapable of all this secret agent stuff? He had every reason to sail to the safety of Scotland and abandon his agreement with the Real IRA.

"To hell with them all!" he spoke aloud. He stood up behind the helm and turned northeast. "To hell with Ireland. To hell with Timothy's terrorist gang, and Fiona too." His voice broke there.

"Oh God, Mary, why did I ever leave you?" He got out his phone and reread Mary's message. Then he tapped 'reply' and wrote.

"Dear Mary, You must not come here!!! Do not!!! What I'm doing here is too dangerous." He paused, not really knowing what to say. Knowing Mary, he realized she might board that plane, come hell or high water. What a fool he had been to give her up to Wade! He sent the message and then put his hands to his head.

"What am I doing, going to this rendezvous? Why am I risking my life?" Then in a moment he sat down. What had he been doing with his life? It was time to succeed at something, stand for something, he turned to port to resume his course to Rathlin. "Because I have to," he muttered. "Because I said I would, and so it is my duty."

With his mind made up now, he realized that, like it or not, he'd have to call Wade again. He activated the phone, and it took a minute or more to connect.

"I'm on the way to a drone training exercise," Wade said curtly. "Can it wait?"

"I'm into something big," Joe said, noting Wade's unfriendly manner. He guessed it was the "having-it-out," as Mary said, that had upset him. "I'm going to a rendezvous to pick up explosives for a gang called the Real IRA," he went on. "I'm supposed to smuggle them into Ballycastle tonight."

"How'd you manage that?"

"Long story. I figured I'd just set up the opportunity and then let you guys figure out what to do next." There was a pause.

"Give me the details."

"Are you familiar with Rathlin Island?"

"Of course, I am. We're about to do this exercise with the Brits real near there. What's that got to do with it?"

Trying to overlook Wade's belligerent tone, Joe explained that he was to meet a ship on the nearly deserted north side of the island where they couldn't be seen from the mainland. He was to pick up weapons or explosives or something and then just go into the marina at Ballycastle, tie up, and spend the night. The IRA members then would give him further instructions about where to take them next.

"I'll figure out something," Wade interrupted. "This op-ex is ready to go. I'll call you back when I can."

"Oh, wait," Joe said. "Mary sent a message saying she plans to come over here. Did you know that?"

"What?" Wade shouted into the phone. "I forbade it."

"I just got her email. I told her not to come." There was a long pause.

"I have to hang up." Wade disconnected.

Joe thought about Wade's tone of voice, realizing the guy was more than sore at him about Mary. "Sorry to mess up your little scheme," he said aloud. *Well, never mind that,* he thought. *Wade is my one and only contact at CIA, and so he is the only one who can help me out of this fix.*

"Okay, here's the deal," Wade said when he finally called. "Just go right on and do as they instructed. We'll work with MI-5 to intercept them at some point in the process."

Joe stopped him. "Look," he said, "I'd like to survive this whole event somehow. How do you plan to get me out of it?" There was another pause.

"After you tie up in the marina, go ashore…like to take a shower or something. Then just get lost somewhere. You'll be okay."

Joe shrugged. "Okay, I guess," he said. "Then what?"

"Don't worry, Sport," Wade said. "We'll take care of your ass." With that he broke the connection.

Joe found he was giving the phone a white-knuckled grip. Of all the people to have to depend on, Wade was the last one he'd have chosen. Again he glanced to starboard at the coastline of Scotland, its cliffs gleaming gold in the sunset, and wondered just how much of a fool he was for not running out on this whole mess.

At 1:45 AM with sails furled, he motored with the now ebbing tide, coming past Torr Head and steering for the north side of Rathlin Island. The lighthouse on the island's eastern end, Point Rue, cast its white beam on the water. It, along with the reflected glow of lights from the mainland, provided the only illumination under an overcast sky. He headed around the dark north side of Rathlin, careful to remain safely a quarter of a mile offshore, and searched the horizon through his binoculars. When he spotted both red and green running lights and white masthead and range lights of a ship heading straight for him, his pulse began to pound.

"I don't even have a pistol," he murmured. *And just how would it help against the whole crew of a ship?* Even under the circumstances, it made him grin.

215

The two vessels converged below the dark and deserted high cliff of the island. Joe put his engine in neutral and waited. He heard the big diesels of the ship slow and then shift to reverse. It coasted to a stop about a hundred yards off his bow. Joe eased *Kittiwake* forward, turning in a wide arc and then coming up beside the ship on a parallel course.

"Say the password," someone called down to him. Joe's heart raced.

"What password?" he yelled back. "I don't know any damn password." *Hell, had that Tom forgotten to tell me some stupid password?* He could hear a couple of voices discussing on deck.

"A southern yank's voice, for sure," he heard one of them say. "Your accent's the password, mate," the man said. "That drawl is all we need to hear."

"So, now what?" Joe called back, irritated by the whole encounter.

"We have a gangway lowered amidships, starboard. Come alongside and we'll throw you a bow line."

Joe moved in closer and peered through the gloom. "I need to rig some fenders." .

"Well, bajezus, be quick about it."

Joe opened the hatch under the seat and pulled out a couple of white rubber fenders. Once he had them rigged, he maneuvered in to the gangway. They tossed him a line, and he made it fast to the bow. Then he got a stern line rigged and tied off. Crewmen already were coming down the gangway with crates.

"Stow them below," the man on the deck above commanded.

Joe stared through the gloom at the big boxes. "What's in this?"

"Plastic explosives," the first man down the ladder said. "And you're welcomed to it." He climbed over the lifelines and the other man began passing boxes across.

"Really! Where's it come from?"

"The States," the man with the box on his shoulder replied.

"Shut your yap," the man on the deck above commanded. "He don't need to know."

"I haven't got room for all that," Joe said, looking at the stack of boxes.

"Look, mate," the first man said. "It's a little late to trouble about that, don't you think?" He elbowed past Joe, climbed down the ladder into the cabin, and the other passed the boxes down.

Joe peered down and saw the crates lying helter-skelter across the sofa, on the table and everywhere. "That doesn't look safe."

The two men climbed out. "It ain't," was the only reply. They scrambled over the lifelines, climbed on the gangway and cast off.

"Luck to ya, matey," one called as they climbed up the gangway to the ship's deck. Joe heard the deep guttural roar of diesel engines easing the ship forward and away. Joe put his engine in reverse and backed down to avoid the ship's prop wash. Silently, he stared as the freighter headed off to the east, its stern light fading in the gloom.

He shined his flashlight down into the salon, studying the boxes piled around. He might as well be sitting on a bomb. The sooner he could get to Ballycastle, the better. Then it occurred to him that with that much explosive aboard, if anything went wrong at the marina, it could blow half the town away. He sure as hell hoped Wade and the CIA had figured out some way to handle this without killing everybody, including himself.

Chapter Seventeen

As he motored around the eastern end of Rathlin Island, the intermittent flashes of Rue Point Light first cast a glow of light reflected by the foggy air. Between flashes he could make out the hulk of a boat with a bright light a half mile to the south and realized it was *Red Dagger*. Of course, O'Leary would be out fishing, he thought, but it always had seemed mighty late even for that. As he turned south toward Ballycastle, he could see that he'd have to run past them fairly close. His first thought was to make a kind of dogleg track, heading out and then coming back around close to Fairhead. But that meant using extra fuel and his supply was getting critically low. It also would mean taking longer to arrive in the marina, and he was antsy about getting finished with this whole task. Gritting his teeth, he turned off his running lights and steered the most direct course toward Ballycastle. With luck they had not spotted *Kittiwake* and would just keep on fishing.

As he passed the lighthouse abeam to his starboard, the trawler's bright fishing light went out. He could make out its running lights and realized the boat was coming toward him, picking up speed. Making seven knots, *Kittiwake* could not out maneuver the bigger, twin-engine trawler. It was on a course to intercept him, and Joe could do nothing about it. The trawler swung around in a wide arc and came up to his starboard side. Seamus' younger brother, Mikey, was rigging mooring lines to port.

"Stop your engine," Seamus shouted. "I'm coming alongside."

"What the hell for?" Joe yelled back.

"A matter to discuss." The trawler was alongside now and bumped up against *Kittiwake*. "Take a line."

Sensing that everything was going wrong, Joe backed down and tied off the line that Mikey tossed over. *Kittiwake* bumped gently against the fenders and settled against the other boat. Joe shut down his engine and Seamus his.

"So you've been to Belfast," Seamus accused, climbing over lifelines and coming aboard. Even in the darkness, Joe could see the pistol he had in his belt. His brother followed.

"How did you know?" Joe tried to keep his voice even.

"A mutual friend told me. A young lady by the name of Fiona. I believe you've met?" He moved in close, getting in Joe's face.

"Look," Joe said, backing up a step. "I'd like to discuss this some other time. I'm in a hurry to get in."

Seamus jerked the pistol from his belt and aimed it at Joe's head. "You'll talk to me now, by damn you will."

"He's got crates down below," Mikey interrupted. He was shining a flashlight into the hatchway.

Seamus glanced down and then back at Joe. "What manner of contraband is that?"

"Tooth paste," Joe said. "What brand, I don't know."

Seamus swung the gun at Joe, hitting him on the right temple. Joe fell to the deck, almost blacking out.

"Think you're pretty clever, don't ya?"

"Look," Joe said, sitting up and rubbing his head. "This stuff belongs to the IRA. I wouldn't be interfering with me right now."

"You think we don't know? Youse is not playing with children here." He gave Joe a vicious kick in the ribs. "And just what wee party did you have planned for your arrival at the dock? Thought you'd just call the peelers to ambush us, did ye?" He stepped on Joe's shoulder. "Well, we know what to do with your sort." He put his weight on his foot, and Joe gasped in pain.

"Keep an eye on him." Seamus handed Mikey the pistol and climbed down into the salon.

Lying on deck in a panic, Joe wondered if there was anything he could do. He tried sitting up again, hoping that in the darkness Mikey wouldn't notice. Slipping his hand down to his belt, Joe felt for the iPhone and tapped the special icon, hoping it would connect to Wade and that Mikey hadn't observed his actions.

"Keep a sharp eye," Seamus said, handing up one of the crates. Mikey gave a quick scan all around and then took the box and set it down in the cockpit.

"Where's your tool box, arsehole?" Seamus called.

"In the bow cabin," Joe said, deciding that being cooperative was the best thing at the moment.

Seamus came up the ladder with a big screwdriver and started to pry open the crate.

"Be careful, for god sake," Joe said. "That's not really toothpaste."

"Shut up," Seamus barked. "Your voice carries out here."

"Sorry. But that's plastic explosives in there." *God!* He hoped Wade could hear all this on the phone and was getting the idea.

Mikey was staring at his brother roughly prying open the box. "Be careful," he said. While his back was turned, Joe had a chance to put the phone to his ear. "Wade?" he whispered

"Got it," Wade replied. "You're in Rathlin Sound?"

"Right," Joe whispered. Then he heard Wade say something muffled—something like "Get a fix on the iPhone signal."

Mikey heard it, too. He wheeled around to look at Joe. "What the hell, you doin'?" he said. "Hey, Seamus, this bloke's on his bloody phone!"

"Gimme that thing." Seamus charged over and bent down to take it away. Realizing the phone's *recent calls* would show who it was last connected to, Joe made a fumbling motion, managing to drop it in the water.

Seamus ran to the rail and peered down in the darkness, watching the shadowy splash circles. He turned around and stared at Joe.

"Damn you," he said, grabbing the pistol from Mikey and cocking it. "I ought to put a slug right in your eye." He aimed the pistol at Joe's face.

"Hold on, Seamus." Mikey said. "Someone'll hear if you shoot." Seamus kept the pistol pointed at Joe, clenching his other fist. Joe managed to shrug.

"The whole world will be hearing it when a wee bit of this Semtex blows him and this boat to kingdom come," Seamus said. He was removing some of the explosive from the crate.

"Listen," Joe pleaded, "I was just doing what I was told. I don't know anything about any ambush."

"You're a lying dog, too," Seamus said. "Foster's told us all about it, right enough."

"Foster?" Joe gasped. "The harbourmaster? I don't have anything to do with him. I don't even know who he is."

"A supergrass, like you," Mikey said.

"Shut the fuck up, both of youse," Seamus spit out the words. He let his breath out between his teeth. "Lie down," he shouted at Joe. "Lie down on the deck, you

223

bastard." Joe did as he was told. "Get on your stomach, and don't move. If you move an inch, I'll blow your head off."

Joe assumed a prone position and held his breath. Seamus told Mikey to get below and pass up the rest of the crates. Seamus watched Joe until he was handed a box. Then he took it and laid it over across on his boat, wheeling around to ensure Joe had not moved.

As the unloading continued, Joe heard a distant whine in the sky and thought it sounded like one of those drones he had heard before. He wondered what the hell Wade was doing to help him, if anything. What could Wade do? It wasn't as if he had much help nearby. If he called MI-5 or the PSNI, it would take a lot of explaining before they even began to move. All Wade had at his disposal was the drone, and what good would that do? Joe caught his breath. What good would that do? Suddenly the truth became crystal clear. It would do everything for Wade. His mission was either to capture or destroy the explosives, maybe at any cost. *At any cost.*

While the O'Leary brothers continued bringing up boxes, Joe turned his head and looked over the side. He was close enough to grab a lifeline stanchion post. If he got his left hand around it, he could pull himself in one swift motion over the side and into the water, and it could be quick enough that they wouldn't know it until he splashed in. Oh, gosh, how cold it would be! And if he did that, would they not be able to see him swimming away? If they spotted him, would it be easy enough to shoot him in the water? Hell, they were going to blow him up anyway. At least this way death would be of his own doing. Escape was his only chance.

How far were they from shore, a mile or two? The O'Learys were about finished unloading the Semtex. It was now or never.

Joe grabbed the stanchion, jerked with all his might, pulling his body as hard as he could. The lower lifeline caught on the backside of his belt as he went under it and made a twanging sound, but his bodyweight carried him on through. He hit the cold water, and the shock knocked the breath out of him, leaving him momentarily paralyzed by its iciness. Coming up, he heard the two men scrambling and cursing. Joe took a deep breath and went under, pulling himself along the keel of his boat, hoping to make it to the bow. Through the water he could hear the men's heavy footfalls on the deck. Oh, it was cold and dark as pitch! He realized the ebb current had increased, swinging the boats into the current. He came up in the space between the two boats, banging his head on *Kittiwake*'s hull.

On deck the two men were shouting at one another, peering over the side, trying to see him in the water. They turned on the deck lights. Joe inched his way over to the far side of their boat. He heard Seamus say, "Douse the friggin' lights." Joe knew his best hope was to swim away underwater as far as he could. He kicked away his shoes and pulled off his pants. Taking a deep breath, he pushed away from the hull, swimming at an angle that would keep the superstructure of the trawler obscuring their view. Thankfully, there was no moonlight. He came up breathless, realizing he had made it about 30 yards away. They were shining flashlights all around, the beams looking like yellow lasers.

He swam the breast stroke, going as fast as he could without making a splash. The wind was calm, which meant his wake was more likely to be seen, but the darkness helped hide him. He was 50 yards away when he heard Seamus speak.

"Aw, hell. Switch off your torch, Mikey. The buggah'll freeze out there. He'll never make it to shore." The lights went out, and the men appeared to be turning their attention to transferring the crates.

Joe could see lights on shore to the southwest and realized the current was carrying him more or less in that direction. He swam as fast and as silently as he could until he was a hundred yards or so from the two boats. In the still air, he heard a faint humming sound. It was in the sky, coming closer. An airplane? Or could it be a search plane? Had Wade managed to get some kind of search and rescue aircraft to come for him? No! It was a drone! It had to be a drone! Then in the sky there was another sound, a dull whistling, like air rushing from a punctured tire. Joe peered up to try and see. He caught a glimpse of something like a flare against the dark sky. The hissing sound became a scream. Then a mammoth ball of white flame engulfed the boats. There was a giant boom, and a shockwave ran through the water, striking him like a giant hammer. It hit his stomach, doubling him up, violently driving the wind from his lungs. Hunks of debris fell around him in the water. His ears ringing, gasping to regain his breath, Joe watched in amazement as the blinding flash dissolved into a huge yellow flame, engulfing the two boats.

"Jesus!" he cried. "Jesus Christ!" Then more explosions threw fireballs into the sky like fireworks. One whistled just over his head and splashed down not far away. In shock and panic he swam as fast as he could away from the inferno.

Breathless, nearly exhausted, he had to stop swimming. Treading water, he turned back toward the conflagration. The burning hulk seemed smaller, the flames subsided, as the boats began to sink. Hot metal and wood crackled as they submerged. A missile had been fired from the drone, he realized. Then it came to him that Wade must have ordered the missile firing. *Who else? It had to be Wade.*

"The bastard!" he yelled, his voice breathless and hoarse. Of course, Wade not only would be destroying the smugglers and their contraband, but by killing Joe he was removing his rival for Mary as well. This man was his enemy. How simple, how neat, how vicious and evil. What a fool Wade had made of him.

Teeth chattering in the frigid water, his shock turned to anger. How to survive now was the issue. Looking at lights along the shore, he could tell that the current was carrying him. The ebbing flow should be reaching its maximum speed, he realized, meaning he would be carried more and more toward the west as he tried to swim south. The crackling and banging sounds of the inferno grew fainter behind him, and then he heard a rushing sound ahead. Raising his head up, he peered out, seeing white waves, the great eddy swirling before him. *Slough na mor!*

In a panic again, he turned to his right and swam hard, trying to get away. It was no use; he was being drawn into the swirl. Having little strength left, he could not resist. The whirl of the water caught him up, carrying him around a wide circle, while white foam-crested, standing waves loomed over him, obscuring his view of shore. The power of swirling torrents locked him in the monster, taking him down, down into the deep dark water. Holding his breath, he knew he was dying, about to drown and be carried to hell in the depths below. He was blacking out, giving up his life to the terrible horror of blackness. As he began losing consciousness, his body totally relaxed. Death would be a cool dark sheath into which he would slip, unknowing.

Controlled by the power of the whirlpool, he dimly felt his limp body being tossed aside, ejected by centrifugal force away from the main swirl. Still being carried to the west, coughing and sputtering, he could see distant lights again along the shore. How far had the current carried him? He guessed the shore was maybe high a mile or so away. Regaining consciousness and shivering violently, he sensed his body heat was going fast, and would soon make him faint again. Realizing that Wade had tried to kill him, his anger rose. Wade, he knew, wanted to murder him in order to have Mary. Not if I can help it, he promised himself. *Not if I can only make it to shore. I'll crush him with my bare hands*, he thought. *I'll smash the eyes out of his head*. The adrenaline from his hatred fueled his efforts.

He heard the dull sound of diesel engines in the distance. Looking west, he could see a large boat coming his way. Then he saw that it was not coming toward him but was headed toward the flaming wreckage. Two hundred yards away, the craft passed by, and he could see that it was the lifeboat from Portrush. He tried to yell but was unable to make more than a groan. No one saw his hand in the air, desperately waving. His hopes dashed, he turned back toward the dark cliffs ahead, barely able to move his arms and legs.

Ahead loomed what appeared to be an enormous rock, blue-black against the gloom of morning twilight. It was not merely a cliff but also the remains of Kenbane Castle—crumbled rock walls standing atop a low cliff. His arms ached now and his legs had no feeling. But he swam toward it, realizing that reaching shore was his only hope. Swimming on with the last of his stamina waning, he got close enough to make out the rocky beach below. With vision dimming into unconsciousness, he kicked a jagged rock beneath the surface, painfully abrading his toes. He eased in closer and found himself on land. Staggering, he fell down just out of the water and passed out.

Sometime later, long before daybreak, Joe awakened, shivering violently. Looking back toward Rathlin, he could make out the lights of several boats and maybe a helicopter, but there were no more flames from the burning boats. He became aware that he was going to die from exposure if he didn't get going. It took all his effort to pull himself up on all fours. He remained in that position for a few minutes until he felt he could stand. Finally, with a huge groan, he staggered upright and took a few steps, but the rocks hurt his bare feet. Gritting his teeth, he stumbled over to the wall of the cliff and found a crevice through which he could climb up.

229

Breathless at the top, he looked at the skeletal remains of the castle and realized he was close to the road to Ballycastle. Clad in nothing more than sodden shirt and underwear, he made his way out to the pavement, turned left and began to walk. He estimated that it was maybe three miles or so to the town, and he wondered if he'd have the stamina to make it.

At dawn, Joe crawled up the stairs to Ryan's flat. He raised a fist and rapped on the bottom of the door. No answer. With the last of his strength he knocked again. Soon there was the sound of stirring and grumbling from inside.

"Who's that causing a disturbance at such an ungodly hour as this?" the big man called out hoarsely as he opened the door. "My God, Joe! What has happened? A half-naked and shriveled apricot ye be."

Joe tried to speak but couldn't. He felt Ryan dragging him inside, and then he knew and felt no more.

Chapter Eighteen

"Well, I see the dead man's awake," Ryan said when Joe suddenly sat upright in bed. It took Joe a minute to realize where he was. He squinted his eyes and tried to focus on the figure sitting in a chair nearby.

"I got to pee," he mumbled, swinging his legs over the side of the bed. Painfully, he stood up and staggered a few steps. He was dizzy and his mouth felt like dry cotton. He also was naked.

"Help yourself," Ryan said, motioning with his head. "Door on the right." Joe tried standing. It hurt. He was sore all over. He managed to stand and stumble to the bathroom.

"The news says you're missing and presumed dead," Ryan called to him as he got up to find a bathrobe. "Blown to smithereens in the sea."

Joe limped out of the bathroom. "What about the O'Learys?"

"The same." Ryan tossed him the robe. "You'll be telling quite a tale, I'd imagine."

"Got any coffee?" Joe asked. He collapsed on the side of the bed and pulled on the robe. "And maybe a good shot of whiskey to go in it."

"Mean to make me wait 'til you've had your coffee, eh?" Ryan grumbled, getting up.

"I just need a minute. Please."

"Next you'll be after rashers and eggs," Ryan fussed as he headed to the kitchen. Joe forced himself to get up and follow, aching with every step. The big man already was digging eggs and bacon out of the refrigerator.

"How about that coffee first?"

"Getting a might bossy in your afterlife." Ryan loaded a drip pot.

Joe smiled. More than once during the swim he had thought it was the end. He eased down into a chair at the table. "You haven't told anyone about me, I hope."

"Nope. I figured you'd rather do the telling."

"Good." Joe was relieved. "There's some people out there that would want me dead." He thought about Wade and shook his head. "And they're not all terrorists."

"It's high time you told me who you really are, Joe Anderson. That is your real name, I hope? I think you must be some government man." He stared at Joe until Joe nodded and began to tell all, including his life with Mary and his reasons for coming to Northern Ireland. Ryan listened with rapt attention, shaking his head from time to time. Joe recounted what happened after leaving Carrickfergus. Ryan made him back up and tell it all from the beginning. Joe admitted to being a spy for the CIA and then tried to explain about Fiona, but it all sounded terribly confused, even to himself. "And who tipped off O'Leary anyway? His brother, Mikey, called Evan Foster a supergrass.

"I knew it," Ryan exclaimed. "Foster's a tout is he? A mole, as you Americans call it. So that's why the government took my job of harbourmaster and gave it to him." The big man looked grim.

Joe gazed at the big man. "I've got to figure out what to do next."

"Do next, bajeezus!" Ryan looked at him with condescension. Then he sighed. "Always suspected you had a loose screw." He shook his head and poured Joe a mug of coffee, adding a spike of Coleraine whiskey. Then he sat down across the table and poured himself a good shot. They sat in silence for a few minutes while Joe sipped the spiked coffee and began to feel a little better.

"I want to thank you for putting me to bed and all," Joe said. "I was so exhausted that I didn't really expect to make it here."

"Quite a swim youse had," Ryan shook his head. "Not many would have made it."

"I didn't have much choice." Joe sipped the hot liquid while trying to assess his situation. "Lost my wallet, my passport, my phones, my clothes, my credit cards and my money—everything I had, even my shoes and pants." He had to laugh. "And now I don't even have my shirt and underwear."

"Like a newborn babe you are," Ryan replied with a chuckle. Then he gave Joe a sober look. "Daft for sure. So what do we do with you now? Wrap you up and send you home before you get in any more mischief?"

Joe thought about that. "I'm convinced that Wade Johnston was responsible for the drone firing the missile, knowing full well that it would kill me." He clenched his fists. "And he was supposed to be my handler and protector, for God's sake."

"What would be his motive?" Ryan asked. "Knew of him before, did ye?"

"I'll say I did. He was Mary's former brother in law. I guess he became 'former' when Mary's husband Earnest died. Anyway, he kept coming to see her while I was living there, and he was jealous of me. I got the idea that Wade wanted to get control of her inheritance from Earnest. But when I thought Mary cared more for him than me, I stopped worrying about it."

"He wanted her but she kept after you, was it? A right and proper love triangle if e'er I heard tell."

"But would he want to kill me for that?" Joe asked. "Would he kill me and the O'Learys, too, just to get at her money?"

Ryan nodded. "A professional spy he was, trained in skullduggery. What else would you expect?" He rose and poured them more coffee. Then he started cooking a huge Irish breakfast.

"So what I don't know is who to turn to at CIA," Joe called out over the sound of rashers sizzling in the pan. "I mean, did they all want to kill me?"

Ryan thought a moment. "Surely there's someone in that bunch you can go to."

Joe nodded. It surely was a paranoid thought to believe the entire CIA wanted him dead. "But I don't even have my secure phone anymore. Do I just call the main number and tell the operator that I'm a long lost agent and please connect me to the first compassionate person you can find?" He chuckled.

Ryan shrugged. "It's your own web you've weaved." He continued cooking their breakfast, and the aroma made Joe's mouth water. He had never been so hungry.

"I should call Mary," Joe decided. "I was going to call her anyway. Maybe she can find out from Wade what the mood is at CIA without telling him I'm still alive."

"You trust her then?" Ryan asked while setting a heaping, steamy plate in front of Joe. "She seems mighty tight with this Wade fellow."

As he grabbed up a fork full of egg and ravenously stuffed it in his mouth, Joe considered that idea. If her last email was any indication, Mary wanted to distance herself from Wade and get Joe himself back. "If I can't trust Mary, then there's no one I can trust? Except for you, my friend, and her, I don't have anyone to count on." He wondered how to call since he had no phone, no credit card, not even any coins to put in the pay phone. "You should have taken that fifty quid I offered," he said, grinning apologetically.

"I'll run you a tab," Big Ryan replied with a grin, imitating Eamon at the bar. He pointed to his telephone on the wall. "You can call from here."

Joe thought about what time it would be in Alabama—six hours earlier. Mary surely would be home, probably still in bed. Then it occurred to him that he shouldn't use Ryan's phone. This flat was his only safe place to hide, and he was concerned that the call could be traced.

"Would you lend me some money?" he asked. "I think I'd better not use your phone here."

"Aye, and some clothes to boot. Can't say it would do to be walking the streets in your skivvies."

"There's a thrift shop down the way. I'll go see if there's a more fitting outfit for you. One thing about Ballycastle. It's a wee, close-knit town, and everyone hears about what anyone sees. Walking the streets would be risky."

"Thanks," Joe said. It also occurred to him that secrecy was his only protection. The last thing he needed was for a member of the Real IRA to spot him. "You know, wearing some disguise is not a bad idea. Would you see if there's a big hat or something."

"A cloak and a dagger perhaps?" Ryan groused as he prepared to leave. "Look at where playing the spy already has got ye."

While Ryan was away, Joe considered his situation. He still did not know how Seamus O'Leary knew about the plan to have the police ready to swoop when the IRA smugglers came to the harbor to take the explosives off *Kittiwake*. He would have expected that Tom, Ned and Timothy were the only ones who knew about his rendezvous with the ship, except for Wade, of course. So who told Seamus? Perhaps as Mikey O'Leary had said, Evan Foster had to be a *supergrass*, a double agent. He recalled the time Foster had his dog sniff out the drugs on the French boat, and then after Foster left, the police had come to arrest the Frenchmen. So if Foster spied for the British government, why would he tip off O'Leary instead of just letting the police nab whoever came to the marina to receive the explosives from Joe's boat? Was Foster trying to insure that O'Leary was trapped in the operation as well? Whatever had happened, Joe realized, nobody cared a flip for saving Joe Anderson. At best, he was considered expendable. God knows, he'd like to get his hands around Wade Johnston's throat.

After about an hour, Ryan returned with some passable pants, shirt, shoes, socks, underwear, and a brown hooded jacket. He also had some cosmetics he had picked up at the chemist's.

"Paint up your face a bit," Ryan said. "Give you a wee bit different look."

Joe eyed the mascara. "I didn't ask for drag. I'm not sure whether this will help me be disguised or just call attention to myself," he said. "But thanks for the thought anyway." He began dressing.

"Look, Ryan," he went on. "I've got nothing. I mean, well, I've got about $50,000 in a bank in the States. But for the moment, I have nothing and nobody to depend on and trust but you. So I hope I can count on you to help me work myself out of this mess."

Ryan stared at him a moment then looked away. "All my life I've avoided all this loyalist-against-republican hell on earth. It was what sent me to sea. I think I told you that. And now you want to get me thrown right in the pot there with you." He took in a deep breath and sighed. "Well, a man can't run from life forever." He gave Joe a long look and then nodded. "I haven't got much, but of course, I'll help you. Of course."

It was past sunset and growing dark when Joe ventured out to find a pay phone, his pocket loaded down with coins from Ryan's stash. There was one of the red structures about a block away, and he hurried to it. He really did not have any idea how to make an overseas call but was able to reach an operator who helped. The connection was tinny sounding, but he was thrilled to hear Mary's voice and told her so. She was astonished to hear his.

"Wade told me you were killed in a terrible accident," she sobbed. "Oh, Joe. I'm so relieved. You don't know how I've been grieving."

"Don't tell Wade I'm alive, whatever you do," Joe said. "It's a long story, but I'm very suspicious of Wade's part in that so-called accident."

"I don't understand," she said. "What do you mean his part?"

Joe explained briefly what had happened and how he had managed to swim ashore. "Wade must not be told any of this. Don't tell anybody. I have a friend here named Ryan who's helping me. He'd be in danger, too, if the wrong people found out."

"When Wade called to tell me you had been...you were gone, he said he was being sent there to make an investigation," Mary said. "He may be on the way by now."

Joe's pulse quickened. "Coming here is he? To see his handiwork, I guess." Joe thought that perhaps he just might have some plans for Wade's visit himself.

"Please come home," Mary pleaded. "I miss you so much, and I'm so worried. Just come on home."

"I'm afraid that's not possible right now. I've lost my wallet and identification," he explained. "I have no passport or anything. But I'll be okay." He paused. "I really need a friend right now."

"Then just tell the CIA to come get you, or something. Just come home."

Joe noticed a vehicle coming down the street and recognized it as Timothy's car in which he had taken Joe to the IRA meeting. Joe turned away and covered his face, putting his left hand to his other ear as if engaged in a call and it was hard to hear. Thankfully, the car went on by.

"I'll do the best I can," Joe said. "Remember now, please don't say a word about me to anyone. It's very important." When she agreed, he said good bye and hung up. As he stepped out of the phone booth and started down the street, his thoughts turned to Fiona, and he was perplexed by his dilemma over allegiance.

When Joe returned to the flat, his host had some news.

"There's to be a memorial service planned for the O'Learys," Ryan announced. "Tomorrow at 1:00 o'clock in the afternoon, out at the docks, it is, where the town can gather to see out in the Sound where it happened."

Joe was immediately excited. "I have to go to it." The prospect of watching what could be considered a memorial service for himself as well was too intriguing to let go by. And, besides, he realized someone else might show up there too. "Wade Johnston's on the way here to see what a fine job he did."

"Not a surprise," Ryan replied. "Like as not someone from your CIA would show up here to pick up what's left of your corpse, or whatever."

"Good point," Joe agreed. "They do need somebody to come make a report on what happened. And if Wade really was trying to do me in—damn! I know he was—well, he'd be wise to come make sure that the story was told the way he wants it."

"And if he were to find that you're still alive and kicking, he might just try to finish what he started." The big man raised his eyebrows and drew his finger across his throat.

"Yeah, but if he comes here, and goes to that funeral service, I just might find some way to cook his goose." He slapped his left hand with his fist. "I would expect my good buddies in the Real IRA would like to meet the man who blew up their explosives."

Ryan cast a dark look. "There's an old Irish saying: A man who would dig a grave for another had best take care not to fall in it himself."

Chapter Nineteen

At noon the next day, wearing the black wig and black moustache that Ryan had found in some novelty store, along with Ryan's hooded jacket, Joe accompanied the big man down to the waterfront. He had not shaved in several days, but it would take a while for his light beard to show enough to change his looks. While being relatively taller than most Irishmen, Joe decided that standing beside the towering Ryan would make himself appear less conspicuously large.

Seeming to be casually out for a walk, they went by the car park close to Joe's rental car that, in order to protect his anonymity, he could never use again. Besides, the keys were on the bottom of the Sound, likely an amorphous blob of burned metal. They sat down on a bench at the beach where they could see the marina. By 10:00 AM a crowd of a hundred or so had gathered in the car park. His heart raced when he saw Fiona and Timothy walking down the street, probably having closed the market for the memorial service. He felt an urge to run to her and an equally strong sense of wariness. What was Fiona feeling, Joe wondered, supposedly having lost two suitors at once? Probably saddened but not shocked, he thought, realizing that life had hardened her to violence and loss. What a beautiful woman and what a terrible life, he thought. Was there any possibility for their relationship? At one point he had imagined marrying Fiona and settling down here forever. Was that still possible? Would she have his child? Would he ever see it? He put his head in his hands and tried to put it out of his mind.

Then when a taxi drove into the marina car park, Joe nearly jumped up when he saw Wade get out.

"Ryan," he whispered. "See the cab. That's Wade Johnston!" His pulse racing, he forced himself to look the other way so as not to be recognized.

"So your lady, Mary, was right."

Joe knew it was logical that someone from CIA would show up, if for no other reason than just to report the event. But wasn't it strange that the CIA had not suspended Wade or something, pending an official inquiry into his death? Well now, here was Wade Johnston here, the inimitable Dr. Spin, apparently all by himself. "On my turf," he thought, "and I'll have him on my terms this time."

The harbourmaster, Evan Foster, was out on the dock, clearing a gathering place where O'Leary used to moor his trawler. He walked up the ramp, opened the gate, and ushered the people in. More people arrived. Joe watched Fiona make her way toward the front of the gathering crowd. She went to an older couple, spoke to and then embraced each of them. When she turned around Joe could see tears in Fiona's eyes. *Those are the O'Learys' parents*, he guessed. Apparently, she had close ties, perhaps through her somewhat rocky relationship with Seamus. Joe's passing thought was to wonder if his own parents had been there, would she have been equally as sympathetic to them? No, sadly, that would not be the case, he realized.

A Catholic priest in white vestments arrived and soon began greeting individuals in the group. When everyone's attention was upon the priest, Joe got up to walk over to the marina. "We shouldn't be seen together," he said.

Ryan put a firm hand on Joe's shoulder. "Don't go off half-cocked." Joe nodded and went on. Shaking his head, Big Ryan waited a minute and then came along.

Joe was glad there was a cool breeze because having the jacket's hood over his head seemed normal. As he walked down the ramp and onto the pier, one or two people he didn't know glanced at him and then back at the speaker. Joe spotted Tom and Ned across the crowd. *How nice of them to come*, he thought. He lowered his head, slipped farther away from them, and stood among some unfamiliar people. One problem was that he was taller than most of the Irish there. Occasionally, he peered out from the hood to look at Wade from behind. He fought back the urge to run over, grab the man around the neck and choke him, break his neck with his bare hands. But, he realized, it was more important not to be spotted by the IRA gang.

The priest stepped in front and introduced himself as Father O'Donnell. "A truly tragic event happened here Sunday night," he said with priestly gravitas. "No one knows why the huge explosion occurred. It was an act only Almighty God understands." He crossed himself and most in the crowd did likewise. "Our brothers, Seamus and Michael O'Leary, good Catholics both, were taken from us in this terrible accident out here in the Sound. Oh yes, and there was this American, too, a Joseph Anderson, I believe. Let us pray for the souls of these departed ones."

Joe felt very strange being prayed for, even if the priest had included him as something of an afterthought. He sneaked a glance at Fiona, recognizing that she was in tearful grief. He did not know if it was for his own death or Seamus'. It had to be for Seamus, he supposed, since he himself was the outsider. Was it possible, he wondered, that she was just using him to make O'Leary jealous? Well, in a sense Joe had been using Fiona and Timothy, too, to get to the IRA. People always use people, he reflected, to get their own way.

Father O'Donnell recited several prayers, some in English and some in Irish Gaelic. Most people crossed themselves at certain points and replied to the 'amen.' While the prayers continued, Joe surreptitiously looked around the crowd and saw that Tom, Ned and Timothy were looking his way and whispering to one another. Then for an instant his gaze met Ned's. Joe forced himself to look away, hoping he was not recognized.

The priest called upon those gathered for a few words about the departed. The gray-haired man, walking stooped over with a cane, stepped forward to speak.

"Yes, Mr. O'Leary." The priest embraced him briefly and stepped back.

"It's known…" The old man's voice rasped and dropped off into a cough. "It's known widely here that in my youth I stood with many a courageous man for the cause. What youse may not have known is that my sons, Seamus and Michael…" His voice broke and he pulled out his handkerchief and swiped across his eyes. "Seamus and Michael carried on in our struggles. They stood very tall as Óglaigh na hÉireann—young volunteers of Ireland." He paused to collect himself. "It was no accident occurred out there at sea. Some dastardly enemy took those brave lads as they fought the good fight." He coughed deeply, stooped over on his cane, and seemed to lose his balance. His wife and a young woman, rushed to his side.

During the pause, Joe dared another glance toward the IRA thugs. They had moved closer to him and were still looking in his direction. He gently elbowed his way closer to the front to separate himself farther from the men.

Near the priest, still supporting her husband, the old lady, clad in a faded black dress, spoke in her crackling, aged voice. "'Twas the American's doing. He bears the blame for the death of me sons. 'Fore God, I know it full well." As Joe listened, he stared at Wade and saw a smirk on his face. Mrs. O'Leary raised her fist. "May the snails devour his corpse," she shouted. "May the curse of curses in sorrow prostrate his kin."

"May the devil sweep him," the younger woman cried. Many in the crowd gasped, fully understanding the women's use of damning Irish oaths.

Here he was taking the brunt of the old woman's curses while Wade stood by, so smug and uncaring. It was all Joe could do to keep from running over and bashing his face in. He began to shake with anger as the old woman finished her rant. To be cursed like that in the face of all that had happened was intolerable.

"Óglaigh na hÉireann forever," the old man cried. He pulled away from the women, standing as tall as he could, and limped back into the crowd.

Father O'Donnell stepped back to the front and held up his hand for silence. Then he turned toward the old man and made the sign of the cross. It was clear the family's grief was keenly felt by all the gathering, and Joe was growing incensed. He took one more glance in the direction of the three IRA members. Tom and Tim were still looking in his direction, but Ned was not with them. Then he was shocked to feel the hood jerked off his head. He spun around to see Ned. The man grabbed Joe's wig and yanked it off, then gave him a malicious grin. Joe pulled away, bumping into a man beside him. He glanced around to see if there was any way to escape but saw none.

"Is there anyone else who would like to speak a few words?" Father O'Leary asked.

Joe gritted his teeth and then stepped forward. "Aye!" He bolted away from the thugs and pushed forward through the crowd. "Yes. I have something to say." He stood beside the priest and turned to see that Ned had not followed. He glanced over to see that Wade's face had grown ashen in surprise. Thankfully, the IRA men were hanging back. He might be safe as long as he spoke.

"I'm the American who escaped from the explosion," he said. "And I have a few things to say about what happened that night." Some people were gasping and exclaiming in low voices. Then Joe looked around and spotted Fiona, standing close by with her brother, shaken and pale. Realizing he was still wearing the moustache, he reached up and stripped it off.

"Last year, someone in the IRA stole my boat in Florida, used it for smuggling and then sank it. It ruined my career, my livelihood. So I came here to find out who did it. That got me involved with the Real IRA. In order to set a trap for them, I was helping smuggle explosives, and that's what blew up. It was their explosives that they were going to use to kill people." As he spoke, he noticed that Ned was making his way toward the front, a vicious frown on his face. Joe hoped the man was not likely to attack him in front of the crowd.

"Seamus O'Leary meant to kill me," Joe said looking at the man's parents. "He accosted me out there in the Sound. It was his own fault he and Mikey were there, not mine." He glanced at Fiona. "And you know why? Seamus was jealous over my relationship with Fiona. I know you all know Fiona. So for his own selfish reasons, Seamus wanted to do me in. But I managed to escape and swim away." The people were in rapt silence.

"Now what the hell were these "brave lads" going to do with all those explosives?" He looked at Mr. O'Leary.

"Set bombs to kill and maim people in the name of politics? What, for the love of God, is so brave about that? How's that going to right any wrongs or fix anything?" He glanced at Ned and they locked in a stare of hatred. Then Joe looked away.

"Now, while I have your attention," he said, *and I'm still alive*, he thought. "Since I've been in your country, I've learned a few things. I came here seeking revenge. It was purely selfish. But last Sunday I saw the parade in Belfast— the Ulster Volunteer Force with their Shankill Butchers being paraded about like they were heroes. Hero butchers, for god sake? And you know what? A person that's here right now was part of an attempt to shoot them as they paraded by." He flicked a glance at Fiona, who looked back a second and then dropped her eyes. "It was for revenge, of course. Vengeance against the loyalists and their butchers."

"Good on whoever," someone shouted. Another one or two shouted agreement.

"And so it goes," Joe said, raising his voice to regain attention. "You try to kill them, and they'll try to kill you. And it will go on and on and on until everybody's dead. Isn't that right, Father O'Donnell?" The priest merely shook his head.

"I was after revenge," Joe forged on. "And, out of revenge, Seamus was going to kill me. And I guess I have to take some of the blame for his death and his brother's."

"And I'll see your soul rot in hell!" the older O'Leary cried, shaking his cane at him.

"I'm sorry about your sons, I truly am," Joe replied. "But who taught them to be terrorists, Mr. O'Leary? Oh God, what a legacy you've passed on to them."

The old man started to shout something out at Joe, but his voice broke into a feeble fit of coughing.

"There's another man here whom I want you all to know." Joe pointed his finger at Wade. "Meet Wade Johnston, Ladies and Gentlemen. He's a real spy, you know, a real agent from America." Wade cringed, glaring at Joe and then looking for an escape.

"This man Johnston and I were in love with the same woman," Joe went on. "So this man, who was supposed to be protecting me, ordered the missile to be fired in order to kill me. But it killed Seamus and Michael O'Leary instead."

All eyes turned on Wade, but it was Fiona who caught Joe's attention. She was making her way between onlookers, moving up closer, the pistol from the day of the parade in her hand. Wade saw her coming but too late. About ten feet away, she pointed the gun and fired several times. His body fell backwards, crumpling into an inanimate bloody heap. Amid screams and people bolting away, Joe was too shocked to move.

"Fiona?" he cried. "What in God's name?" He started over to Wade's body. But then he saw Ned coming at him, a switchblade knife in his hand flicked open. Joe dodged a thrust of the knife and shoved him back. Realizing he had nowhere to run, he spun around and dove off the dock into the water.

Diving down as deep as he could, he swam under the floating dock. He spotted a place between floats where he could come up. He surfaced as quietly as he could. There was too much commotion and shouting above for anyone to hear him. It seemed that no one was making much of an effort to find him. *They probably hope I drowned.* He hoped Ryan had the good sense just to walk away and not let on that he had anything to do with him. He wondered what was happening to Fiona now. Were they having her arrested, or helping her escape? Did she feel that, having killed Wade, she had avenged Seamus? Then it occurred to him that the water was awfully cold, but not nearly so bad as it had been on that terrible night of the explosion.

After about ten minutes or more, it seemed as if most people had walked off the dock. There was the whooping sound of police cars coming. Joe decided it would be better to move away from the place he had gone in. Between the floats he could see another opening beneath another dock about 40 feet away. He thought about kicking off the shoes and pants but decided to keep them on to retain a little body heat. He might be under there for a long time. He took a deep breath and submerged, swimming to the other safe spot and coming up as silently as possible.

From this shadow-obscured vantage point, he could see the parking area. An ambulance had arrived, along with some police vehicles. Then he saw Evan Foster heading toward the marina with his dog, Bounder, tethered on a leash. Foster took him from dock to dock, apparently hoping the dog could smell him out. When they came to where he was, Joe took another breath and forced himself down, holding on to one of the anchor cables under the dock. When he could stand it no more, he surfaced back underneath and was relieved to see man and dog had moved on.

After a couple of hours, he was really cold. Even though he kept moving his arms and legs as much as he could without creating any sound, he began to shiver violently. Knowing he would have to do something, Joe decided to swim for it. He took several deep breaths and went down, heading toward the harbor entrance. He came up once, got a breath without being seen, submerged and swam on. At the end of the jetty, he climbed up on the rocks, hoping not to be spotted. Out of the view of the car park, he peered over the jetty and saw that a van had arrived. The doors were open in back and there were two men donning scuba gear, doing more talking than anything, obviously in no hurry to get in the cold water to hunt for a dead body.

In the gloom after sundown, Joe slipped back into the water again, wincing at the cold. He swam to the ferry dock and climbed up the concrete ramp on the far side of the moored ferry. Moving from shadow to shadow, he stole his way across the street, heading toward Ryan's flat.

Being certain no one was around to see, he stumbled up the stairs and fell at Ryan's door.

"For the love of God," Ryan exclaimed when he opened up and saw Joe. "It's the bad penny keeps turning up, I see."

Chapter Twenty

Joe remained in Ryan's flat for several days, desperately sad and worried about Fiona. Most certainly she was in jail, perhaps being arraigned for Wade's murder. He ventured out only late at night, just to get a little exercise. He wore a new disguise, much better crafted than the first, but Ryan told him it was foolish to go out at all.

On the third night, unable to resist any longer, he decided to slip out and walk down the street past Fiona's market, curious about whether Timothy was still running the place. Peeking in the front window, he gasped. Fiona was inside at the cashier's stand. His pulse racing, he backed off around the corner to think. His first impulse was to go to her immediately, but he realized she was, if nothing else, dangerous. Had she not killed Wade? Did she despise Joe just as much for being a spy? A young man and woman were walking down the street toward the store. Joe turned and walked casually in the opposite direction. Once they entered, he eased back toward the front window to peer in. The couple picked up a few items and took them to the register. Fiona smiled pleasantly as she accepted their money and made change. They exchanged a few words with her and then left, walking back down the street from the way they had come. Joe took a deep breath, went to the door, looked around quickly to see that no one was around, and went in.

Busy with some kind of paperwork, Fiona did not look up immediately. But when Joe approached her and removed his hat, she glanced at him, stared, and then gasped. "I thought you were dead, drowned." She leaned over the counter to touch his arm. "Oh, the saints be praised."

"I'm still here," he said, heartened by her response. They looked at one another in silence.

"Oh, I'm so glad," she said, tears in her eyes. She came around the counter. Joe hesitated and then embraced her tightly. Her head against his chest, she sobbed a moment, and finally looked up and stepped back.

"I thought you'd be... in jail."

She shook her head. "They haven't come for me."

"What? There were police all around within 15 minutes or so. Didn't someone tell them it was you who...?"

She looked away, then turned back and met his gaze. "It was a gathering of our republican friends, it was, there to honor the passing of the boys..." Her voice broke. "... from a good Catholic family."

"But still, I don't see why," Joe stammered. "Why haven't the police come for you?"

Fiona smiled a sad, cynical smile. "The man I shot, you said yourself, was the one killed Seamus and Mikey."

"And he was out to kill me, too," Joe said. "I was his real target." His feelings about the justice of Wade's death was ambivalent. "But what about all the witnesses? So many were there."

She shrugged. "These are my people. Not one of them would ever say."

Joe was amazed. "But, I mean, there were more than a hundred people there. No one will go to the law?"

Fiona stepped behind the counter, found a tissue and wiped her eyes. "You never really understood, did you, Joe? I tried to tell you what it was like living through The Troubles. The O'Learys and all the other people at the service know that the police are for the Prods, the loyalists. When it comes to fairness, to justice, we republicans have to provide our own."

They gazed at one another in silence. While he had been hiding under the dock that day, Joe sadly had realized that, if called upon, he would have to testify against her. Now it seemed that he would be the only one. There was a motion toward the back of the store that caught his eye. He looked just in time to see a door close.

"It's Timothy," Fiona whispered. "I hope he hasn't recognized you." She came toward him and beckoned toward the door. "You'd best leave."

Joe glanced toward the back again, and then put up his hand. "I've got to know, Fiona. Timothy said you, well, you might be pregnant." He took her hand. "Are you? Is it mine, I mean, is it ours?"

She regarded him for a moment, looked away, and then looked at him again, tears forming in her eyes. "Aye," she said. "It would have to be yours."

Joe pulled her to him and held her, trembling as he realized the truth of their circumstances. "I love you, Fiona," he whispered, nearly breathless. Her arms to her side, she allowed him to embrace her for only a moment.

"It's no good, Joe," she said, and gently but firmly pushed him away. "I have no time to have a child." Her voice broke as she said it. Grasping what she meant, Joe felt a cold chill run through him.

"You can't… You're Catholic. It's ours… We can be married," he said desperately. "We can get away. We can go hide somewhere until we can figure out what to do."

She shook her head. "I am sworn to the IRA," she said. "I cannot turn back now. Not for you, not for…" And then she moaned deeply. Joe reached out to embrace her again, but she backed away and wiped her eyes with her hand.

"That's just crazy," he said. He gestured in frustration and put his hands to his eyes. Then he looked at her again. "Why would such a lovely, sweet girl like you be so…fanatical?"

Fiona met his gaze and sighed. "Did you ever hear of Unity Flats? I suppose not. It was the housing section where our family lived in Belfast when The Troubles began. You cannot imagine what it was like to have loyalists throwing rocks, breaking every window. Or having soldiers invade your home, ripping up floors, tearing the upholstery, dumping everything out of drawers and closets, all on mere suspicion and hearsay." She shook her head. "One night my poor Da was out in the street with the other men, trying to defend our homes, they were. The Prods came in a wave, police among them. While we watched from the window, Da was beaten to death in the fray."

"That is so terrible," Joe said, "And a policeman did it? Unimaginable."

"Timothy and I were wee tots, and Mum made us stay inside. But Peter, who was 12, grabbed up Mom's fry pan and ran out to attack the policeman. She screamed for him to come back, but Peter whammed that copper in the head from behind and sent him sprawling. That night, Peter swore into the IRA."

"I can see how angry he was."

"Oh, aye, he was. Six years after the death of me Da, Peter was tortured and murdered by the bloody butchers of the Shankill."

Joe was overwhelmed. "Come home with me, Fiona," he cried. "We'll go to my home in America. Please let me take you away from this terrible place." She looked at him strangely, as if somehow what he was saying was beyond all possibility.

The door in the back opened. Joe looked in that direction and saw Timothy coming toward them, a pistol in hand. "Freeze, you bastard," he commanded, pointing the gun at Joe. Joe glanced at Fiona and raised his hands.

259

"No Tim. It's Joe." She stepped in front of him.

"Aye, I can see for myself," her brother replied as he came closer. "A right bloody spy he is for sure in all that get up. A real enemy to our cause."

"I was an enemy, Tim. But now I know better."

"I trusted you, and you betrayed me, you did." Tim looked at Fiona. "I have to kill him." He extended the pistol toward Joe's face. "He will go to the police."

Joe stepped back and put up his hands. "And how could you ever get away with it?" he stammered, trying to think of some argument.

"We'll say you were robbing the store," Tim replied, addressing his sister but keeping his eyes fixed on Joe, "threatening my sister and all."

Joe looked in Timothy's eyes and sensed that the boy was unsure of what he was doing. He turned toward Fiona. "Let me take you away from all this. We can go live in the U. S., in Florida maybe, and I can fix up my boat and start chartering again." He warmed to the idea. "Maybe I could get the CIA to arrange a visa for you…" He paused, realizing that he was talking unreasonably. Fiona was a murderer, and even in this topsy-turvy world she lived in, ultimately she'd have to stand trial.

She shook her head. "You, Joe, you and your miserable CIA. Why did you have to come here and get in our way?"

"Oh, Lord, Fiona," he wailed. "You're right. I was a fool, a stupid fool. I came here knowing so little about anything that had happened here, or what you've been through. I had no idea. I just didn't understand."

She looked up at him and wiped her tears. "How could you know? You'd have to live in this hell to understand."

Joe held his embrace and kissed her forehead. "I love you, Fiona. We can get away from all this." She looked in his eyes and shook her head.

"Move away from my sister," Tim growled, brandishing the pistol.

"It's not love, Joe," she said. "It's not love." She gently pushed away and stood back. "I don't want your pity."

"If there was any way, I swear I would take you away from this."

She gave him a sad smile. "You're not in this," she said. She reached out to take his hand. "Go home, dear Joe. Go home while you can, and good on you."

"He'll not be going anywhere," Tim said. "I have to shoot him, Fiona. It's the only way."

"No, Timothy," she said and moved toward him. "Give me the gun." He stepped back from her, still pointing the gun at Joe.

"I will shoot him, Sis. So stay back." He cocked the pistol. Joe glanced around quickly, trying to find some escape. Timothy began to extend his arm to fire.

"No, don't!" Fiona screamed and lunged at her brother's arm to stop him. They wrestled for an instant and the pistol fired, striking Fiona in the chest. Tim dropped the pistol, grabbed his sister, and they collapsed together on the floor. Joe knelt beside Fiona. Blood came from her mouth. She looked up at him with an astounded expression, gasped in several spasms and then was gone.

Joe watched in shock as Tim sobbed uncontrollably. Then he looked up at Joe with great hatred. Both of them grabbed for the gun. Joe managed to shove it away. He sprang up, grabbed the nearest shelf, a rack of canned goods, and pulled it over. It fell on Timothy, knocking him down. Joe ran for the front door, shoved on it, but it opened inward. He pulled it back to run out, just as he heard the pistol fire and felt a terrific slam of pain in his left shoulder. He staggered, got his feet back under him and reeled out of the doorway.

On the street, he turned and ran, half-stumbling for a block or so. Sobbing and gasping for breath, he leaned against a wall and looked back. Tim was not following. He reached up to feel his left shoulder and came back with a handful of blood. Then from near the front of the market, he heard Timothy shout one mournful wail, followed by a single gunshot. He peered out into the street, and in the ambient light saw the young man's body crumpled on the sidewalk. Joe's knees buckled, and he fell into a kneeling position, crying. Lights came on in windows on the floor above him. In minutes a police siren whined in the distance. His vision blurred with tears; he realized Fiona had died to save his life. Now her brother, in shock and grief, had committed the mortal sin of suicide.

Joe got up and staggered on, getting his bearings, heading for Ryan's flat. Nearly blacking out while sneaking along the distance of six blocks, he half climbed, half crawled up the stairs, banged on the door, and sank down in blackness.

Chapter Twenty-One

It was around three in the morning when the old Jeep arrived, and they could hear its poorly muffled putt-putt as it idled outside. Ryan helped Joe up out of the easy chair where the big man had dragged him, threw a blanket around his shoulders, and led him down the stairs. He appeared both hideous and clownish, once again wearing some of Ryan's huge pants with a shirt with the sleeve cut off to accommodate a crude bloody bandage. When they walked, Joe half stumbled to the car. He could feel a light, cool mist hitting his face. His shoulder throbbed and burned, but Ryan had done a fair job of bandaging it. The bullet had skimmed through muscle and no bone, so there was no serious damage. Ryan's niece, Breana, was behind the wheel. As quietly as possible, the giant helped Joe into the front seat and then folded his own huge frame into the back. Breana eased the vehicle around and drove on.

The car climbed the hill and turned right, heading down the coast road in darkness. Heavy fog reflected a nearly impenetrable glare from the headlights so that she had to drive slowly. Breana asked Joe how he was keeping, but he didn't feel like talking. Ryan uttered a few words of appreciation that she had come, and then the only sound was the poorly muffled engine and the slap of windshield wipers. Passing the turn to Kenbane Castle, Joe shivered, remembering that horrific night, the explosion, the terribly cold water, the desperate swimming to get free of the chaos of the whirlpool, and the long hike to Ryan's apartment. And then there was the last horrible event—Timothy with the pistol, Fiona grabbing Timothy's arm, the wrestling, the gunshot and Fiona's blood splattering all over him. Through it all there had been an adrenal reaction and struggle to survive, suppressing his ability to feel anything. Fiona was dead; their unborn child was dead. Now in the calm and safety of friends he was more dazed, confused and deeply morose.

Breana drove them in and out of rain showers and patches of fog. Despite his shivering, Joe felt himself going in and out of consciousness. Awakening when the car hit a bump, he felt sharp pains in his wounded shoulder. He kept seeing the image of Fiona shot and falling to the floor. He realized dully that he was still in shock.

The car turned up the steep climb toward Moss Side. Breana found the turn and steered through the brush-covered fence line, down the unpaved lane toward the farm. Soon Joe could see a small lamp on in the window, casting a blurred glow through the mist. The car stopped near the doorway, Whelan ran up barking her greeting, and a man came out to help them in. Joe realized it was Father Jack, the fallen priest, Ryan's brother. When Joe stumbled out of the car, the man took a firm grip on his arm and led him into the house.

"You're safe here," the priest said. Joe noticed that his voice was gentle, but sounded clear and authoritative.

They took Joe back to a room and had him sit on the side of a bed. He winced in pain as Breana began taking the bandage off his shoulder, and she berated Ryan gently for his poor first aid work.

"He did not bleed to death, anyways," Ryan countered.

Shaking her head, Breana went off and came back with a pan of water. She cleaned Joe's wound, said it did not look too serious, and then applied gauze and tape. The priest came in with a steaming cup of tea and offered it to Joe. Joe nodded, took a few sips, coughed, and said he would really just like to sleep a bit. The young woman covered him up, and Joe, despite the dull ache in his shoulder, soon succumbed to a fitful sleep.

While it was still dark, he became aware that he had been dreaming and possibly that his own restless murmuring may have awakened him. Terrible images of Fiona lying in blood faded from his mind, leaving only a sense of grief and despair. Then he remembered where he was and realized someone was there in the room with him. He opened his eyes and saw the silhouette of the priest, sitting in a chair by the bedside.

"I knew you were a spy," the man said evenly, "and I knew you had your own evil intent within it."

Joe tried to focus on the priest, but in the gloom he could not see his face, only that he wore his white collar. "I don't know what you're saying." Joe's voice was hoarse and raspy.

"You came here to meddle in our affairs," the priest said, "is that not true?"

Joe struggled to raise his head and prop up on his elbow. "I came here because...I wanted..." It seemed strange now to be saying it. "They stole my boat. The IRA or somebody. And I wanted to get... get even..."

"Revenge?" The priest laughed humorlessly. "Oh, revenge. Of course. That's what we all want, isn't it?" He locked his eyes on Joe, his gaze piercing the darkened room. "Isn't it?"

Joe sat up. "I don't know. I thought I knew, but then..."

"How many died?" the priest demanded gruffly. "How many because of you?"

"Five," Joe whispered.

"Name them."

"Seamus and Mike. There was the explosion..."

"Who else?"

"Fiona shot Wade Johnston. He was trying to kill me..."

"I don't care about that. Go on. Who else?"

"Fiona," Joe cried now. "She was trying to save me. She was trying to save me." He sobbed. "Then Timothy her brother shot her by accident..."

"And he killed himself?" The priest shook his head. "Five lives lost. Five souls not yet in hell or heaven. All because you wanted to get even?"

Joe put his head in his hands, his chest heaving. "I never meant for any of this... It never, never should have happened." He cried as he had not cried since childhood.

The priest motioned toward the floor. "Get off bed and kneel beside it," he commanded. Joe looked up through bleary eyes at the silhouette of the man seated beside him.

"Do as I say." The priest spoke through gritted teeth. "Kneel here, now."

Joe obeyed. He sat upright, his head spinning in dizziness. When it stopped, he slipped down on his knees. The priest put his rough farmer's hand on Joe's head.

"Say 'Forgive me, Father, for I have sinned'."

Joe tried to look up, but the man pressed his head down, so he could only see the dark floor. "You will do as I say. Speak."

"Forgive me, Father, for I have sinned," Joe whispered.

"Tell me your sins, my son." Father Jack's voice was kinder.

Joe hesitated. "I don't know where to begin. I don't know…"

"There is no hurry. We will be here until you do."

In silence they remained as they were. Slowly, Joe began to recall his anger at seeing his ruined boat, his desire for revenge, his resentment toward Mary and her way of life. He began to tell these things aloud, haltingly and with confusion, but it began to grow clearer. He thought about his animosity toward Wade, his jealousy over Wade's relationship with Mary. He recalled his encounter with Seamus and Mikey, and Timothy and the IRA gang and how they used one another. But most of all he thought of Fiona and how he had become obsessed with her, and finally had betrayed her and used her, and caused her to conceive a child.

"It was all pure selfishness," he admitted, his voice choked. "Nothing I did was for the benefit of anything, not my country, not justice, not for any cause. It was only for myself." He put his hand to his face in pain. "Oh my God! Fiona! How could it be?" He slumped forward, almost prostrate on the floor and cried once more.

They remained there in the dark silence for a long time, until the first light of dawn created a dull grayness in the room. Then he felt the hands of the priest taking his uninjured arm, gently pulling him up. In the early light, Joe could see the man's worn face, tears running down gaunt cheeks.

"When you came here to our troubled island, you opened the door and looked in upon this hell on earth." He paused. "I too have seen it."

Joe looked up, trying to make out the man's face in the dim light.

"It was that same hell—the hell you saw, the evil you did. But I too, I too..." Father Jack cried. Joe realized he now was hearing the priest's own confession. They were confessing to one another.

"Most who've seen it have not survived its deadly curse," the priest said. He shook his head. "I've hidden in the bottle. I have tried to drink myself away from it all. I do not know why I am allowed to be here still." He sighed deeply. "But if we can understand what it does to us—not the liquor but the hate, the violence, the revenge. If we can see the harm it does to ourselves and those around us, we may yet live."

"I understand," Joe whispered. He was not certain at that moment that he completely understood, but he did comprehend the feelings. The priest knelt beside him.

"Father, forgive me," the priest said, "for I have sinned." In the silence that followed, Joe could hear the man's quiet sobbing. Then he was still.

"Say the Lord's prayer with me," he commanded. He began, and Joe followed along, tentatively at first but then growing stronger in its comfort. They finished. The priest put his hand on Joe's shoulder.

"Rest, now, my son," Father Jack said. "Rest." He pulled himself up, made the sign of the cross over Joe, and then left as quietly as he had come.

After a few moments, Joe crawled back in the bed, pulled up the cover and turned on his side with his knees pulled up. His tears finally ceased and he slept as he had not slept in a long time.

Chapter Twenty-Two

At noon, Breana drove Ryan along with a once-again-disguised Joe down a road on the southerly side of Knocklade Mountain. They turned up a narrow road to a small outpost of Corrymeela Center. Consisting of a few buildings nestled obscurely near the mountain top, Corrymeela-Knocklade was a remote retreat for smaller more-intimate gatherings. The director, Reverend Jackson Barnett, and his wife, friends of Ryan, agreed to shelter Joe and protect his anonymity until such time as he could sort out his situation.

Wounded, physically exhausted and emotionally drained, without money or passport and uncertain of his status with CIA, Joe did not know which way to turn. Was he to be arrested and sent home in chains? Or, to protect the CIA's secrecy, was he simply to be annihilated by another covert agent? Or, if he let anyone in Northern Ireland know where he was, then would the Real IRA kidnap, torture and kill him? He remembered how Ned brandished the knife, clearly out to cut his throat. He had read news articles about people being brutally maimed, and those victims merely were former IRA who had erred. There was little doubt what they would do if they found an American spy.

"I hope my being here doesn't cause you trouble," Joe said when he, Ryan and Reverend Barnett met and took a walk around the grounds. "I'm sure the Real IRA would like to find me, or the police might say you're abetting a criminal or something."

"No one knows you're here," Reverend Barnett replied with a confident smile. "I think we're safe enough for the present."

"I'm so thankful, and to you too, Ryan."

"Over the years I've picked up a few strange things from around the world." The big man winked at the preacher. "But an exotic piece of work ye be, Anderson, so I decided I'd just collect you in."

Reverend Barnett was called away to the telephone, leaving Ryan and Joe in the yard where they could see the view of farms and villages in the rolling valleys below. Green pastures filled with grazing sheep abutted fields of amber hay, interrupted by small villages, with the city of Coleraine and a range of mountains beyond, blue and misty beneath raining cumulous. As seen from here on Knocklade Mountain, Ulster could not have been more picturesque. But Joe continued to fixate on the confused, twisted, tragic reality of republican Catholics pitched against equally brutal loyalist Protestants.

"Ryan, my friend," Joe said. "How could it be that there's so much ugliness and suffering going on amid all the natural beauty of this island?"

"Because it is men that inhabit God's world," Ryan replied. "Eire is an Eden, and we have no snakes. But man himself is the serpent."

Joe nodded, gazing at the view in contemplation. "Do you think there will be an inquest into Wade Johnston's murder?"

"Likely there is an investigation well underway. But nobody in that republican crowd would testify against Fiona," he replied. "Of that you can be sure."

"What about you?"

"For my part, I can honestly say that, from where I stood behind all the people, I saw nothing of the shooting," Ryan said, raising his right hand symbolically. "All I know is hearsay." Then he gave Joe a long look. "And as for you?"

Joe had not fully decided where he stood on that. He certainly saw Fiona shoot and saw Wade go down. It was hard to think that she, in killing Wade to vindicate Seamus, had carried out Joe's revenge on Wade—a strange and twisted gift to give him. Did he now have a moral obligation to speak against poor dead Fiona?

"I don't know. I'll have to think about it. I am bound to secrecy, after all. I couldn't testify without telling the whole truth, including the drone attack and everything. What is my duty anyway? It's very difficult to know."

"And are you not now the only witness to her death?" Ryan asked. "Where do you stand on that?"

Joe put his hand to his eyes. It was all so painful. "Since Timothy and Fiona and I were alone, no one but you and Father Jack know I was there. In fact, the public still think I drowned under the docks." He shook his head. "Maybe I'll simply report the events to CIA and let them make the call." He paused. "You know, it's very strange being alive but presumed dead at the same time. To the people here, I don't even exist." He breathed deeply and let it out with a shudder. "But Poor Fiona. For her to go that way... What a horrible life she had." He thought a moment. "And her brother Timothy. Until he killed Fiona, it was as if he thought the whole thing was a game." He shook his head. "I don't know what I'm supposed to do."

Big Ryan stepped closer and put his hand on Joe's good shoulder. "There's an old saying. Let the dead bury the dead."

Joe reached across his chest and put his hand on Ryan's big hand. "Where is the law? Where is civil justice? What right does my government have to send me here? Am I above the law of the land because I acted in accordance with my duties as an intelligence agent? What is my place in all of this?"

"I suspect you'll be called upon to declare yourself soon enough," Ryan replied. "But I can't say that there'll be any justice."

The preacher rejoined them, apologizing for having run off to handle a matter on the phone.

"We were just discussing duty and justice," Ryan said.

"I imagine that it will all be sorted in due time," Reverend Barnett said. "Up above, if not here."

"Through all that's happened," Joe said, "it's so difficult to know to what rules or alliances or moral viewpoint I am to be committed."

"That's what I told myself when I went off to sea," Ryan said. "Well, what are you? they asked when I was 20. Catholic or Protestant? Republican or loyalist? I did not choose to answer, and so I signed on a freighter bound for nowhere." His voice broke, and he looked sad. "And that's what's made me the man I am today," he added in a tone of self-condemnation. The three of them stood silently. Joe was trying to think of something reassuring to say. Then the preacher smiled and spoke up.

"Sounds to me like you have the right qualifications for volunteering at Corrymeela." Ryan looked at him uncertainly. "A man who grew up with one Catholic and one Protestant parent," Barnett continued, "a man who's seen the world rather than spending his life immersed in the difficulties of Northern Ireland..."

"And a man who is very, very wise," Joe added.

"I cannot imagine a more perfect individual to join our staff. So, why don't you?"

Ryan glanced at Joe, who nodded encouragement. The big man looked off down the valley. "No doubt I have not liked the life of an old age pensioner," he said. He looked at the director and nodded. "If you think I'd be of help, nothing would suit me better. Aye, oh aye, I'd love to."

"Done," Barnett said, extending his hand. Ryan took it and they all smiled.

"I wish there was something for me here, too," Joe said. "I'd be willing to sweep the floors, cut the grass, anything. Lord, I'd give anything to join in here and try to make a difference."

"So be it," the director agreed, giving him a hardy handshake. "For as long as you are able to stay."

"Of course, I'd have to wear my disguise when people are here," Joe said.

"And keep your bloody southern American drawl to yourself," Ryan laughed. "It would not take an Irishman two words to spot you."

As it turned out, within a couple of days the CIA did find the missing Joe Anderson and order him home. It was Evan Foster who tracked him down. He appeared at Corrymeela with Agent Adams, who had flown over to take him in custody.

"I've got to know one thing," Joe asked Foster when he had a private moment with him. "Are you the one who tipped off Seamus O'Leary?" Foster hesitated, studying Joe's expression, then nodded.

"For years, O'Leary had been in the drug-trafficking business, to finance IRA terrorism," Foster said. "We knew he wasn't making a living fishing on all those nighttime excursions. But he'd never been caught. So it was a perfect opportunity to have his ass."

"And mine," Joe added. "But I guess that part didn't matter, huh?"

"You're merely a soldier, Anderson—a wee price to pay, weighed against the damage done by cocaine to a people already oppressed by violence and injustice."

"The Catholic Irish, you mean?"

"There's drug users on both sides. Abuse. addiction, ruined lives—that's not a sectarian issue here. It's just another sort of war that goes on and on."

"When I saw you call the police on those French sailors, I guessed that you're a British agent," Joe ventured to ask. "But when you told O'Leary about the trap being set for seizing the explosives, I thought you were IRA?"

"I never comment on my affiliations." Foster gave Joe the smile of the Sphinx. Then he took him to his car and pulled a flyer from the glove box. "Read that, when you're a mind."

Joe scanned the paper and stared at one line. "Republican Action Against Drugs (RAAD) proudly operates in cooperation with the RIRA..."

"We've got to get you out of here before somebody else dies," Adams said, as the two of them waited in the

279

concourse at Belfast International. "Man, I hope I can be at your debriefing to hear you explain it all. It ought to be a show."

Thankful Adams hadn't wanted to handcuff him, Joe looked at the newly printed passport Adams had produced. "What do you think they'll do to me?"

"Where should I begin?" Adams laughed. "Reprimand you for insubordination or maybe just charge you with treason. Hell, your ass is grass at CIA."

"I was just trying to do my job," Joe said. "I wanted to find out who was responsible for stealing my boat a year ago." He paused. "The problem is that, knowing what I know now, I don't really have any idea who to condemn as the bad side."

"Trying to do your job, eh?" Adams laughed cynically. "You never did get it, did you? Why they sent you to this god-forsaken place?"

"What do you mean?"

"Why were you sent here? To help sell a bunch of drones and missiles to the Brits, man. Who do you think we're working for, really?"

"What?"

"The military-industrial complex of the United States, you idiot," Adams said. "Maybe you've gotten out of touch, ole boy." He laughed. "You didn't think having your oar in the water there was going to make any difference to the Irish problem, did you?"

"Well, I'll have a few questions of my own to ask at CIA," Joe shot back. "I'd like to hear Hankins expound on CIA's picture of the truth and justice of this whole situation."

Adams gave his usual smirk. "I won't hold my breath waiting for that."

Looking out the window as the plane made a left turn after takeoff and flew briefly north, Joe had only a quick look at Rathlin Island, Ballycastle, and Rathlin Sound between. The memories of Fiona and all the tangle of what had happened came back to him in a rush. He had come to seek revenge, but he realized he had known nothing about revenge. Vengeance, he had found, was the poison in the wound that festered in Northern Ireland. It was a tribal heritage, born of sad history, and likely to go on and on.

Just before the plane turned west and flew into the clouds, he saw a sight that seemed to sum up his experiences in Northern Ireland—the swirling, turbulent eddies of Slough na more.

Chapter Twenty-Three

As the marine guard drove them through the gates at Langley, Joe's pulse jumped 40 beats. They drove up to the same building, entered the same door, and passed the same guarded entry point where he and Wade Johnston had come in several months ago. Wade now was dead, and Joe was here to answer for it, along with a few other "blunders," as Adams described them. Not since they had left Corrymeela, driven to Belfast International, flown to Newark on United and then connected to Baltimore's BWI, had either of them had a chance to bathe, shave or change clothes.

"We don't know what sort of prison garb you might be putting on anyway," Adams replied to Joe's complaint. Adams, Joe realized, was enjoying trying to make him squirm. Not so long ago, Joe would have let Adams have it, but now he was more subdued.

"You really have a wonderful way about you, Adams, you know that?" Joe told him anyway.

They went to the same conference room where Wade had taken Joe on his first visit. Deputy Director Hankins entered, along with an official-looking stenographer, and finally even the staff psychologist, Dr. Olwert. *Everybody's here,* Joe thought, *except the executioner.* As they all sat down, this time with no greetings or handshakes, Hankins turned to Joe with no more than a humorless nod.

"Our purpose here is twofold. We will debrief you and inquire into the death of Wade Johnston. I want you to give us a summary of the events leading up to the shooting, and then we will follow up with a number of questions concerning the incident."

"Am I to consider myself on trial?" Joe asked. "Or am I here to explain what happened?"

Hankins gave him a long intense look. "You are here to explain to your superior why one of our own was murdered in your presence. This is not a court of law. I want to hear your full and complete explanation, and I want it now."

Joe met his gaze. "I will be happy to tell you exactly what happened, and then I will have a few questions of my own." He paused to be sure he kept his voice calm. "I was sent over to spy on the IRA and learn anything about weapons smuggling operations. I suppose I should begin by saying that I infiltrated a group called the Real IRA."

"And how did you accomplish that?" Hankins asked.

"I befriended a young lady named Fiona, who ran a wee... a small store in Ballycastle. Her brother Timothy took me to a meeting with two men at a farmhouse somewhere near the little town of Cushendun. He blindfolded me so I wouldn't know where it was. There were two men, Tom and Ned, and that's all I know them by. Tom, the leader, was fiftyish and this Ned was an ugly young thug with a tattoo of a cross that looked more like a dagger. Anyway, they said that, because I was a foreigner with a sailboat, they needed me to rendezvous with a ship at sea, pick up some explosives, and deliver them ashore."

"And you agreed?" Hankins asked.

Joe nodded. "That's right. I was to be paid to do it. Of course, I never intended that the delivery would actually be completed. That's why I informed Wade Johnston as soon as I could."

"Why do you think these Irishmen trusted you?"

"It was because of Fiona, I think. We sort of had a relationship." Thinking back, he realized that perhaps she only meant to use him all along, at least until the fateful day aground in the River Bann. In any case, he had been a great chump through it all. Well, perhaps everybody was trying to take advantage of everybody; that was human nature, wasn't it? He looked down at the table so they would not see his expression.

"And this woman is the one who shot Wade Johnston?" Hankins asked.

Joe knew there was nothing else he could say. "That's right."

"How did she learn Wade's identity?"

285

Joe realized that this whole explanation was going wrong. A simple answer now would cast all the blame entirely on himself.

"I heard that you exposed him," Hankins pressed. "At some kind of public gathering, you named him, and then this Fiona woman pulled out a pistol and shot him. Is that it?"

Joe fixed his gaze on the deputy director. "That is not *it!*" Joe said, raising his voice. He glanced momentarily at Dr. Olwert, recalled the psychiatrist's admonishment six months ago about temper, and forced himself to calm down. "As I was heading for the rendezvous with the ship, I called Wade, told him what was going on and asked for his help. He said he would set up a trap of some kind for the IRA and that I merely was to go right on with the whole smuggling operation and then slip away when I got into port."

"Did you get the name or registry off the ship's hull?"

Joe shook his head. "*The Bonnie* something, maybe. I don't know. It was pitch black dark at the time, and I didn't exactly go shining a light on the stern to read the name." Hankins gave a look of disapproving disappointment.

Maybe you think you could have done better, Joe kept himself from saying. He paused and cleared his throat to keep his voice even. "After receiving the explosives in the middle of the night, these O'Leary brothers, who turned out to be members of the Real IRA, or maybe some other faction of the IRA, I don't know. Anyway, somehow they found out there was to be an ambush or whatever by the police when I arrived in port, and all the explosives would be seized and

286

the IRA people caught taking them from my boat. I'm pretty sure it was this Evan Foster, the harbormaster, who told Seamus O'Leary about the police trap. And I thought Foster was MI-5 or maybe even CIA. Is he CIA?"

"I'll ask the questions," Hankins said.

"Yeah, now I'm sure he works for you," Joe shot back. "Anyway, so O'Leary motors out in his trawler to accost me out in the sound. He pulls a gun on me, holds me hostage, and starts loading the explosives on his boat. I manage to call Wade on the phone and tell him what's happening. Then Wade somehow orders a goddam drone to shoot a missile that blows up both boats and the O'Learys. It would have blown me up, too, if I hadn't escaped."

"We'll get into the matter of the missile in a minute," Hankins interrupted. "Right now, the question is, how did you escape?"

Joe looked at him hard. "I managed to swim away," Joe said.

"Swim away? How far?"

"A mile or two, in the dark, in freezing water with a powerful current and even a whirlpool."

"That's hard to believe," Hankins challenged.

"You're damn right it is!" Joe finally lost it. "The question is, the question is, why the hell did Wade Johnston and you and the CIA and the whole fucking government fire a missile at me. AT ME! And who authorized killing the O'Learys? Those are my questions, Mr. Director. Do you know why Wade Johnston wanted me killed? Because he was in love with his sister-in-law, who was in love with me. That's why. And I don't think he was really in love with her anyway. He just wanted her money. So does that give him the right to order a missile that was meant to kill me, and never mind that it might take out a couple of IRA men in the process?" Joe stared at the director, who stared back a moment and then looked away.

"An incredible story," Hankins said, exchanging glances with Adams. Joe noted Adams wearing his usual cynical smile.

"Yeah, it felt pretty incredible watching a huge explosion from a drone missile fired where I was expected to be, and by my own country. You ought to try it sometime."

Hankins shifted his gaze to Adams. "Stan, what do we know about this?"

"As you know, we have been conducting exercises with the British Navy," Adams said, "training them in the use of drone warfare and intelligence. Our drone control team was engaged in drills with their submarine fleet out of Holy Loch, Scotland, which conducts exercises in the sea north of Rathlin Island." He went on to explain that exercises were held in which the drone operators were to search for surfacing submarines and to simulate firing upon them. In fact, there had been several actual firings of dummy-warheaded missiles at surface practice targets.

"And my boat just happened to be one of those practice targets, huh?" Joe said.

"I'll ask the questions, Anderson," Hankins snapped. He turned to Adams. "So how did one of these missiles become targeted on the boats in Rathlin Sound in the middle of the night?"

"We had on-going exercises. Somehow the message came in that there was a target in Rathlin Sound that was to be immediately engaged and fired upon." Adams paused. "The missile did not have an explosive warhead, so we're not sure what happened."

"That's easy," Joe said. "You shoot a supersonic missile into as much explosives as were on that boat, and the mere concussion would set it off." Hankins shot Joe a look of warning, but Adams looked at Joe and nodded.

"That's entirely possible."

"Damn right, it's possible," Joe said, nearly rising from his chair. "I just happened to have seen it myself... knocked the breath out of me while I was swimming around in freezing water and sprayed one hell of a lot of shrapnel and junk near my head. You guys nearly killed me."

Dr. Olwert put up his hand, gesturing to Joe to just cool it.

Hankins gave Joe a measured stare and then turned to Adams. "Do we have any idea how this could have happened?"

"I read the log books and other records," Adams replied, almost with a sneer. "Miscommunication between MI-5, CIA, and the two Navies. Because there was a naval exercise underway, there was no need for approvals from

289

higher up." He smiled cynically. "Seems that there was some mix-up about the target. Mr. Johnston's urgent call somehow was understood as a drill intelligence report or something—like a pop-up target for practice." Adams laughed. "Typical bureaucratic SNAFU."

"Maybe we should offer to carve a couple of tombstones for Seamus and Michael O'Leary—write *Situation Normal All Fucked Up* on them," Joe said.

"Watch yourself, Anderson," Hankins said. "You've still got plenty of explaining to do." He was not sympathetic. "I want to know what happened to Johnston. You still haven't answered my question. How did Wade Johnston's identity become compromised?"

"Wade went to a memorial service that was being held for the O'Learys," Joe explained. "I was there in disguise. IRA people were there—Tom the leader, Ned the thug, Timothy the apprentice terrorist bomber, if you can imagine, and Fiona. Everybody thought I had died in the explosion until Ned recognized me and pulled off my disguise. In order to get away from him and buy some time, I went up in front of the crowd and told everybody the true story. I knew that this Ned character was going to stab me right then and there. Then all of a sudden, to me the whole situation seemed so absurd. I mean, here were members of the Irish Republican Army, trying to overthrow the loyalist government and unite Ireland when they could all be at home living sane, happy lives. And here I am after revenge for something they did to me—thought they did to me. And here's CIA and MI-5 and a harbormaster who's a double agent, and drones spying on everybody. And then here's

Wade Johnston pretending to be a nobody at the memorial service when he was the one who had murdered the O'Learys. And why did he do that? Because he wanted to win over Mary Johnston by killing me. So yes, I did point Wade out at the funeral, to expose him for what he was. And yes, Fiona did shoot him because he had caused the death of her lover, Seamus O'Leary. And there's the truth as plain as I can tell it." Joe ended his story, breathing hard and exhausted by the telling.

There was a long silence. The director exchanged glances with Adams and Dr. Olwert. The stenographer had taken her hands off her machine and was staring at Joe incredulously.

Hankins looked at Joe again. "And what happened to this Fiona?"

Trying to be calm, Joe recounted the final encounter with her and told how she had tried to stop Timothy from shooting him and was shot in the process. By the time he reached the part of the story about Timothy committing suicide, he was so choked up he could hardly hide his feelings. Everyone stared at Joe and sat in silence for a full minute.

"We'll take a break," Hankins said finally, pushing his chair back. "We'll reconvene..." he looked at his watch. "Let's meet back here after dinner. Make it at 1900."

"It would not hurt to sleep on this," Dr. Olwert suggested. Hankins looked at him a moment and nodded. He then looked at Joe.

"Let's have Anderson stay in one of the rooms in building B," he said to Adams. Then he gave Joe one last look, turned and walked out.

"Is that a jail cell?" Joe asked Adams as they went down the hall.

"Nope," Adams said. "Just a dormitory." They walked on a few steps. "I suppose it means you came out okay."

"What do you think's in store tomorrow?" Joe asked.

Adams made his typically cynical smirk. "There's already an inquiry underway about the drone missile firing that Hankins is stuck with. He's going to have to answer to the White House and maybe Congress if it gets that far. So far there's been no leak to the press—about the drone being ours, I mean. But eventually somebody over there's going to repeat what you said at that memorial service." He shook his head. "By having that missile fired, Wade Johnston left a big thorn in the side of CIA, let me tell you."

"I see," Joe said. "And what about me?"

"He probably will give you a good wrist slapping and send you for some R&R. You're just in the way right now."

"R&R?" Joe repeated. "Send me packing, you mean?"

Adams grinned. "The way I read it, Hankins probably will give you another assignment."

"What?" Joe stopped in his tracks. "Another mission? You're kidding."

Adams smiled. "After all of that, congratulations. You're finally trained. I expect the next time you'll make a pretty fair man in the field."

Joe looked at Adams with surprise. Maybe this acerbic old agent has some kind of humanity after all.

"So where're you going for your R&R?" Adams asked.

Joe grinned. "To Birmingham, I guess. I need to see if Mary will allow me in the door."

Chapter Twenty-Four

It was late afternoon two days later when the taxi stopped in front of Mary's house. Except for the box of Cadbury's chocolates he had bought for her in the airport, he had no luggage and only an envelope from CIA containing a very nice check. As he walked to the entrance to the kitchen, he wished he had taken time to buy more presentable clothes. But he had lucked out on getting an airline reservation right away, and he was anxious to see Mary.

There was no sign of her outside, but both her car and Earnest's roadster were visible in the garage. Seeing Earnest's sports car made him recall his first run-in with Wade. He had not called Mary since the brief phone conversation from Ballycastle, so he had yet to know for sure how upset she was over losing her brother-in-law. Now that he was standing at her door, he began to doubt his decision not to call and tell her he was coming. He had not phoned because he was afraid she might have told him not to bother coming. Well, for better or worse, here he was.

Mustering his courage, he rang the bell, and then fumbled around with the box of chocolates, trying to decide whether to be holding it when she first saw him. It seemed so inadequate a gift. As he heard her footsteps inside, he quickly bent down and put the box and his envelope to the side. Then the inner door opened, and Mary was there, peering at him through the screen. She had on a white frilly blouse and dark gray pants that complemented her blond hair. She was stunning.

"Hello," he said. "It's me." He suddenly was at a loss for words.

Mary did not open the screen door but merely looked at him, not with a smile or a tear, but with contemplative neutral expression and a long silence.

"Say, Mary," Joe tried, "gosh, you're looking great."

Her expression did not change. "I suppose you expect merely to show up here and have things go on as if you'd never left." There was no anger in her voice, no reproach, no excitement, no emotion. It was as if she simply was recognizing and stating the obvious. Joe was caught by surprise.

"I don't know whether to come in and hug you or just run," Joe said, trying to joke but was more than serious.

"I'm wondering if you'll ever grow up," Mary said evenly.

It made Joe grin. "Lord knows, I've tried," he said. "Just doesn't seem to be in me."

Mary shook her head. "I guess not." Neither of them had moved.

"Oh, Mary," Joe said. "If I had known what I do now, I never would have gone." His feelings from last winter came back to him briefly, the sense of not belonging in Mary's social world, the desire for revenge he had felt about the loss of his boat, Wade's intrusions into their lives, the fear that Mary was more in love with Wade than with him. And now here he stood in limbo, hoping above all else that she would forgive him and accept him back into her life.

"Why do men go?" Mary asked. "Like Odysseus and Aeneas and all the sailors and soldiers and adventurers who leave their women behind? No, it's not a matter of growing up, Joe. Too late for that. You'll just be a wanderer in search of something...I don't know what. But it's something that not you or any other man like you was ever able to find."

Joe considered silently what she had said. Grimly, he sighed. "I know you've had enough of me." He gave her a long look and realized he should have told the cab to wait.

"Women like me are doomed to endure your absence," Mary went on, "angry at your leaving, angry when you return." She shook her head. "But we have to take you as you are... because... there is nothing else to do..." She turned away and her words broke off in a silent sob. Joe took a deep breath and opened the door.

"We need each other, dearest Mary," Joe said. He took a step toward her. "I missed you so much."

Mary fell into his arms. "I missed you, too. Oh, Joe, please don't leave me again." She put her head on his shoulder and wept.

"Oh, Mary," Joe cried. "I love you." Joe felt her strong embrace and was filled with a great sense of relief that swept over him like a huge, gently breaking wave.

She led him into the kitchen and they sat at the table under the daintily painted strawberry wallpaper with pale yellow background. Everything looked so beautiful to him. She began making a pot of tea but went in the den and brought back a bottle of scotch.

"After your plane ride you must need something," she said as she put the bottle beside him. Then she brought the cups of tea, and Joe added a stiff shot of whiskey to his. She took some in hers, too, and they sipped and asked about one another.

"You know," he said. "I thought I was justified in going to Ireland to seek revenge." He paused, thinking. "What I came to realize was that everybody wants vindication for something that has happened to them, but no one has a right to revenge. It only brings more suffering."

She shook her head sadly.

"It's so good to see you," he said. "I can't even tell you how much." The image of Fiona lying in that pool of blood flashed through his mind. "It was hell over there."

"What are they fighting for, anyway?" Mary asked as she brought the drinks to the table and sat down. "Seems to me they would spend their energies on more profitable things."

"I've been mulling all that over, Mary," Joe said. "It's tribal warfare, feuding, sins of the fathers passed to the sons and grandsons—that kind of senselessness." He shook his head. "The majority of the people live their lives peaceably, but there are the few who still harbor their hatred. It's as if they thrive on it, as if it gives them some cause to live for, provides some meaning or direction to their everyday lives. They latch on to some past wrong done to them or to their families and make it a justification for violence and cruelty. There is something basic and primal welling up in them, overcoming reason, and driving them to all sorts of irrational acts."

"Well, don't think the Irish have any monopoly on irrational acts," she replied. "While you were over there dealing with their problems, more and more crazies have surfaced in this country. One of the scariest things is that more and more hate groups seem to be forming."

Joe wiped his hand across his eyes. "After what I've seen in Northern Ireland, I can't believe people want to stir up that kind of divisiveness here."

"What is the saying? Those who don't know history are bound to repeat it? Something like that?"

Very soon the discussion came to Wade and how he died. In an effort to push away the image of Fiona with the pistol in her hand, Joe gave Mary a brief, thin summary of what happened, admonishing her not to tell anyone anything he was saying—that it was all very secret and that he knew he could trust her. He apologized profusely for Wade's death, saying it was his own incompetence that led to it. He did not say that Wade had tried to kill him with the missile.

"Poor Wade," she said. Apparently, she had had days to get over the grief and shock. "I knew he was in a dangerous business, but his motivation always was difficult to understand."

"It's very hard to explain," Joe replied. "The circumstances were pretty complex."

She sighed. "I don't know how you survived all of that. Oh, Joe, I'm so happy to have you back home and safe." She reached across the table and held his hand firmly.

"I know you had strong feelings for him," Joe said sadly. "I'm so sorry to have had a part in his death."

Mary gazed at Joe intently for a long moment. "Strong feelings?" she repeated. "Joe? Well, of course, I cared about Wade in that he was Earnest's dear brother. But, no, Joe. If you mean did I love him, certainly not. I mean…" She hesitated and bit her lip.

"He kept coming to visit you while I was gone," Joe said. "He took you out, and stayed here with you, I guess. I mean, that's your business. But anyway, I thought you and he…" He paused because she was shaking her head. She squeezed his hand and held on.

"Oh, my dear foolish Joe," she said. "Don't you realize? I was playing the woman's trick of letting him court me in order to make you jealous and come home again." She paused to read his expression. "I am an actress, after all."

Joe blinked then closed his eyes tight for a moment, trying to comprehend what he was hearing. He thought about how Fiona had used him to make Seamus jealous, and now here was Mary having done the same thing. And both Wade and Seamus were now dead, and Fiona as well. He looked at Mary as if more or less thunderstruck. In tears he laughed, squeezed her hand and blew her a kiss.

"Over there in Rathlin Sound, the bay right off of Ballycastle," he said, "there is a big whirlpool that forms at ebb tide." He sighed and fought away the image of Fiona and Timothy struggling over the gun. From their childhood in The Troubles, he understood now, neither of them ever really had a chance. "Northern Ireland, Ulster, is all at once the most beautiful and the most terrible place I've ever been. I now believe that my entire experience there was one gigantic Slough na mor."

Afterword

Having recently spent the better part of twelve summers in
Northern Ireland, I fell in love with the northern coast with
its magnificent natural beauty and wonderfully friendly
people. My dear wife, Sumter, and I made many friends and
enjoyed their great hospitality. Through my association with
members of the Rotary Club of Coleraine—as a Rotarian one
has the privilege of visiting any Rotary Club in the world—I
developed some true friendships there. This, in turn, led to
my acquaintance with a group of recreational sailors, who
dock their boats on the River Bann. They welcomed me as a
fellow enthusiast and adopted me as one of their own,
allowing me to crew with them on many sailing adventures
in the Atlantic, including passages to Rathlin Island and over
to the Scottish Hebrides. It is to these fine friends that I
fondly dedicate the novel.

With as much exposure to life in Northern Ireland as
I have been fortunate to enjoy, however, I also have become
very conscious of the history of sectarian strife that disturbs
the social fabric. Even though the violent period of The

Troubles supposedly ended in 1998, many citizens still carry the emotional and physical scars of that era. Religious intolerance and political differences remain unresolved, creating an undercurrent of prejudice, hatred and discontent that divides the population. The urge for revenge of past wrongs remains a powerful motivator among many who lost their fathers and mothers, brothers and sisters, provoking some to carry out acts of murder, mayhem and terror, even as the majority of the people lead normal lives.

Because the recent "Brexit" vote is expected to remove Britain from the European Union (EU), there likely will be significant consequences for Northern Ireland. Separating the six counties from the remainder of Ireland was a long-fought and bloody campaign between loyalists and republicans, which quieted after the Good Friday Agreement in 1998. During the period of Britain's EU membership, open borders and free trade between the Republic of Ireland and Northern Ireland have provided a period of relative, if not complete, accord. Should Britain actually withdraw from the EU, however, all the old issues of political representation, economic parity, religious toleration (albeit never with ecumenical agreement) will come into question again. There presently exists a very delicate balance between sectarian and political factions, which will be highly disturbed, if not overturned, by movements either to remain with England or to join the Republic of Ireland. At this writing, Sinn Fein's Gerry Adams already has called for another referendum on the question of a unified Irish State*. The issue likely will cause a rearming of at least a few underground units on both sides, making the situation created in this novel ever more realistic.

My intention has been to illustrate the history of this ongoing conflict and to reveal the corrosive effects of hatred and revenge. To accomplish this, I have employed a main character, Joe Anderson from a previous novel**, placing him as an outsider who comes seeking revenge for his personal and selfish reasons. He succeeds only in becoming embroiled in dangerous intrigue. *Slough na mor*, a whirlpool which forms during the ebbing tide in Rathlin Sound, becomes an ample metaphor for the morass of troubles Joe creates for himself.

This story is fiction, told to illustrate the real problems facing Northern Ireland. The characters, the plot and places are fictional. Any likeness to actual persons, either living or dead, is strictly coincidental. I have chosen to use the real names of cities and towns, not because these communities deserve to be singled out as settings for the often violent actions that are fictionally described, but because their geographic locations are important to the plot. It is not to be implied that the beautiful seacoast town of Ballycastle, for example, actually harbors the crime and violence that is set there in the novel. In fact, Ballycastle is the home of Corrymeela, a privately established service organization that works to resolve and reconcile sectarian and political differences. It is my hope that all those who live in Northern Ireland will find the peace, harmony and happiness for which all mankind strives.

I hope you have enjoyed my novel. It would be most appreciated if you would go to the book's webpage on Amazon and write a review. Thank you.

Steve Coleman

P.O. Box 130524

Birmingham, Alabama 35213

sbcolemanjr@bellsouth.net

www.captstevestories.com

* Gerry Adams, "Brexit and Irish Unity," *New York Times* (July 12, 2016): A23.

**This novel is the second in a series following *The Navigator: A Perilous Passage, Evasion at Sea*, which is available in paperback and Kindle formats at Amazon.com, Amazon.co.uk, and other online booksellers.

Bibliography

Annaidh, Seamas Mac, *Irish History; From Prehistoric Times to the Present Day*. Bath, UK. 1999.

Bardon, Jonathan. *A History of Ulster*. Belfast, UK. 1992.

Haywood, John. *The Historical Atlas of the Celtic World*. New York, 2001.

Hume, John. *A New Ireland: Politics, Peace and Reconciliation*. Boulder, CO., 1996.

Mallie, Eamonn and David McKittrick, *Endgame in Ireland*. Hodder & Stoughton, London, 2001.

Nutting, Wallace. *Ireland Beautiful*. New York, 1925.

Uris, Leon, *Trinity; A Novel of Ireland*. New York, 1976.

Winn, Christopher. *I Never Knew That About Ireland*. New York, 2006.